THE MAN WHO WAS A TREE

Goran Baba Ali has written and published various literary and journalistic works in English, Kurdish and Dutch. *The Glass Wall* (Afsana Press, 2021) was his debut novel in the English language. Since he left the Kurdistan Region in 1994, he has lived in various countries. He studied sociology in Amsterdam, where he was also the editor-in-chief of *exPonto Magazine*. After fifteen years living in the Netherlands, he moved to London in 2012 and has since spent most of his time writing, including a part-time job reporting news from Iraq for the English language outlet *Insight*. In 2019, he completed an MA in creative writing at Birkbeck, University of London.

For more information, you can visit his website:
www.goranbabaali.com

The Man
Who Was a Tree

Goran Baba Ali

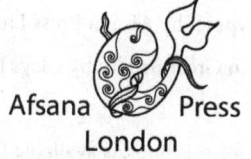

Afsana Press
London

First published in 2025

by Afsana Press Ltd, London

www.afsana-press.com

First published as a novella in Kurdish in 2011 by Afsana Press

The Man Who Was a Tree is a work of fiction. All the characters and events are
the products of the author's imagination, and while certain organisations and
institutions are mentioned, the characters involved are wholly imaginary. Any
resemblance to actual persons, living or dead, is purely coincidental, except for
the well-known persons. Places and times may have been rearranged to suit
the purposes of the book. The opinions expressed are those of the characters,
and should not be confused with the author's.

Typeset by Afsana Press Ltd

Printed and bound in Great Britain by Clays Ltd, Elcograf S.p.A.

A CIP catalogue record for this book is available from the British Library

ISBN: 978-1-7385552-9-1

MIX
Paper | Supporting
responsible forestry
FSC® C018072

To all the young women and men who feel stifled
by the societies they inhabit – those who are
misunderstood and feel unheard and unseen,
those who struggle to understand the communities
around them, and those who feel compelled to
remain silent about what they witness in the world
surrounding them.

1

The Photographer was the first to see him. Initially, he thought he had caught a glimpse of Jesus, dragging a large cross on his shoulders, wading naked in the river current. But he could never be sure of what he saw that day at dusk. The naked creature was wrapped in a long leaf resembling that of a palm tree, but much longer, creeping around his body, hanging over his shoulders. And then in a sudden, the man turned into a tree, so before his very eyes – or was he imagining it? – only to vanish amongst the other trees at the edge of a stream just outside the city.

From that day forth, the young Photographer began an obsessive search for the tree-man. He wanted to capture him in a frame in order to prove his existence and convince everyone that he himself was not a deceiver or just a crazy lad who wanted attention. He also wanted to justify the turmoil it would later create in the city. And the love of his life; didn't he lose her because of this manic chase of a creature whom he wasn't sure if it was not an illusion after all? Or was it rather that possessed man, the Asayish Director, behind the unfortunate loss of his love? The broken but powerful head of the security forces who tried to seize control of anything that happened in Slemani. The Iago of a man who tried everything to stand between him, a simple young Photographer, and his love, a modest young girl from the neighbourhood. The frustrated little megalomaniac who also barred the Photographer from catching the tree-man, thwarting all his efforts to prevent an irreversible catastrophe.

The Photographer later regretted that he hadn't kept quiet but instead had allowed his story to travel around the city. Though first he had only told a few friends about that vision-like appearance. They in turn told others and within a few weeks the story had even reached the *Khatib*, the head imam of the city, who included it in his Friday sermon. From that day, the genie was out of the lamp.

The day the young Photographer spotted the tree-man, he also got fired from his job as an assistant photographer in a studio and released from his 'crazy' boss, as he had always described him. That day, he appeared half an hour late for work and found himself confronted by a crowd of angry customers in the doorway, waiting for the photos that they were supposed to get back immediately. In fact, some of them were still waiting for someone to take their picture.

The Photographer was still in the doorway, greeting the cranky customers, when his boss ran out of the darkroom, his hair dishevelled, swearing at him. Drops of sweat trickled down his cheeks, behind his ears and his neck, dripping from his chin. His white shirt was also steeped in sweat and stuck firmly to his body, accentuating a wad of dinar bills hastily stuffed into the pocket of his shirt. He shut the door of the darkroom and stepped into the office, made his way through the many customers in the tiny space and came directly to his apprentice who was about to stride into the store. Instead, the boss gave the Photographer a hefty shove and stood at the entrance of his studio watching his sidekick roll down the set of three steps, shouting at him, 'Don't you dare enter, you lazy bastard! Go away! I never want to see you here again!'

The young Photographer sprung up immediately from the pavement, embarrassed, yelling back defiantly, 'Yes, I'm a lazy bastard, but now I'm gone.' He raised his arm. 'And forever, mind you! Now I am a free man!' he shouted harder. He dusted himself off, crossed the crowded road, bounced onto his bicycle and rode away, elated. When he turned his head over his shoulder, his boss still stood on the doorstep of his shop, open-mouthed, his fingers scratching through his scraggly hair, as he always used to do.

He was the only apprentice who had been able to endure this confused madman for such a long time, the young Photographer would tell anyone who experienced an odd encounter with his boss. He saw himself more as his slave than his assistant. And now, after five years working there, 'I suddenly feel free,' he would say. It was not the only time he had shown up that late for work or had done something so wrong that his boss felt compelled to throw him out for a few days before begging him to return. This time, however, he never returned.

Back at home in Pirma Sur, one of the city's oldest neighbourhoods, the Photographer grabbed all his savings out of a small cardboard box designed for postcard developing paper and left home again. He walked downtown to Maulawi Street and went to the only camera shop that had a few Polaroid cameras on display, too expensive for most of the people to buy. He bought one with a large number of instant film packs and rushed back home like an excited child who couldn't wait to unpack his new toy.

He spent an hour playing around with the camera. Then went out and took some pictures of his family house and the alleyway, after which he walked down to King Mahmud's house. During the British mandate, the abandoned house had been the residence of the only official king his nation had ever had. He had revolted against the colonialists shortly after the First World War, which had led to his exile in India.

Walking through the alleyway, the Photographer thought that capturing the sites of his beloved city would be much more exciting and certainly more creative than shooting faces that would only end up on some official document. Already, he felt that he had begun to see the city with a different eye.

He wanted to get inside the king's house, but the huge iron gate was thoroughly locked. He jumped but could not reach the edge of the high wall. He mustered his strength and jumped again, caught the edge with one hand, suspended along the wall, then tried again and got hold of the edge with his other hand. And it was all worth it, as he managed a glimpse. The two-story mud house was at the far end of a wide courtyard, almost dilapidated.

His hand slipped and he fell to the ground. A group of children playing in the alley laughed. He sighed and shot them a reprimanding glance. He then sat upright, leant on the wall and examined his camera. It was intact.

He imagined the king returning home from the *Serah*, the palace that was home to the British troops and, at the same time, the king's office. He would then enter the wide courtyard, which, at the time, might have been a lavish garden. The king would then walk through the garden to his mud house, which must have been a prestigious residency, escorted by his generals and guards in Kurdish clothes, daggers at their waists and rifles hanging over their shoulders, some of them with bandoliers, shoulder belts with little pockets full of cartridges, crossing their chests.

How would the king have been welcomed home? Would his children have dared to run to him with open arms or would his wife have waited for him on the doorstep? Or would he immediately have gone to his *diwakhan*, the guesthouse, to meet citizens, elders, family or members of his tribe? For the first time, the Photographer became curious about the history of his city and thought how shameful it was that no one had given any attention to this treasure hiding in this ordinary little alley. The politics, of course, he thought. Especially the regime would have disliked any attempt by the people to rehabilitate this house or revere that period in history. Politics, indeed. Anything in this city, in the country, all life was defined by politics.

As there was nothing to photograph there, he thought it was maybe better to take a picture of the children. He stood up and took a position. The children interrupted their game immediately and posed for him in a line, except for one little girl who leant back on the wall, putting her thumb in her mouth.

The Photographer instantly took a picture of her from over the shoulder of one of the other children. The camera chugged and pushed out half of the picture, a piece of square cardboard. He pulled the cardboard out and held it between two fingers to get ready for another take.

The children all ran to pose beside the little girl, laughing and imitating her by putting one of their fingers in their mouths.

The Photographer took another picture of them and pulled out this piece of cardboard too. He shook the two cards for some twenty seconds, grabbing the attention of the children.

'What are you doing?' asked one of the boys.

'He took pictures of us, silly,' another boy said, pushing him away, lifting his head up to the Photographer. 'My uncle's got one of those cameras as well.'

'Just wait and see,' the Photographer said and tore the shiny black cover from the pictures. The photos appeared before the kids' own eyes, and they started yelling, hurrahing, and shouting at him to give them the photos.

The Photographer put the picture of the small girl in his pocket and gave the other one to the oldest child, a girl of about nine years old, while the boys were shouting, 'Me, me, me!'

The Photographer said that they should take turns keeping the picture, each for one week or so.

'Shush!' shouted the older girl at the other children, forcing them to be silent. 'I have a better idea. I'll cut everyone out and you will each get your own bit.'

Walking back home, thrilled by his encounter with the children, the Photographer thought he could start his new endeavour as a street photographer immediately. *Why wait?*

Just as he pushed open the old wooden gate that he had left ajar and was about to rush inside, his neighbour girl came out of the house opposite, making him turn round.

'What is all that rush about?' the girl shouted. 'You look very excited. What's going on?'

'Hi Neighbour!' he said, a wide smile crossing his face. 'Oh, you can't imagine; I've got this new camera, and I am about to start a new life!' He then bent his left knee a bit and stretched his right leg backwards, getting ready to take a picture, holding his camera with both hands firmly, and warned, 'Don't move! Just stay like that. Very beautiful!'

'Oh, don't. I'm not dressed for a photo,' the Neighbour-Girl said and walked away hurriedly. But the Photographer had already clicked, and the camera made the wheezy chug, pushing the square cardboard out.

'Tear that up please. I'll come to the studio one day soon for a proper photo.'

'I quit my job there,' the Photographer shouted.

'What? Are you mad?' the Neighbour-Girl shouted back, turning towards him. 'I hope that's temporary, just as always, you mad man. Tell me later. I've got to go now.' She dashed down the alley.

The Photographer tore off the shiny black cover from the card and the picture of his neighbour appeared before his eyes: The Neighbour-Girl was moving sideways, looking over her shoulder directly into his eyes, a smile revealing her perfectly carved white teeth. He glanced round, then kissed the picture, put it in his pocket and went inside. His father was in the garden, leaning on a crutch, examining the blossoms of a huge *Yengi Dunya* tree, a Maltese Plum.

The Photographer tried to sneak in.

'Would you come here for a second, *kurm*?'

'I'll be with you in a minute, *Baba*,' the Photographer said and ran inside the house, rushed to his own room, put all the film packs he had just bought into a bag, slung the bag over his shoulder and again tried to sneak out of the house. But just when he had reached the front gate and taken a step outside, his father shouted, 'Come on, my son, I saw you. Why do you always run away from me? I just want to show you something.'

The Photographer stepped back into the garden and sauntered towards his father, who remained standing under the tree, the crutch under his right armpit.

'Look how beautiful it is, *kurm*. Look at the blossoms! It looks like it'll give a good lot of fruit this year. I was afraid that it would never bloom again after that damned black rain last year.'

The Photographer touched one of the flowers indifferently and said, 'I see. They're gorgeous, aren't they, *Baba*?'

'I know you don't give a damn, Son. But you will be the one who will pluck a kilo every day soon, not me. *You* are the one who loves them and—'

'Dad, I do give a damn. I really do,' he said, putting his hand on his father's shoulder. 'I know this year will be a good year for your garden, Dad. I've already noticed that. Come and take a rest,' he said, taking his father to the bench, and let him sit, helping with putting aside his crutch.

'You know, *Baba*, you've told me this story a hundred times. And I know it. I have lived it myself, haven't I? So, please stop complaining and enjoy your beautiful garden. I've got some work to do.' He kissed his father's cheek and rushed out to the street. At the gate, he turned his head and shouted, 'I will be late tonight, Dad. Don't wait for me. Have your dinner.'

Outside the house, he got on his bike and rode towards Serchinar, a picnic area on the outskirts of the city.

2

Riding through the alleyways of the old neighbourhoods in the city centre, the Photographer was certain he was about to embark on a prosperous future. And the fast-turning wheels of his bicycle were steadfastly taking him there. For Serchinar was going to be the starting point of his new endeavour. He was going to work for himself as a street photographer and build up a business of his own. He had all the right to be optimistic about it, just as many others were about their future, ever since they revolted against the regime over a year ago. It would not change so much in his father's life anyway, except that it might make him happier that his son was becoming somebody. As for the Photographer himself, he would then be a responsible man who was thinking about his future instead of being a sidekick who spent his petty wage solely on beer and cigarettes with the lads. His father never understood what their aim in life was except to play the artist. 'But we're only young, Dad. We want to have fun,' the Photographer would say to end the long discussions with his father, any time he would try to give his son a lesson in life matters.

A responsible man who thinks about his future. He thought about his father's phrase, contemplating the word 'future' in his mind. He smiled. Is this how growing up feels? But his smile was gradually replaced by a frown as a sense of guilt began to emerge. If he only was a bit nicer to his father. But it was difficult to be reminded of an event over and over again when you've lived every bit of it yourself. The black rain his father complained about every time he was in the garden, which was every day, hadn't only destroyed his father's precious trees and affected the environment of the whole region, it was also symbolic of the end of an era; a black curtain closing on a tragic scene in a theatre, to be followed by a more promising one. This is how the Photographer saw it, hoping that it was not just wishful thinking.

It had rained crude oil. An ominous black substance poured down from the sky the whole morning of that late winter day, creating surreal scenes, which the Photographer would never forget. Pedalling slower, he remembered how his late mother woke everyone in the house, screaming that it was Doomsday. The rattling rain on the windows of the bedroom had awoken her in the early morning. She had left her bed, gone to the bathroom, and taken *dastnwezh,* ablutions – the ritual washing before prayer. After praying, she had gone to the kitchen to make tea for breakfast. While pouring water into the kettle, she had noticed through the window behind the sink a strange reflection on the puddles in the courtyard and had looked outside, only to be shocked by the black rain.

'Go to the window and watch... Watch what's happening! It's Doomsday... It's Doomsday!' she was yelling, running through the house, room by room, waking up all occupants: her husband; her son, the Photographer; her other newly married son and his wife, who were waiting for their own house in a new suburb to be finished, as the construction work had been halted due to the winter and the war; and her eldest son, who for the past few weeks had had to sleep in the living room with his wife and two daughters because he no longer could afford to heat his own house.

The Photographer was now cycling on the pavement, in the opposite direction of the traffic of the busy Mawlawi Street, pedalling carefully through the crowd. But the memories were overwhelming. He remembered how a few weeks before the black rain, late in the evening, his eldest brother had appeared at the door with his family, put down two large bags in the courtyard and said, '*Baba,* I can't cope anymore. I have not even enough money to buy a single tin of kerosene. I thought we could...'

The Father would interrupt him, grabbing one of the bags and nodding to his son the Photographer to pick up the other bag, saying, 'Come in, son. You're most welcome! We're going to keep our heads together and see how we'll manage. Everything is going to be all right.' He would then put his hand on his eldest son's back, leading him in. 'Everything is going to be all right, *kurm.*'

8

The little girls would run into the arms of their grandmother, and the wife would greet everyone with an embarrassed grin. The family would then go inside quickly as it was freezing, and the clouds had become thicker, threatening heavy rain.

The Photographer and his middle brother, the newlywed, had already been hiding in the house for about six months. They barely went out, except sometimes at night or whenever they could arrange false papers such as well-forged military leave permits for a couple of days. The Photographer had just finished school so had not yet appeared for military service, despite the conscription rules and a recent general emergency call for anyone who could carry a gun. The middle brother had deserted shortly after the war began with the invasion of the southern neighbouring country, Kuwait.

The long-standing dictator had thought that invading a small oil-rich neighbour would help him boost his immense popularity in the Arab world – as from the Levant to the Maghreb millions of people saw him as the saviour of the Arab nation. Only two years before that, the country had come out of an eight-year-long war with another neighbour, Iran. But the dictator was already threatening other countries, ignoring warnings of world powers. He was even bluffing that he would free the Palestinians from the Israeli occupation; had hosted thousands of Palestinians in the country and was trying to bully Israel, claiming he had mastered the production of nuclear warheads. But he took the world by surprise, invading Kuwait one day overnight.

Like many other Kurdish men, the Photographer and his middle brother refused to go to the frontline. Except for those who served in military bases inside the cities, as the Photographer's eldest brother had done, most Kurdish men who were sent to the front had either deserted and hidden in the cities and small towns or they had joined the *peshmerga*, the Kurdish guerrillas stationed in the mountains and remote villages, who had already been fighting the regime for nearly two decades.

The Photographer and his middle brother had made a hiding place in the pantry room behind the many food containers, casks, and barrels, separated by a false wall, so they could hide whenever there was a raid or mass search for deserters. Female neighbours would warn them when they noticed any soldiers, police or suspicious security members in civilian clothing in the neighbourhood, for any deserter who was caught would be executed in front of their own house, and their family would be forced to pay the government for the price of the bullets.

Day by day, the Photographer would notice how the sacks of grain, rice, beans, and other dry food in the pantry diminished without being replenished. And since his eldest brother's family had moved in, he'd noticed that meals had become smaller and smaller, with only plain bread and sweet tea for breakfast. After a few days, even the tea became less and less sweet. He would see the same hunger in the faces of the whole family. Even the two little girls understood that food had become scarce, and you could not expect any more than your ration, and certainly no sweets.

In the evenings, they would hear on the radio how the war was developing, mostly from Arabic language international broadcasts such as the Voice of America or BBC Arabic. The country's state-owned radio and television would only yell about victories that did not occur. The regime's calculations were apparently wrong: an international allied force had gathered to rescue Kuwait. The small country was an important crude oil supplier to western countries. As bombs were falling over the cities and hundreds of thousands of Iraqi troops were lethally hit in the southern desert by scary science-fiction-like aircraft and heavy artillery never seen before, the President ordered the retreating army to set fire to the oilfields of the neighbouring country. Soon, dark clouds covered the region around the Persian Gulf, causing the black rain that destroyed vast swathes of agricultural fields that were intended for cultivation in the coming spring.

Life became harder and harder in the dark rooms, lit only for a couple of hours in the evening by a single candle; batteries were worth spending your last pennies on. And that had indeed happened to them one evening. The radio stopped working. So, just before the shops closed, the Photographer risked his life to go to buy batteries. He had also surprised his nieces with two lollipops. The news that came out of the refreshed radio, as they gathered around it, came over them as salvation: Kuwait was freed by the allies, and their own country defeated.

After this, most of the news became about black rain that was caused by the burning oilfields. It had even reached the Indian Ocean and parts of India. In less than a week's time, the clouds had also come to the Kurdish North and started to rain oil there too; a sticky tar that was not easy to remove, especially from the soil that had to wait for more and more rain in the coming months to wash it away.

People tried everything to remove the tar from the tiles in their courtyards, the outside walls of their houses and the trees in their gardens. As if they were cleaning off a gloomy past. For a whole week, the Photographer's father would only do one thing: spray the trees with water that itself had become scarce. He would then scrub the tree trunks and branches with a sponge, especially his three most beloved trees: the Maltese plum and two figs; one of them a black fig and the other a so-called "seven-season" that would fruit throughout the spring until the end of autumn. His sons would beg him to stop this madness and leave the trees to be washed off by cleaner rain that should come as Spring was approaching. The persistence of their father, however, and the sight of their mother scouring the walls and the concrete of the courtyard with soap and hot water would push them to join their parents, followed by the two daughters-in-law, then by the little girls. After a week, the garden and the façade of the house were shining.

The effect of the black rain would deepen the emerging poverty, but people soon forgot about it. Other major issues preoccupied them. Mass uprisings had enflamed the country. Encouraged by the weakened army, people took up arms. First in the Shiite South. Then in the central provinces and in the largest Shiite neighbourhood of the capital Baghdad. Lastly in the North. By this point, the news hardly came through at all, as no international media were allowed into the country, and the regime had disrupted all radio broadcasts.

In March, just before the spring started, the Kurds revolted too. Although it was the most crucial moment in his nation's history, the excessive use of violence he witnessed during the short period of the uprising, for the first time in his life, made the Photographer as depressed as he was cynical. It was different to hear about it on the radio than to go through it himself. He had taken part in the uprising, as most people did, though there was nothing for him to do but to watch the locals slaughter the regime's men and women. Most of the government buildings and poorly guarded institutions fell into hands of the people. Police left their offices and went home. Even after bombarding the city at random from the government's many fortified bases, the hundreds of security members in the city's main office, a long-time feared bastion, were only able to resist for about three days.

As the merciless presidential guard and the security forces cracked down on the revolting people and crushed their uprising in the southern and central provinces, the troops were deployed towards the North. The Kurds fled in millions to neighbouring countries, the Photographer and his family included. The mass exodus forced the international community to declare large parts of the Kurdish region a no-fly zone to protect them from further attacks. Kurdish political parties reached a peace agreement with the central government and the Kurdish people returned home. After a few weeks, they revolted again and could this time finally free large swathes of the land they claimed as their own. They managed to prevent the regime from returning.

The loss was huge for his family; the Photographer came back home only with his disabled father after losing his mother, his two brothers and their wives, and his two nieces.

The crystal teardrops in his eyes now blurred his sight, and as he pedalled faster and faster through the town, passing rows of houses on both sides, his memories faded.

3

When he arrived at Serchinar, the Photographer chained his bike to the railing of one of the tea gardens and started to walk about. His camera dangling from his neck, he wandered by the lake for almost an hour, among the orchards and the many bars and teahouses. But he was too shy to ask anybody if they would want to record their day with a photo. There was a big difference between being asked by customers in a studio for a photo and trying to tempt them on the street to be photographed. He was thinking about the right way to approach people when five drunken young men suddenly blocked his way and asked him to take a group photograph of them.

Trying to hide his nervousness, the Photographer found a suitable background and the right angle to make sure that the sunlight was not behind his subjects and asked them to stand in a line and pose for the camera. The guys were too drunk to be able to stand straight, each trying to hold hands with the person next to him, while the two at the ends of the line put their arms around the shoulder of the friend beside them. The Photographer clicked the button and quickly pulled out a square piece of dark grey cardboard covered with a shiny black paper on one side. The guys started laughing.

'What the hell is he doing?' said one of the young men.

'Ah, shut up. Just pose and let him do his job,' said another. 'Oh hold… Hold my arm, little shit… Oh, I think I'm going to vomit.'

'Just hold a second, please,' the photographer pleaded and clicked once more, pulled out another square piece of cardboard, and repeated the process rapidly three more times. Then, while the young men were still trying to form a straight line, laughing, falling on the ground and standing up again, clutching at one of their friends' arms, the Photographer shook his bits of card for half a minute. He would raise one corner of the cover and have a quick look at the picture to check if it was well developed, then shake it again for few extra seconds before tearing off the black covers from the surface of the cardboards.

When the guys noticed that the Photographer had finished shooting, one of them let go of his friend's hand and came to him to ask when and where they should go to pick up their photos. The Photographer gave him five developed photos and said, 'Here and right now. I hope you like them.'

Looking at the pictures quickly one by one, surprised and amazed, the man started laughing and ran back to his friends, swaying, holding the pictures in the air above his head, shouting to them, 'Watch, watch! Oh my God, how shameful we look... Look at you.'

Not believing that their pictures were there right away, his friends attacked him and ripped the photos out of his hand. They started fighting about who would get which one and who was better in which photo.

The Photographer was looking at them amused. It was wonderful to see that these guys liked his pictures. But would they pay him? Did they even have enough money? They seemed like they had drunk themselves to their last pennies.

One of them came to him and asked, 'How much do we owe you for the photos, my friend?'

'Half a dinar per photo,' said the Photographer, hesitating, not knowing if he had asked the right price.

'Ah, come on! Others take only a quarter dinar,' shouted one of the guys in a drunken tone.

'They even do it for two hundred *fils*, man!' said another one, raising his voice aggressively.

The Photographer was looking at them, calculating the seriousness of the situation, when the guy who first saw the pictures stepped in and said, 'Hey, hey, come on guys. Put your hands in your pockets. Can't you see how amazing it is to get your photo back right away? These are different. These are instant photos. Of course they're worth more.' Then he collected the money and gave it to the Photographer, thanking him for his patience. 'Go, enjoy it man! It was a bit... too expensive. But go, enj... Go enjoy... it, man. Go enjoy it,' he slurred.

As the Photographer put the money in his pocket and walked away, the guy called him back, put his hand on his shoulder and said, 'For...

for... forgive us... for being... for being... rude. They're drunk, you know!'

The Photographer said that he didn't mind and shook hands with him. As he was about to leave, the guy lost his balance and fell on the ground. The Photographer helped him get to his feet and handed him over to his friends who all hurried to the rescue, staggering, swaying, and laughing at him.

Roaming around for a few hours more, the Photographer took as many as thirty-four photos of people who were impressed that they got their pictures back straight away without waiting a few days as they would have to with the other street photographers who would have given them a receipt for a studio to go to pick up their pictures – sometimes only to hear that, unfortunately, their photos hadn't come out well.

It was the anniversary of the uprising. The day had been declared a public holiday, and by noon most of the shops in the city had already started closing. The streets had become full of people dressed in traditional Kurdish clothes, who walked in groups through the city, danced the Kurdish *shayee* in the squares or went for picnics.

The photographer looked round. Just a little bit over a year ago it would not be possible for him to walk around with a camera dangling from his neck without being summoned by a security agent who would interrogate and request for him to show his permit. And look at these people now: happiness radiating from them, as if none of the horrible things in the past had happened. Or were they also in doubt, as the photographer was, not believing they were now free from the dungeon their former president had created for them? Only a year ago these people were being liberated from a dictator who held them for so long in the grip of his regime that all paths to a normal life were closed. Besides the two wars that spanned an entire decade, they had also survived two decades of a bloody, terrifying conflict between the Kurdish *peshmerga* and the central government. They had been shocked by the mass murder of the rural population and the destruction of almost the entire countryside. They had experienced arrests, torture and displacement. All this had robbed a large part of two generations of their life and stolen the best years from the younger generation, the Photographer being among them.

He could see with what delight people were approaching one another, making their way through the crowd, singing, dancing, jumping in the air and shouting. The people were still caught up in the euphoria of the uprising, and they had every reason to be happy, didn't they? They were allowed again to go out in the evenings and hang out in the streets until late in the night. Everyone seized the opportunity, particularly frustrated young men who no longer had to worry about war or the enforcement of army service. They were to be found in pairs or in groups of three, four or more on every corner of the city; in the many fields and hills on the way to the mountains; and especially in the recreation area of Serchinar, one of the most beloved leisure places of the city.

The young men went to drink and tell each other about their failed romances or the disappointments of their one-sided loves. They talked about the heartlessness of women and young girls who dressed up, wore heavy makeup, and strolled through the streets without even a glance at all those frustrated men. It was as if there were clean polished glass surrounding each of these women; you couldn't see it, but it was there. A glass fence that only those men who dared to approach them would encounter. And to work out all these frustrations, the men went to the outskirts of the town to drink in groups.

It was mainly these men who asked the Photographer to capture them hugging; to record their eternal friendships. Some wanted him to take their photos while they were jumping in the lake with their clothes on or when they gave one of their friends a kick in the bum. He had to try to show in the picture how much the kick would hurt. It had to be an unforgettable kick. They asked him to sit in a tree and shoot them from there while they lifted their glasses towards the sky, clinking them together in a toast. He had to take the picture just as the drops of *arak* or beer were splashing out of their glasses, like they saw in spaghetti Westerns.

After some hours walking around, he felt tired and disappointed by how people treated a street photographer. His excitement of the morning, when he had just bought the camera and started shooting on the street, thinking about the prestige of registering people's lives and their intimate moments, was gradually taken over by a rancorous feeling towards the people he was shooting.

He sat on the railing around the tea garden, to which he had chained his bike, and watched how the area became more and more crowded. He saw full buses come one after another, halting at the last stop on the Serchinar main road. He watched groups of people of various ages, wearing colourful, mostly Kurdish clothes, getting off the buses and out of all other kinds of vehicles that parked at the roadsides. They would then walk into the recreation areas around the lake.

Oh, wasn't that his boss – or rather his ex-boss – making his way amongst the crowd towards the orchards? It was indeed him, holding his youngest son's hand. His wife and older son behind them. All well-dressed. Each held a bag full of food and drinks or rugs and barbeque stuff. The ex-boss carried a thermos box, which must contain ice and drinks.

When the family was closer, some meters away from the railing on which the Photographer sat, the ex-boss caught his gaze and frowned immediately. The Photographer kept staring at him triumphantly, trying not to blink. The ex-boss looked at the Polaroid camera in his ex-apprentice's lap and frowned further. When his younger son saw the Photographer, apparently not knowing that he by now was his father's former assistant, he raised his free arm and wanted to tell the rest of the family about him. But his father pulled at him and quick-ened his steps.

The Photographer looked at his Polaroid that rested on his lab, then stood up and started walking around again, staring at the people with an enquiring look of: 'Would you like me to take a picture of you?'

The teahouses and casinos around Serchinar lake were crowded with families drinking tea and cola and eating ice cream, baklava and other sweets. They were lazing about, cracking pistachios, sunflower- and pumpkin seeds. Children were screaming, running around, playing on the few swings, seesaws and slides. In the many bars, hundreds of men sat to drink beer and *Arak*. Many others, especially the young men, just bought their alcohol from one of the kiosks and sat to drink it around the lake, in the bushes at the foot of the Serchinar hill, where the residential area was. Some would walk further into the trees that stood on both sides of the Qilyasan stream.

By the end of the afternoon, he had used all his stock of Polaroid films, and his pockets were full of money. Maybe it was the start of a prosperous life. It was strange that most of his customers were happy to pay whatever he asked just because they could have the photos in their hands right away. It was the magic of recording the moments that enchanted his customers. They would look at their pictures with amazement, comment about it and ask the Photographer to take another from a different angle. It seemed that people felt happier about their life when they could look at it from a distance, on the surface of a piece of paper. Now he was enjoying his job even more.

He thought he should try to find a place in one of the bars to crown his enjoyment of the day with a drink. The smell of *arak* now dominated his thoughts: a recognizable odour that excited and invited him to drink. It was his favourite drink as it was for many of his countrymen; the most famous strong drink in the whole region. Everything in Serchinar, even the trees it seemed, emanated that irresistible fragrance, with the sharp scent of aniseed. As he looked at the men, indifferent to what was happening around them in a rapidly changing society, he envied them for their laid-back approach. At the same time, he blamed them for their apathy and for letting things go in an undesirable direction.

One thing prevented him from joining the other men in the teahouses and bars, and that was their moral code that permitted them to drink and smoke while forbidding their wives, daughters and sisters to do so. Even in the family lounges, where some hours ago he had been allowed to enter as a Photographer, the men were drinking and smoking, talking and laughing hard, making erotic jokes or commenting on the breasts and buttocks of the women on other tables. Meanwhile, the women at their own tables, even the small girls, had to remain modest and lower their voices so as not to laugh, but to be happy drinking their soft drinks and cracking seeds.

Actually, he would enjoy his *arak* more alone than amid a crowd of men. On his own, he would be just fine. Other men around him would strengthen feeling the absence of a female companion even more. If he had a girlfriend, he could bring her here to drink together, challenging all the others. What about his neighbour? She could be a perfect companion, as she was open-minded and so much different from so many other people. Maybe he should try. He smiled, pondering about the idea.

He walked to a kiosk and bought a quart bottle of *arak* and asked the shopkeeper for a plastic cup and some ice cubes. He walked down through the willows and *chinar* trees to the edges of the Qilyasan stream and sat under a large tree. Lighting a cigarette, he began to drink and unwind.

His exhaustion, after all that had happened that day, and a consequent sense of indignation had left him with a feeling of humiliation from his new job as a roving photographer. With each sip of *arak* and puff of the cigarette, he looked at his camera and thought about the sense and nonsense of his work. The longer he thought about it, the more he lost the enthusiasm and determination of the past few hours. So much so that he now began to hate the camera, to which he was starting to get attached. He stared again at his camera and sighed. He then looked at the clear water in the creek in front of him; how confidently, unceasingly it flowed over the gravel and sand, and how all the sticks, tins, bottles, caps and lids under the transparent surface of the water sparkled, half-immersed in the sand, left behind in an eternal silence, waiting for the mercy of a stronger flow to banish them mercilessly away.

As his eyes roamed across the scenery, he remembered the photo he had snatched of his neighbour this morning. He smiled and took the last puff from his cigarette and stubbed it out in the sand beside him. He took a sip from the *arak*, savoured it in his mouth, and as he gulped it down, feeling its warmth through his throat and then in his stomach, he took the photo out of his pocket and stared at it for some time.

Wasn't it strange that he was just realising that he had a special kind of affection towards this girl, without ever having considered it? He always felt comfortable and cherished in her presence but had never tried to go a step further in his feelings for her. Wasn't she actually the only person he wanted to be with all the time?

He took another sip, lit another cigarette, and decided to put aside his gloom and no longer think of his frustrations. He had a wonderful person in his life, no matter what the relationship was. Maybe he should look at the events of this morning from a different perspective. To lose his job was for him a first step towards liberation from the bonds of a society from which he was beginning to feel alienated.

He reached out his hand, grabbed his camera and laid it on his lap. This camera could in fact provide him with the distance he needed to protect himself from his environment; a society in which he, as a young man, felt unwanted. The political changes happened so rapidly that people had lost sight of what was happening, especially the youth. This was the source of his malaise and that of so many other people of his generation. Politicians and government officials, of whom the greatest majority was until a year ago nationalist partisans struggling for the liberty of the whole Kurdish nation, had now become greedy power hunters, seeking control of all lucrative businesses and projects. As a young man, he was forced to realise that he had nothing to do or to say. He kissed the camera and put it back on his lap.

For the Photographer, Qilyasan was an other-worldly place in the city, where he came often to run away from the daily lives of other people who, to him, looked as if they came from another planet. He could not bear the way they thought about life and themselves and their relationships. Although, in fact, it was he who seemed to them as if he were not of this world. He smiled at the thought of it. But he immediately realised that it was not easy to live in such a society if one was not like the others. However, when he came among the trees of Qilyasan, he could be completely himself. He could connect with his inner world and forget the others with all their ideas, religious thoughts and political beliefs. The hissing wind through the trees, the burbling stream and the smell of the *arak* strengthened that feeling so much that he forgot himself and became more and more a part of the world around him – a part of the trees, the river, and the gravel and sand under the clear water.

Every time he got drunk, he would undress and lie in the shallow water, gazing at the blue sky that changed colours fluidly in the early evening: first to a pale orange that would slightly penetrate the blue, then to a darker colour between brown and navy blue, before gradually fading into black. Then glittering stars would appear, followed by the muffled sound of the birds getting quieter little by little until a heavy silence dominated the orchards. At times, it was so still he would think that he could hear, through the darkness and the tempered flow of the stream, the stars singing.

But that evening, when it gradually became dark, and he peered into the stream, waiting for it to invite him in, he was too tired, too sleepy and too drunk. He leant against the tree, stretched his legs and propped his feet on its huge roots, which were jutting out of the ground and stretching towards the water. Through his tired eyes, he saw many plastic bags, soggy papers, rags and empty cigarette packs stranded between the roots. His eyes fluttered at the gravel and sand that sparkled under the orange light of the sunset at the bottom of the river, bewitched into a deep sleep.

As he startled by a strange noise that he couldn't quite place, the young Photographer felt a severe hangover swarm around his head like a handful of iron filings. Did the sound come from outside or did it echo inside his skull? He rubbed his eyes and saw in the water before him a strange creature crouching between the huge roots of the tree. He rubbed his eyes even harder and saw that it was a naked young man trying to detach himself from the roots. As he managed to release himself, wrapped in weeds and algae, the creature crept in the water to the other side of the creek.

A new eddy of pain whirled through the Photographer's head. He closed his eyes and screamed. He then pressed his palms to his temples in order to soothe the pain. When he opened his eyes again, the naked man had disappeared. Holly… What was that? Should he believe his own eyes or was that only a vision? No, he was sure of what he just saw. He grabbed his camera, hung it around his neck, gathered his strength and stood up. The photo of Neighbour-Girl fell from his lap. He picked it up and put it quickly back in his pocket. Reeling, he stepped into the water and floundered to the other side of the creek. He ran, drunkenly, in all directions but didn't find a trace of anyone in the dusk.

It was getting darker when he returned to the streamside and saw in the water, a little further away, the naked man trying to get out of the stream and reach the bushes. He was carrying a large wooden cross on his shoulders, which in the dark could have been a tree stump or a very big leaf. The young Photographer opened his eyes wide to get a better view. Quickly, he raised his camera and tried to take a picture; a picture that could become a masterpiece; a picture of the crucified Jesus, or a new Jesus with a big leaf on his shoulders.

As fast as he pressed the button, he remembered that there was no film in the camera. Immediately, without thinking about it, he ran into the water towards the naked man. Just a few metres away from the fading silhouette, which now seemed more like a tree than a man, his foot slipped on a rock, and he fell forward. First his camera and then his face sank into the water. At the exact moment that his eyes reached the surface of the water, he saw the silhouette disappear between the birch trees in the small grove.

4

For the last few days, everyone in the village of Qilyasan had been talking about a strange tree that would suddenly disappear with the sunrise, only to be found again at dusk, just before darkness would fall, here and there, each time in a different spot. Sometimes it was discovered to be on the edge of the stream, with its roots torn from the ground but without its fresh spring leaves withered or faded at all. At other times it was replanted in one of the orchards between the other trees, horrifying the farmers. At first, they thought that someone might have pulled it out of the ground, in jest or malice, and carelessly thrown it down. Then, it seemed that they had taken the trouble to replant it again.

One evening, the farmers found it in one of the orchards, neatly replanted. They surrounded it with barbed wire and paid one of the villagers to guard it overnight.

Early the next morning, with the first light, when the village imam called for the morning prayer, in a sleepy voice through the single speaker of the village mosque, the guardian of the tree ran back to the village uphill, screaming around, confused. The villagers thought he'd gone crazy. They laughed at him when he claimed that he had seen the tree suddenly, with the first morning light, turn into a naked man and in the blink of an eye leap over the barbed wire fence and disappear between the other trees. They were sure he was lying and because he was such a lazy man, they guessed he was asleep and hadn't seen the trespasser tear the tree again from the ground. But even after they had spent the whole day searching in and around their orchards and alongside the river, the Qilyasanies could find no trace of the tree.

As soon as the Photographer heard about the incident, he bought a second-hand camera, got on his bike and rode to the village. He was one of the few people in town who used a bicycle as a means of transport. Cycling in this city was traditionally seen as something for ne'er-do-wells, street punks and paedophiles. Only during childhood, until the age of eight or nine, was it normal to ride a bicycle: a three-wheeler, mostly during school holidays. Once you learned to ride a two-wheeled bike, you entered the world of evil knife-fighters. Only teenagers who couldn't be controlled by their parents, who skived off school or left education at an early age and carried a knuckle-duster or a flick knife in the pockets of their *sharwal*, the wide Kurdish trousers, hung around the bicycle shops or rented bikes and motorcycles to drive around the city.

Since his childhood, the Photographer had loved to cycle. But that was one of his father's many taboos. 'If you learn how to ride a bike,' he would say, 'you'll quickly learn how to smoke too.' As a young boy, the Photographer could not understand the relationship between cycling and smoking or why his father and most residents of the city hated bicycles so much. When he was about sixteen, he secretly learned to smoke, but not only was he still unable to ride a bike, he had not even had the opportunity to try it. In the meantime, he had understood that the particular aversion of the inhabitants of the city towards cycling was because the most famous – and for years the only – bike shop in town was owned by a notorious paedophile. And when he eventually learned to ride, he also learned that, unlike in other parts of the country, cycling was impractical because of the many hills in and around the town.

Cycling offered the Photographer the chance to go to the most attractive places around the city to paint landscapes. Now that photography had become his passion, it came in even more handy. And handier it had become with his new obsession to find the Naked Young Man, or the Tree for that matter, so to take a picture of him. But when he returned to the village, however hard he searched, in Qilyasan and the surrounding groves and orchards, until late into the night, he found no trace of the exotic tree or the naked man.

Only when he cycled back to Qilyasan early the next morning did he finally find, at the very spot where the villagers had surrounded the Tree with barbed wire, a small clue: an unusual green leaf that did not look like any of the leaves from the neighbouring trees. He quickly picked it up and put it in the top pocket of his shirt. But he was still desperate to find real proof that would convince people of his story. That single leaf would not be enough; it could give his friends more reason to laugh at him or even label him as crazy, as people had done with the man from Qilyasan who had been left to guard the Tree.

Try as he might, the Photographer was not allowed to meet that guard. An old man even advised him to leave and never come back again because the family of the guard, who since the morning of the incident seemed to be possessed by the devil and had been locked in a room, might hold the young Photographer responsible for his predicament.

'Just go away, son. You have no business here. Leave us the hell alone,' the man said, surprising the Photographer with his vehemence.

'Who cares about us? Do you know who the inhabitants of this village are and what they have gone through? Is it not enough that we are living this damn miserable life? And now you also want to drive us all crazy?'

The man then put his wrinkled hand on the Photographer's shoulder and continued, 'Go away, *mamme gyan*, we don't want to vote for anyone.'

The young Photographer noticed that the old man's eyes were fixed on the pocket of his shirt. He looked down and saw the green leaf sticking out of his pocket and understood what the man meant by his last comment. Green was the colour of one of the political parties participating in the upcoming election.

On his way back to town from Qilyasan, a small boy waved for the Photographer to stop. He got off his bike and listened to the boy, who asked him if he was the man who was looking for a naked tree. The Photographer squatted down and looked the boy in his eyes.

'Be careful,' he warned the boy. 'You shouldn't be talking about that. But tell me, did you see something?'

The boy told him that, although nobody wanted to believe him, when he was playing in front of his house the previous night, he had glimpsed, in a sudden flash, a tree running swiftly through the alley. Then, he took the Photographer to where he had seen this apparition. But despite scouring the little street, the Photographer could not find any trace of the Tree. Nevertheless, he decided not to despair. He felt that looking for the tree-man was like looking for truth. You know that you might not find it, but you should never stop searching, as he remembered a philosopher had once said.

5

The Tree had left Qilyasan and headed towards the city. After three days crawling through the night and hiding in little alleyways and half-built houses during the day, it reached the Rizgary neighbourhood early one morning. In the light of dawn, it could see a large building on the other side of the street, decorated with colourful flags, blinking little lights and large faces on huge boards on the walls. Loud music and song spread far and wide into the distance. Gradually, people came and lined up in front of the gate, waiting to be let inside.

With the first morning light, the Tree transformed again into a naked man. He immediately crept back behind the remaining walls of a demolished building and hid under the broad, long leaf that enfolded him. From behind the stone slabs, the Naked Young Man saw the line of people getting longer and longer. A moment later, the gate opened, and the people began to go inside, a few at a time, only to come out again a couple of minutes later. They showed each other their forefingers, which were stained with purple ink right up to the middle knuckle. After some hours, they started to dance and sing in separate groups, waving coloured handkerchiefs in the air.

Suddenly, two men entered the abandoned building in which the Naked Young Man was hiding, and crouched behind a wall opposite him. Without noticing him, one of the men removed the lid of a tin that was full of soap scum. He added some white powder to the scum and stirred it with a stick. Then, they both started to scour their forefingers with a coarse rag, soaked with the foam they had just made, trying to wash away the purple ink. When their fingers were completely clean, the two men quickly left the ruined building.

For the rest of the day, the Naked Young Man slept amidst the ruins. He was woken late in the afternoon by the voice of one of the men who had come in the morning with the tin of soap. From under his leaf, Naked Young Man saw that the man was this time accompanied by a different guy, and again they quickly began to clean their inky forefingers. When they were done, the man with the soap said to his companion, 'Don't worry, no one will notice it. This is my fourth time today. But be careful, don't go back to this polling station. There is another one in the Ashty district. Hurry up. You still can make it. You've got time!'

The last orange rays of the setting sun had disappeared when the second man hid the soap tin and left. Not much later, the Tree stood up in the dark. The early evening breeze stroked its leaves. Carefully and quietly, it slipped away from the dilapidated building and stood at the side of the street. It stayed for a while there, watching the crowds of people: women, men and children who passed along the street on foot or in cars. They waved their different coloured banners and flags – yellow, green, red, and blue – shouting and singing. Now and then, they would fire shots into the air with their guns.

That night, and a few other nights after that, the Tree wandered through the streets in the neighbourhoods of Rizgary and Sheikh Muheddin. In the daytime, as a man, naked but wrapped with a green leaf, he would look for places to hide or cautiously observe with bewilderment the unfamiliar daily lives of the people. Confused as he was by their doings, he knew that he looked like them, but he felt no affiliation with them. Nor did he dare to engage with them.

Occasionally, people would spot the Naked Young Man walking through the backstreets, making them angry and embarrassed. Children thought he was a crazy man who had tried to wrap himself in a leaf. They were afraid and would quickly run home or throw stones at him. Or they would run after him and try to catch up with him and, if they succeeded, they would grab the tail of his long leaf from behind and pull on it. And he, with his lightning-fast movements and giant leaps could get away within seconds of being sighted. But while this had all become a naughty game for children, for their parents it was a source of resentment and discomfort. Parents tried to scare the young by saying that if that naked fellow caught them, he would bite them and tear pieces of flesh from their arms or leg. They might end up dead. If the adults got the chance to see him themselves, they would redden with anger or shame. The men would throw a reproachful glance at their wives, daughters or sisters when they gazed at him from their doorsteps and would order the women to go inside at once.

Within weeks, the Naked Young Man had been seen in so many places in town and there were so many different stories about that eccentric creature that nobody knew what to believe. Even those who had seen him began to doubt their own stories. What made people more suspicious of all these mysterious tales was that even people who hadn't seen him claimed they had spotted him in the street, strolling in the gardens or running on the flat rooves of their houses. But the arguments of those who denied his existence were much stronger than those of people who swore by everything they revered that they had seen him and were certain of his existence. The trouble for the last camp was that they themselves got confused and did not know whether they should believe their own eyes or listen to those who dismissed it as a fable. The encounters were so swift that in the end, they could not say with any conviction that they really had seen this naked creature. They would just say that they could swear they had seen him but admit that it could also have been a vision or hallucination. And people who believed in ghosts and *jinn* wondered whose restless soul it could be that was haunting the city. A small group of mystics had even gone so far as to declare that it was not only one ghost but that hundreds of awoken souls of the slaughtered men of the regime were now trying to terrify the city.

A few people however, mainly young people who had already started to claim different ways of life, defended the Naked Young Man. They themselves were wearing clothes that even a year ago would have been quite unacceptable. Although they also faced lots of rejection, the relative freedom that had emerged with the disappearance of the regime from the Kurdish region and the chaos it had created, made them more daring. Some even ventured to proclaim the right of nakedness and demanded that the Naked Young Man should be let alone. A friend of the Photographer, also a young man who had started writing about sexual freedom and had called for a sexual revolution in one of his pieces, even to the extent of reading it in public during a symposium, had published a column in one of the new daily papers to defend the nudity of the Naked Young Man. 'And by the way,' he had written, 'that young man is not completely naked. A large leaf covers his shame, doesn't it? Nobody sees his balls, do they? And isn't that what counts?'

6

'No,' shouted the *Khatib*, the chief imam of the city, through the speakers of the Grand Mosque in the centre of the city, during the Friday sermon. 'The problem is not only the fact that the boy is naked. And whether he is completely naked or half naked or a leaf covers his shame or not. All that doesn't make any difference. At the end of the day, he's not Adam who was thrown out of Paradise. He doesn't live in a jungle, does he? What counts is the influence of his illicit behaviour on our children and our youth, the implications of it for our future and our faith and the resulting decay of the community.'

Nobody could argue against the *Khatib*'s words except *kafirs*, infidels and pagans, as faithful people would say. For many of the residents of the city the sermons and statements of the *Khatib* were as important as *hadith*, the sayings of the prophet of Islam himself. For at least the *Khatib* was speaking in Kurdish and had translated many of the Arabic hadiths and verses of the Quran into their mother tongue. He also interpreted them for the people and tried to establish a link between those complicated verses and the problems and events of their daily lives.

However, the *Khatib* was not without enemies. Some of the funda- mentalist believers thought that simplifying religious matters was a big insult to the hadith and the Quranic verses. The power and influ- ence of the sacred texts were, they would say, in the mystery of those writings and in the very fact that the ordinary man could not under- stand them. They knew very well that the more enigmatic and myste- rious the religion remained, the more intimidating they themselves would be. Then, people would fall much more easily under their spell. If man reduces the words of God and his prophets to ordinary human language, those words will lose their magic and strength. It is that magical power of religion that makes people aware of their actions and behaviour. Man must constantly live in fear of God, otherwise he will turn his back on faith and religion.

Other believers said that it was precisely this demystification that brought people closer to the faith. If religion is simple and accessible, it has more application to daily life, and that strengthens the faith. For human beings remain human beings and always look out for their own benefit and self-interest. That is why God gave us the world in this beautiful form, full of lust and temptation, their argument ran. They thought that the extremists and fundamentalists were worried about their own religious and political position, not about the faith itself. They were afraid they would not be able to mobilize people for jihad and realise their plans and political agendas, all of which were the antithesis of the essence of faith.

The *Khatib* paid no attention to criticism. 'As long as those critics are themselves believers, let them think and say what they want,' he always replied to people who confronted him with those arguments. For him, the opinions of intellectuals were more important, especially those of the disbelievers and atheists among them – those who usually were hostile to religion and criticised faith or humiliated it, directly and indirectly. He referred to them in turn, during his Friday sermons; to their publications, their radio and television programmes, and to most of the debates that were taking place that week. Often, he would intervene in politics and political matters as well. That was one of the reasons many people went to the Grand Mosque in the centre of the city for the Friday prayers. Finding a place to pray in the Grad Mosque, even in the large courtyard, was for many a challenging undertaking.

Every Friday at noon, when the *Khatib* issued the call to prayer and began his acclaimed sermon in the large, well-lit hall, a huge crowd would gather in the wide square in front of the mosque and in the surrounding streets. His preaching rang through the speakers on top of the high minaret, over the whole bazaar, dominating all the din and clamour of the market, and echoing in the streets and alleys of the city centre. Buses, taxis and other cars quickly parked along the streets; shopkeepers pulled the iron shutters of their shops half-way down; fruit and vegetable vendors covered their carts with plastic sheeting, and all rushed to the mosque. Only a couple of shops remained open to receive those few customers who were hurrying to do some shopping at the last moment before they went home. Other than the noon prayer at a mosque, most people traditionally went home on Fridays to join their families for lunch. They usually held their feasts on Friday afternoon, particularly civil servants, for whom Friday was their day off. After about half an hour, silence dominated the bazaar and the entire city centre. People were praying.

The day the *Khatib* elaborated on his sermon about the Naked Young Man and the consequences of his behaviour for society, a large crowd gathered after prayers in the courtyard of the Mosque, around the *hauz*, the high round concrete basin in the middle of the quad, which was encircled by a low concrete wall on which the mosque-goers could sit, by the many taps surrounding the basin, to perform *dastnwezh*, the ritual ablution, washing their hands, arms, face and feet, before the prayer. Instead of going home for lunch or leaving the mosque to open their shops, they hung around in the courtyard to discuss the *Khatib's* sermon. So it was true: *Ahriman,* that devil, was real! He existed. And as the *Khatib's* fatwa, the religious ruling, pronounced, it was the duty of every believer to deliver him to the authorities if they managed to catch him. Some went further and said it was even *halal,* legitimate, to kill him. A few people called it a *jihad* and a religious mission. They interpreted the words of the *Khatib* as an indirect fatwa for *jihad,* a holy war against the Demon. But, of course, the *Khatib* could not openly express that because even the religious leaders couldn't open their mouths for fear of political backlash, the believers would conclude.

'For it is a democracy! Huh! Democracy! They have screwed us all with their democracy,' said an elderly man in a small group beside the basin.

A shopkeeper, who put his right foot on the edge of the low wall around the *hauz,* bending over, with his elbow on his thigh, observed the nagging man, while stroking his own jet-black moustache. He stared at the older man, scolding, 'Dear uncle, I think you're taking things the wrong way.'

The old man flung his hand over his shoulder in a sign of 'oh, never mind' before quickly walking away. He pushed through the large crowd that had surrounded the whirling Dervishes, the Sufi Muslim friars, blocking the gate of the mosque.

Another man patted the jet-black moustached shopkeeper on his shoulder and said, 'Let him go. It doesn't help. I know him very well. He is always negative about everything, and just whines.'

Suddenly, everyone looked back. The *Khatib*, accompanied by two other imams, came out of the prayer hall. He greeted a group of *hafiz*, blind Quran reciters, who sat in a row on the low concrete wall in front of the toilets, performing the *zikr*, reciting the names of God while they slid one by one the beads of their *tasbehs*, chaplets, between two fingers. Using their sticks, the blind reciters stood up simultaneously and answered the *Khatib*'s greeting in a chorus.

'Oh, please sit down, God be with you,' the *Khatib* said to them, motioning for them to "sit, please". But the blind reciters, missing his gesture, only sat down again when they heard the steps of the *Khatib* and his two companions disappear into the din of the crowd.

When they reached the crowd at the exit, people made way for the *Khatib* and the two imams. The Shopkeeper saw the *Khatib* shake his head, avoiding looking at the Dervishes who were whirling in a trance, their cheeks pierced by *zerg*, a large needle, with only a drop of blood seeping out of the wound onto their cheeks. Like most people, the Shopkeeper knew that to the *Khatib* Dervishes and Sufis were heretics. He passed them by, followed by the two imams, and left the Mosque, maybe to rush home and take his afternoon nap after having lunch and a strong black tea.

Just before the crowd closed the circle around the Dervishes, the men at the basin saw the three Dervishes spinning around, waving their swords in the air in a rhythmic motion. They turned their heads in circles, their long henna-dyed hair swaying in the air, and chanted loudly, 'Hay, hay, hay Allah… Hay, hay, hay Allah…'

The Shopkeeper said to the other men that he had to go take care of his business. 'I got a lot to do,' he said, and left with fast strides, elbowing himself through the crowd. Once outside, on the pavement, a row of old beggar women raised their hands, thrusting their money bowls at him, but the Shopkeeper hurried by without looking at them, heading towards his shop on Mahkama Street, right opposite the city's main court, just a few hundred meters from the Grand Mosque.

When he reached his shop, he pulled up the half-closed shutters and was about to enter when he stepped backwards and came out again. He pulled down the shutters once more, closed his shop, locked it with two large padlocks. His neighbouring shopkeeper watched from his store in amazement at how quickly he left his business. He must have seen in his glistening eyes that he was planning something. For it wasn't like him to close the shop so early on a Friday afternoon. The neighbour raised his eyebrows. But the Shopkeeper didn't respond. He took to the road again, walking quickly up the street. On the way, he tightened his *cummerbund,* the thick cloth belt around his hips, and stroked his black-dyed moustache. From that day on, the Shopkeeper belonged to the people who were searching for the Naked Young Man.

7

'Have you heard about the election results?' the Photographer's father asked him, when he came out of the house and into the front garden. The Father stood under one of the pomegranate trees, his crutch under his right armpit, pruning some overgrowing branches with an old pruner.

'Ah, leave it, Dad. It wouldn't change anything for you, would it?' said the Photographer, and sat on the weathered bench at the edge of the lawn, leant back, put his hands behind his head, and closed his eyes to enjoy the morning sun of the late spring day.

'They're going to share the seats equally and form a fifty-fifty parliament. Isn't that outrageous?' the Father said, sounding genuinely upset.

'Oh, who cares? I wouldn't, for sure,' the Photographer said, sitting upright, staring at his father.

'But you should care, my son,' said the Father without looking at him. 'It's your future. I'm going to die soon. I might not need to care. But you...' he turned to him. 'You know what? These two parties will fuck up the people, you'll see. They claim that they're democratic and so on, but they can't even accept each other's winning. Now, we'll never be able to know who really won.'

'Dad, please! I'm really not interested. I didn't even vote. Of course they will fuck us all up. They already did. Not only these two parties, but all of them.' He slouched again against the bench's back, and said in a sad voice, 'No one is decent. I don't trust any of them.' He leant forwards and stared at his father again. 'Tell me if there is anything left in the country. They have smuggled everything, even all the electricity cables, out to Iran. Dad, leave them—'

'You see?' the Father said, looking at him with wide open eyes. He laughed, while pointing towards him with the rusty pruner in his hand. 'You care too. Of course you care. It's great to be angry, my son. You should be. That's what I mean.'

'Dad, I'm not angry. I really don't give a damn who wins or loses. Let's not talk about this, okay? I would like to talk to you about something else.'

'Oh, wait, wait… Let me tell you something before I forget again,' the Father interrupted him, while continuing to trim the trees. 'Your boss came along yesterday afternoon. He wants you back.'

'He is no longer my boss, *baba gyan*,' said the Photographer, annoyed. 'But what did you tell him?'

'I tried to be polite. I said I'd talk to you and—'

'Dad…' the Photographer interrupted his father furiously. 'Why would you say that for heaven's sake? Didn't I ask you say that I'd never work for him again? I knew he would come. You see?'

'Wait, wait, son… Let me finish,' said the Father, waiving to him with the pruner, before leaning on his crutch. 'I said that you were very busy with other stuff and that you are now working for yourself. Are you actually? I haven't seen you with your camera lately.'

'Dad, I am… But now—'

'Wait… You know what he said? He said he would buy a poly camera or something.'

'A Polaroid.'

'Whatever!' said the Father, back up with the trimming. 'And he said it will all be as you wish.'

'Dad, forget it. I won't go back to him. But don't worry, I will handle it.' He bent over and put both his elbows on his knees, staring at his father who had just finished pruning the trees and put down the pruner. He was standing, leaning on his crutch, watching the trees that had started to fruit.

Staring at his father, the Photographer smiled as he recalled what his former boss had said about buying a Polaroid. The thing was that lack of efficient equipment was not the only issue in his studio. The main problem was the boss himself. The man had been in this business since childhood, shooting people's faces and developing their photographs in a dark room, but had only halfway through his life discovered that he had chosen the wrong profession because he just didn't have enough patience for the job.

But the Photographer was no longer mad at him. He rather felt pity for him, although a Polaroid camera would help his former boss a lot now that he had no apprentice. That morning though, when he was late, the boss had had the right to be angry. The poor man had had to welcome all those hurried customers on his own, ask them what kind of pictures and how many copies they needed, bring them quickly to the studio and then take their picture.

After having photographed a few customers in a row, the boss had had to lock himself in the darkroom, quickly pull the negatives out of the camera and submerge them in the developer liquid. Then, when the negative picture had appeared on the celluloid, he had to drag them between two of his fingers to get rid of any drops and dry them quickly with a hairdryer, then print them with the projector, then put the small square cards in the developer liquid again until the positive pictures appeared. Then, he had to put them in another liquid to fix them. After doing all of this on his own, he'd had to run out of the darkroom, drenched in sweat, give the printed pictures, still wet, to the customers who were waiting in the shop, take their money, bid them goodbye, and go through the process all over again on his own. And all because his apprentice was late. But also because of the very fact that he found it too expensive to buy a Polaroid camera with which they could take, within a few minutes, four or eight photos of each customer without them having to wait for long, sometimes even up to half an hour. It was all in vain, however, because this suggestion always fell on deaf ears.

The boss found his own cheaper solution a much smarter one. He had transformed his Swedish Hasselblad into a fast-operational camera. Originally, the camera worked with rolls of the so-called 120-film, a film roll with which he could take twelve square photos. But he cut the film in the darkroom into twelve loose squares and kept them in a separate box protected from light. Then, when he or his assistant had taken a picture of a client, they would put the negatives one by one in a template that the boss had made out of cardboard. After that, they would put the template with the negative in it into the camera. If they had to photograph a few customers in a row, they would take the negative rapidly out of the camera in the darkroom, put another negative in the template and put the shot negatives in a box to the left of the developer so as not to confuse them with the raw negatives. With the new negative in the camera, they would go back to the studio to take the picture of the next customer. Then, they would develop a couple of negatives at the same time and print them. When they were both in the shop, they would divide the tasks and everything would usually go well, like an assembly line. There were never any problems with the process; everything went very smoothly. Except for when one of them was on his own in the shop and had to help several customers at the same time, as had happened on that 'damn day', when the boss lost his assistant forever.

'So what did you want to say?' asked the Father, startling his son who was submerged in deep thought.

'What do you want me to say, Dad?' answered the Photographer, upset. 'I told you, I will not go back to him.'

'No, not that. You wanted to talk to me about something else, you said,' the Father replied, walking towards him on his crutch.

'Oh, right,' said the Photographer, making space for his father to sit beside him.

'Tell me, Son, is there anything I should be worried about?' the Father asked, after he sat, his amputated right leg dangling over the bench. He put his crutch between both legs, put both his hands on it and rested his head on his hands, looking at his son.

The Photographer stared at the lawn under his feet, waited a few more seconds. He then said, without looking at his father, 'Listen, Dad, you don't need to be worried, but I think I need to hide for some time. I mean, there is nothing serious, but—'

'Hiding? What hiding? What on earth do you mean?' the Father asked, more surprised than worried.

'*Baba*, I told you, nothing serious.' He then turned to his father, put his hand on his shoulder and continued, 'I don't know if you have heard about a walking tree or a naked guy causing trouble in the city—'

'It's not you, is it?' asked the Father, even more surprised, now looking right into his son's eyes.

'No! Of course not. What do you think, Dad?' said the Photographer quickly and pushed himself back a bit to lean against the arm of the bench. 'But apparently some people do think I am.'

The Father remained staring at him, mouth agape.

'It is not me, Dad. I assure you. But someone warned me that the police think I have something to do with it. They might be looking for me.'

The Father stood up, leaning on his crutch, and walked away again towards the trees, saying, 'This is ridiculous. If you haven't done anything, why then would you hide?'

'I haven't, Dad. But explain that to them.'

'Listen, Son. Just stay home. I will talk to them if they come.'

'Ah, come on, Dad. Even the *Asayish* is after me. You know how they are. I really don't want to get involved with them. Better to hide. Then they will forget me. It all looks just like a joke, anyway. I'm sure things will clear up soon.'

'But you make it worse, Son. If you hide, they will then think you have something to run from.'

Suddenly, there was bang on the front door. The Photographer jumped from the bench and ran through the courtyard towards the house. Then he came back quickly to his father, kissed him on his jaw and whispered, 'I'll run away via the roof. Just try to delay them as much as you can.'

He ran inside, looked through a window in the living room and saw his father walk slowly on his crutch towards the door, shouting, 'I'm coming... I'm coming.'

The banging continued until the Father opened the front gate.

The Photographer's former boss rushed inside and started begging him to let him see his son.

The Photographer cautiously opened the window ajar and stood behind the curtain.

'I'm sure he is hiding inside, sir. I Just saw his bicycle outside. Did you talk to him? I really need him. My whole business is in ruins,' said the Photographer's former boss, almost weeping.

'Come and sit, sir,' said the Father, leading him towards the garden bench.

The Photographer stepped back from the curtain and the window, and sat on the floor, sharpening his ears.

'Try to find someone else,' the Photographer heard his father saying. 'I talked to him. He really is resolute and will not come back to you. I know my son. When he says something, that's it. And by the way, he's found another job. I'm so sorry, sir.'

The Photographer crawled back to the window and raised his head above the window sill. He saw his former boss sitting on the bench with his back to the house. He was staring at his father in disbelief. Then he suddenly stood up, saying, 'It's really a shame.'

The Photographer retreated back again from the window, but could still see him walking towards the main door, leaving his father on the bench.

'It's more a pity for him. He lost such a nice, proper job. But never mind,' the Photographer's former boss said and opened the front gate. Just before he went out, he shouted, 'I'm sorry, sir, for bothering you. But your son will never become anything in his life. Such a jerk. Goodbye.'

Ten minutes later, as the Father sat on the bench looking at his beloved trees, the Photographer came out of the house with a bag on his shoulder and went directly to his father, hugged him and said, 'You don't really need to be worried, *Baba*. I'm sorry to leave you alone. But I'm sure you will be okay. The neighbours will help. I'll be in touch with you. Love you, Dad!'

His father only shook his head, tears beginning to fall from the corners of his eyes.

The Photographer walked slowly away, leaving his father behind in the middle of his garden. As he was out and closed the old wooden front gate, he leant back on it for a moment, before he walked down the road.

8

The *Khatib*'s last Friday speech obliged the Governor to make a move to arrest the Naked Young Man. The police and security guards had started searching for him, although they were not sure what they were looking for – a naked man or a tree that walked around in the city at night. The second option seemed to them not to be very appropriate, embarrassing even.

The city's Police Chief told the Governor on the phone that he really could not make his men believe that such a thing would even be possible. 'I mean, I'm sure many of them already believe in it, just as lots of other people do,' he said while doodling with a pen on a paper on his desk. 'But come on, such a thing is just... I mean—'

'Are you trying to explain to me that this is a myth? I mean do you really think that I would believe it?' The Governor laughed over the phone.

The Police Chief interrupted him, apologising that that was absolutely not his intention, but he wondered if he would consider whether there could be any scientific explanation possible for such a thing. 'I mean, we as the police have to take all options seriously, even when we are sure it's absolute nonsense. Ah, but... Oh, no, leave it... I mean, I really cannot convince any police officer...'

The Governor was still laughing in the background. 'Listen, the answer is no. I don't think there would be a scientific explanation for such a thing. Let's not ridicule ourselves. And no, I don't think you should take everything people say seriously. You know how superstitious our people are.'

Over many years, both men had built a noble reputation in the city. The Governor used to be one of the most famous secondary school teachers of physics who was dismissed from his job and imprisoned by the security services of the regime two years before the uprising for his political activities as an underground member of the Patriots, one of the main Kurdish political parties. He was released in a prisoner exchange deal between the central government and the newly formed local administration a few months after the uprising. Soon after that, he was rewarded with the post of the Governor. His rival, a member of the Democrats, had had to accept the post of the director of the security forces, the *Asayish*.

The Police Chief was one of few powerful government officials who had withstood the temptation of a prosperous life provided during the regime and all the pressure that was put on him to become an active member of the Baath party of the dictator – The country's sole official political party at the time. Although this gained him respect, many saw his clean hands as a problem. Especially criminal bosses, gangs, and former commanders of the security services and militia-like forces from the time of the regime, considered him as an obstacle in their way to ascending in the ranks of the new Kurdish political parties that had now taken over the power.

'But what about this Photographer guy?' the Police Chief asked the Governor, now with a more serious, self-confident tone. He left the receiver on his shoulder, right under his ear, and wrote down the word "Photographer" in a circle in his sketch plan he already had made on the paper before him.

'I'd rather leave that to you to decide,' said the Governor. 'But I'd like to remind you that we should treat people gently,' he added. 'Let's not spoil the party for them. They have just given us their votes. We should do things differently now, you know!'

'I like your softness, sir. But yeah, leave that matter to me. I don't think he has anything to do with this. There is only one thing: the Asayish Director is also after him.'

'What's the problem with that?'

The Police Chief dropped his pen on the paper, and slouched in his comfortable chair. 'It's actually him who's been trying to accuse this Photographer of all kinds of things. The rumour is that the Asayish Director is trying to get to this Photographer boy, because he has an eye on a girl that is in a relationship with the Photographer. This is how the gossip goes. But I'll try to get to the bottom of it. Of course, we—'

'I can imagine he would do anything to undermine my authority, and yours,' the Governor said. 'He doesn't understand that in a civilised world the police should handle these civil cases. But he—'

'That's exactly what I'm trying to explain, sir,' said the Police Chief. 'But the problem is we don't have the power he has. He's got his party behind him, but also the support of all the other parties.'

'Well, as long as you and I work together—'

'Don't worry, sir. I'd never let you down,' the Police Chief reassured the Governor and as soon as he said goodbye, he snatched a clean sheet of paper from his desk, looked at it for some seconds before putting it back. He slowly grabbed a red pen and scratched the word "Tree" in one of the circles with different options in his sketch plan. Under the word, he made a childish doodle of a tree with two legs wearing military boots. He smiled and scratched a cross on that too. Then, he stared for a few more seconds at his plan, dropped the red pen on his desk, picked a green one and drew more circles around the existing blue circle with the word "Photographer" in it.

He grabbed the phone again, used the pen to dial a number, pausing a second with each turn of the round disc on the phone. The dialling process gave him more time to rethink his plan. While waiting for the other end to pick up, he looked again at the paper before him, put the receiver on his shoulder to free his hand for writing, then drew two lines from the circle with the word "Photographer" to the circle with the word "Tree", and then to another circle with the words "Naked Man" beside the circle with the tree.

When the Asayish Director at last picked up the phone, the Police Chief went immediately to the subject without waiting for a response to his greeting. 'There is this young guy people talking about. I think he is a photographer, and they say he's been—'

'I know who you're talking about,' the Asayish Director interrupted him. 'I'm working on this case already. I think it's better for you to leave him to me.'

'Ah,' said the Police Chief, 'that's why I called you.' He paused, then continued, 'I was just talking to the Governor who suggested—'

'I know,' the Asayish Director interrupted the Police Chief again. 'I talked to him too. I was just on the phone with him. So, as I said, better to leave this to me. That's what I told him as well.'

'So I think we are all sorted then. Good luck with it, I'd say! Bye for now,' said the Police Chief quickly, and hung up. When he replaced the handset, he shook his head and said, 'What a jerk!'

9

In another life, the Asayish Director could have been a dentist or a scientist or professor of chemistry at a university or at least a teacher at a secondary school, just as the Governor had been. He had instead devoted his life to the struggle of his nation, he would say so often to friends or the comrades with whom he usually drank, whether at the office, at the home of one of his party leaders or in one of the old clubs that were now open to the public. He was feeling especially gloomy about his past and his – as he himself would say – 'lost youth', since the Governor had been appointed to his post. Both men's posts were agreed upon in a political deal between their parties for sharing out the government posts. It was the Asayish Director's ambition to achieve the top post, but the Governor's degree weighed heavier.

When he hung up with the Police Chief, the Asayish Director apologised to his guest, one of his party's senior leaders, who sat across from him on a comfortable sofa in the lavish office.

'No worries,' said the guest. 'You're a busy man in this post. I understand that. But anyway, I was going to say you shouldn't be worried about the Governor. He's a good guy. Although he is one of the Patriots, but he is very much different from the others.'

'Is he?' said the Asayish Director, frowning.

'He is a real patriot, if you know what I mean. I know him from the early sixties when we were both in politics. I mean before our parties split. We're nearly the same age.'

'Oh, I didn't know you knew him so well, sir. But anyway, I don't have anything against him. I just don't like to be under him. And maybe I envy him too. You see, these civil people who have never fought in the mountains see us old guerrillas as savages who know nothing of city life and governing.'

'But I'm sure he doesn't think that way of you,' the guest reassured him, putting one leg on top of the other before slouching in the sofa.

'What I mean is they've had all the privileges of the civil life and now they get the best opportunities just because they were so-called underground members of the parties. And now we have to deal with all these—'

'Ah, come on!' the guest interrupted the Asayish Director, laughing. 'You don't want to be in his position. You don't want to wear a suit all the time, do you? At least in your post you can still wear your Kurdish cloths as proudly as you do. And you have more power. You have gunmen.'

'Well, what power!' the Asayish Director said, standing up. He took a cigarette pack out of his pocket, pulled out two cigarettes, stepped off his desk, and limped towards his guest. He offered him one, and lit it for him. He then lit his own cigarette and sat on a chair next to the sofa, leaning forwards on the sofa's arm, gazing at his guest. 'You see, most of the gunmen under my leadership are not from our party. That bothers me as well.'

The guest blew out a puff of smoke and tried to say something, but the Asayish Director nagged further, complaining about the Patriots who had controlled the most important posts in the city, and as a result were now trying to make better alliances with other parties in order to weaken his own Democratic party position. 'I'm struggling, trying to operate as a commander of all the forces, but in vain. They all obey their own parties rather than the Agency. And honestly the whole *Asayish* is just a gathering of all those different forces and not one united force. I hope things will not go wrong one day. But I'm certain they will. We will then be at each other's throats.' He took a deep drag and leant back in his chair.

A few knocks on the door made both men turn and watch as an attendant came in with two *piyalas*, tea glasses, on a small tray. Without a word, the man put both teas on the coffee table in front of the guest and collected another *piyala* with a few sips of tea left in it. He also cleared the empty *piyala* from his director's desk and went out the room.

'You know, that is precisely the point I want to come to,' said the guest, breaking the silence to confirm the Asayish Director's concerns. 'Slemani is not our city. The Patriots are way too strong in this city. I know I'm not making myself popular in our party when I say this, but I really think we Democrats should leave this city to the Patriots and the others and focus on Hawler. We have the whole of Badinan and the city of Duhok. So let's take Hawler from them, our capital.'

'I understand you, sir. But this sounds a bit—'

'Don't get me wrong,' the guest said, leaning forward, shaking his hand with the cigarette, 'I'm not proclaiming another civil war or anything of this kind. But we shouldn't let the Patriots fix their feet in our capital.'

'They can't. We have our main headquarters there. And our leader's residence,' the Asayish Director said with a slight discomfort, shifting himself in the chair.

'Well, not inside the city, we don't.' The guest took another deep drag and slouched again in the sofa, blowing out smoke.

The Asayish Director scratched his forehead, then perched on the edge of his seat and stared at his senior comrade. 'Yes, I totally get your point, sir. But we can't kick them out from Hawler. Just as they can't kick us out from Slemani. This is my city too. I was born here, raised here, fought for this city. I mean I've fought for the whole of Kurdistan. But I'm most loyal to my own city, to be honest. And that's the source of my annoyance. I want us to be strong here, in Slemani.'

'I'm also from this city and hope to die here, you know? And—'

'I know. But—'

'No, listen. This is my point: we should leave sentiments aside. We have to work for our party. That's all: *our party.*'

'And that's what I am exactly doing,' the Asayish Director hollered animatedly. He stood up, opened his arms wide and wanted to say something else, but didn't know how to put his emotions in words.

The guest opened his arms as well and shrugged, eyebrows raised. 'So?'

The Asayish Director limped back to his desk, but instead of sitting, he turned again to his guest, while stroking his thick moustache. He halted in the middle of the room, took a step back and perched on the edge of his desk. 'I want to make our party stronger *here,* in Slemani,' he finally said. 'That's all what I want.' He put out his cigarette in an ashtray on the desk.

The guest noticed that his cigarette was also burning out, a long mass of ash dangling from it. Cautiously, he took one last drag, then put out the cigarette in the ashtray on the coffee table before him.

'I want the *Asayish* to be ours in this city. We need to put more of our *peshmerga*s in this force. I want to make it one force, loyal to me, rather than one for each party, with each party and leader having their own gunmen. Please don't forget, sir, the security forces can achieve more than even an army. And when these forces are loyal to us, we will gain the upper hand,' the Asayish Director made his point.

'That's wasting time and energy, my friend,' the guest said, struggling to stand up, taking support from the sofa's arm.

The Asayish Director rushed towards him, dragging his feeble leg, and gave him a hand. 'You need a cane, sir. I can't believe you still don't have one.'

Standing upright, the guest put his hand on his comrade's shoulder and continued, 'What you're aiming at is an impossible mission. I mean realistically we can't have both cities. Don't waste your time, my dear. That's all that I'm trying to say all day long.'

The Asayish Director nodded, and putting his arm under his guest's arm, he walked him to the door, himself limping.

'Thanks for giving me a hand, but I can manage on my own,' the guest said, holding to the door frame. 'And canes are for losers. We're old *peshmerga*s. A little back pain shouldn't cripple us.'

Holding the door open with one hand, the Asayish Director shook his comrade's hand with the other, then warned him with a smile, 'You really don't make yourself popular with your stance, sir. We should be working for both cities. We will have Hawler as well as Slemani. Trust me. I'd die for that. And by the way, it looks as if no one cares anymore for Kirkuk. That's what we should all be concentrating on. We should retake it from the regime.'

'Oh dear, oh dear. Don't you have a life? You just try to make things more complicated and your own life harder. That's another—'

'I gave up my leg for it, you know. I don't want that to have been for nothing. But that's another issue, indeed.'

When the guest stepped out of the room, shaking his head, the Asayish Director asked his guard who stood at the door to send one of the guards to the building next door 'where those artists and thugs are stationed, you know? Tell the guard to ask that girl to come here for a chat. You know which one I mean? The one who shouted at us the other day.'

The guard looked at him, confused, not understanding what the Asayish Director exactly wanted.

'Don't stare so foolish. You don't remember? When we went there the other day to convince those youngsters to vacate the building, she shouted at us so bravely. That girl. But tell your fellow guard not to threaten her or anything. Just have him tell her that if they want to keep the building, I would like to have a conversation with her.'

When the guard hurried off to carry out the mission, the Asayish Director shut the door, looked at his pistol that was about to fall out of his *cummerbund,* pushed it back inside and then limped back to his desk.

Sitting that evening in the garden of *fermanberan,* the Civil Servants Club, the Asayish Director sat with the commander of his guards, drinking *arak,* sip after sip, as if in a hurry, while chain-smoking and moaning about the unfortunate course his life had taken. They both wore suits instead of Kurdish clothes, as the Asayish Director had insisted. Many educated people and intellectuals were visiting this club, since it was now open to all members of the public. They should look representable, the Asayish Director has been insisting since the start of his appointment as the director of the force. When in duty, *peshmerga*-style Kurdish clothes was just fine – until they would come up with special uniforms. He was still resentful of the way his conversation with his comrade went in the morning and then his brief encounter with the girl from the next building, which hadn't gone well either.

He told the Commander that he had survived several battles as a *peshmerga* against the regime forces in the thirty-two years before the uprising. Then, during his last battle fighting for the liberation of the oil-rich city of Kirkuk, he injured his right leg. He had devoted the best part of his life to the Kurdish cause and his people's dream of Independence, he said. He knew that the poor man had heard this story so many times but had to listen to his boss as if it was the first.

'I was only eighteen when I joined the liberation movement,' the Asayish Director said, then took a deep puff from his cigarette and breathed it out with a sigh. 'I had such good marks on my final exams from secondary school. If my father weren't imprisoned that same year, I could have had even better results. My marks were not enough for dentistry, but I was enrolled for chemistry at the university. I heard that from my family when I was already in the mountains with the *peshmerga*.' He took another sip of the *arak* and yet another puff from the cigarette and stopped talking for a minute.

The Commander entertained himself by stirring a spoon in the tzatziki bowl.

'But let's leave this all aside,' the Asayish Director said abruptly. He looked around, then lowered his voice, 'This girl I'm in love with, you know? The one from the youth centre next door. She came to my office today. Can you please stop doing that? It makes me nervous.'

The Commander left the spoon in the bowl, withdrew his hand swiftly and looked up at him. 'Aha, sorry... Yes, I heard.' He leant back in his chair, straightening his blazer coat.

'I mean I sent for her,' the Asayish Director relayed. 'I probably shouldn't have done that. Maybe it was better if I had gone there myself instead, don't you think?'

The Commander shrugged. 'I don't know, really. I don't think I'm the right person to ask that, sir. You know what I am good at.' He smiled.

'Yeah, beating up people?'

The Commander burst out in laughter.

'She's a Patriot, you know? She must hate me,' the Asayish Director said in a sad voice.

'Oh, that shouldn't be a problem, sir,' the Commander said, leaning forwards over the table, taking now a serious tone. 'I mean if she were to want you too. But, eh... I mean, is she not a bit too young for you?'

'How in the hell can you say that? You mean I am too old?'

'Not so much, but maybe only some thirty years older than her?' the Commander teased, bursting in another laugh.

'Ah, fuck off!' the Asayish Director said loudly with a smile. He looked at the customers on the table next to them, then lowered his voice and commanded, 'Give me your pack.' He pointed to the Commander's cigarette pack on the table.

The Commander took out a cigarette and handed it to his boss.

The Asayish Director slapped the cigarette with the back of his hand, tossing it off the table to the grass. 'Give me the whole fucking pack, I said,' he said with a drunken voice.

The Commander gave him the cigarette pack, looking around. He then bent over and picked up the cigarette from the ground, put it in his own mouth and lit it. But he noticed that it was broken in the middle. He put it in the ashtray, staring at his boss, looking worried.

The Asayish Director took a cigarette from the pack, rejecting with a nod of his head the Commander's offer to light it for him. He grabbed his own lighter angrily, lit his cigarette and said, while blowing the smoke out, 'The problem is that she apparently has something with this bloody Photographer we are after.'

'Okay, you shouldn't be worried about that, sir. We can work on it,' the Commander said, raising his hand over the table, reaching for the pack of cigarettes in front of his boss.

The Asayish Director pulled out a cigarette and handed it to him, then said with the seriousness of an order, 'And make sure you start tapping her home phone and all the phones at that bloody building next door to us. Do that first thing in the morning. Or, you know what? Why not go now and do it immediately?'

10

To have or not have seen the Naked Young Man had become a matter of respect in the city. Those who really had seen him experienced a sense of pride, even if they did not believe their own eyes. Those who had not seen him but only repeated the stories of those who had – or might have – seen him, tried to pretend that they belonged to the camp of the believers, although they were pretty sure that it was nothing more than a myth. It was embarrassing to admit that they had not seen him in such a small city where rumours spread more quickly than even the nastiest flu. How could something that the whole town was talking about escape their attention – such wise men and women as they were? It was one of the characteristics of the people of this city, especially the men, to always pretend that they knew everything and were aware of all events. As the young Photographer had put it once to his friends: Tell people in this town about anything, and most of them will say, 'Oh, yes! I know that.' But when you ask them to tell it, they ask you, 'Um… how was it again?'

The news soon reached other cities and areas in the country. People came from far away with the hope that they might get the chance to admire the Naked Young Man who, it was said, covered his shame only with a single leaf – a leaf that did not look like the leaves of any other tree in the country.

Since some remembered that a few weeks earlier a roving photographer had said that he had seen a naked man crawling out from under the roots of a tree on the edge of the Qilyasan stream, a rumour spread that the Naked Young Man was actually the young Photographer himself trying to cause trouble in the city.

Some said that the Photographer had been driven mad because he was fired and could not bear the loss of face. Others said that his father had thrown him out because he had become unemployed and expected to be supported by his parents. In revenge, they said, he roamed naked through the city to shame his family. Others said that one day he had surprised a political leader in bed with his mother, and when he protested, the politician's bodyguards beat him so badly with the butts of their guns that he lost his mind. Still, others even started the rumour that all his indignation was the result of the outrageous behaviour of his three sisters, who each day went to bed with different politicians, as they had done during the rule of the regime. And some went so far as to claim that they were mistresses of the Baathist intelligence officers.

Indeed a few other people tried to go into more detail, claiming that they were sure one of his sisters was assassinated in the wave to cleanse promiscuous women who allegedly had slept with the powerful men of the regime; a campaign that was led by one of the prominent leaders of the Patriots a short time after the uprising.

Every now and then someone would say, 'What the hell are you talking about? Do you think he cared what his sisters did? He's a faggot himself. Otherwise he wouldn't behave like that!' And if someone else responded disapprovingly and wondered why anyone who was slightly different from others would, sooner or later, be labelled a faggot or a whore, the person who had made the remark would reply defensively, 'Oh, don't make me admit that even I myself have so many times did him.'

There were also people who defended the Photographer. His mother, they would say, had already died in last year's mass exodus. And anyway, he never had any sisters, only two older brothers. When they left the city with almost the entire population, the whole family was hit by a grenade fired by the tanks that were trying to take back the liberated city. They were in a tractor-trailer with many others and had just reached the edge of the city, on the highway to Arbat, a small town nearby. Only he and his father survived the attack. The Father was wounded in one of his legs. He sits now at home alone, they would say, with an amputated leg maintained by his son. He does not even accept the small pension to which he would be entitled every few months. He says he doesn't want money from a government that expects him, after forty-two years of service as a civil servant, to beg for the money he was entitled to. Family and friends tell him not to be so negative but instead to show some understanding of the situation. Even when it was suggested to him that a child could replace him in the queue for government aid while he waited in the shade, the old man would become angry, shouting, 'Understanding? What understanding? Why should I? Have understanding for a bunch of *sharwal*-wearers, coming from the mountains to rule us? It was their fault. They brought us to these perilous, miserable times, drove us out of our houses, forced us to leave the city and lose all our property. And now I'm sitting at home, poor and defenceless. Look… Look around and see what they have made of this country. See if there are any electricity poles, cables or even any shovels and bulldozers left. Haven't they sold all that to the Iranians? You'll see what they will reduce us to.

On the other hand, people who had not seen the Naked Young Man and did not believe any of the stories thought that it was the Photographer, that bastard, who had spread all those rumours to confuse people. Some, especially jealous artists, would say that he started the rumours because he wanted to become famous and attract attention to his photography. Others accused him of being a spy who wanted to cause uproar in the city; he might have been hired, they speculated, by enemies of the nation and the new-born government. Most people in this camp were furious and cursed him. Since the *Asayish* wasn't doing anything about it, some were even looking for the Photographer themselves so they could teach him a lesson and stop all this wickedness forever. Even more, they argued that the reason he had been hiding for the past couple of days was because he was aware of the threatening situation.

One friend had warned him that some of the young communists were even accusing him of being a mercenary of the Israeli Zionists and saw the commotion as part of an imperialist plot to prevent the spread of communism in a country where so much oil and other resources were hidden under its soil. That friend was himself a member of one of the few communist groups that had been established after the uprising. Although there was no manufacturing in the city and the only three factories – cement, sugar and tobacco – had been closed for many years, they tried to educate the proletariat to raise class consciousness and mobilize against the new government. They also appealed for a maximum of thirty-five hours of work per week, although most of the people were unemployed.

Criticising the communists, a small group of emerging young intellectuals said sarcastically that one could talk about any phenomenon in this country except the class struggle. This group was actively publishing tracts and giving seminars and analyses of their society. The young communists could not stand them and considered them to be supporters of capitalism and imperialism, repeating western theories and methods, and thus their enemies. The young Photographer was friends with these intellectuals and had often been seen with them in the teahouses and on their perambulation of the street, always absorbed in debate and discussion. The Photographer's communist friend had told him, under an oath of silence, that one of the members of his group had visited the old Jewish quarter a couple of times to collect information about the Photographer, suspecting him of being a Jew and in the pay of the *Mossad*, the national intelligence agency of Israel. This member had already discovered that the Photographer was born and raised in that district and that his father had spent his youth there in the late forties, during a time when many Jewish families were still living there, before they emigrated or were deported to Israel.

When the defenders of the young Photographer heard these allegations, they could not do or say anything other than shrug and shake their heads or smile scornfully. All they could do was prove that he had nothing to do with the Naked Young Man other than simply be the first person to have seen him.

11

One early evening, halfway on its nightly journey to the city, the Tree stood beside the town's main museum on the corner of Salim Street, which divided the north and south of the city. On the other side of the street, it saw hundreds of people, men and women, young and old, wandering among the small restaurants, takeaways, baklava and sweet shops, teahouses and other stores. The Tree tried to cross the road but didn't dare to go through the heavy traffic.

It walked back towards the Sheikh Muheddin district through the dark alleyways, careful, as so many people, especially children, were now out, playing. When it reached the neighbourhood cemetery on a hill, it went in and stood there amongst the other trees until the streets became less busy.

Early the next morning, the Young Man woke up with the first sunlight, naked, between two graves. Thinking now was a good moment to try to cross the main street, he walked cautiously out of the cemetery, down the hill and along the walls of the old houses in the poor neighbourhood. He saw how rubbish, empty bottles, plastic bags and food remnants littered the alleyways or heaped beside the doors. From under the doors of some of the houses wastewater and excrement flowed into the alleys.

Suddenly, some people spotted him and started shouting and threatening him. When they started chasing him he ran and ducked out of the alley, only to be faced with more people coming towards him from other alleyways with steaks, shovels or iron bars.

He jumped over the hedge of a house into its courtyard, then climbed over a wall to reach the rooftop. From there, he jumped onto the roof of another house and then to another. Once he arrived at the back, he jumped into another alley and got away. He ran until he reached Salim Street again.

This time, as a man he didn't mind the traffic and spurted through the beeping cars, dragging the tail of his leaf behind him. On the other side, he faced a group of men who were rushing up the street. He didn't know why they were in a rush so early in the morning. Equally, the men were taken by surprise to see a naked man, wrapped in only a leaf. They jumped out of his way, staring at him in astonishment and started swearing at him.

'But wait,' one of them said, halting, then turned to his companions. 'Was that not...'

But the Naked Young Man had already disappeared into a side street.

12

It had been a while since the Photographer had slept at home. He stayed at a friend's house and spent most of his time there. He only went out at night in order to search for the Tree. He would then quickly visit one of his friends to get an update on all the rumours that they might have heard that day in the teahouses, on the street or from their family and neighbours. To avoid anyone from turning him in, he visited a different friend unexpectedly every evening. He would then sneak to the places where people had claimed to have seen the tree or the Naked Young Man that day. He sometimes cycled to the locations, but most of the time he walked or took a late bus so as not to attract attention.

His friend's house was the only safe place for him because nobody was aware that they knew each other. In the earlier years of primary school, they had been classmates and shared the same desk. It was only a few years ago that they had found each other again. The Photographer had studied painting at the Institute of Fine Arts, but since he had graduated, he hadn't painted or drawn anything. His only aspiration was photography. His friend had attended a technical school and now had an electrical repair store on Kawa Street, downtown. Because he was the youngest child in his family, he was still single and lived with his old mother who could barely see. She never interfered in her son's affairs and rarely went out. All her other six children were married with children, and didn't have time to visit their mother and brother.

'So,' the Friend told the Photographer, 'even if you stayed for a year in this house, nobody would notice.'

Only the Photographer's Neighbour-Girl, whom he could trust unlike anyone else, knew where he was. Not only was she a good neighbour who cared so much for him and his father, the Photographer had also just recently realised that he was in love with her. He hadn't dared tell her about it, but he was sure she must have sensed that as well.

Every evening when it got dark, the Neighbour-Girl would visit him in his hiding place and stay there for an hour or so. Sometimes she brought him news that she would receive from her contacts at the political party, the Patriots, of which she was an active member. It was also she who advised him to hide, and had told him that the Asayish Director himself had asked about him and the nature of their relationship. More reasons for the Photographer to be worried. Although she assured him indirectly that this man in no way could win her heart, the Photographer had started to feel jealous. What soothed his worries was the girl's untiring loyalty. Despite her busy life, she continued to visit him every day and even helped his father, cooking for him and keeping him company for a few hours.

One morning at breakfast, the Friend asked the Photographer if he had something with the Neighbour-Girl because it was obvious that she liked him.

The Photographer blushed and tried to deny it. 'You must have misunderstood, my friend,' he said, then explained that they had known each other for a few years, since her family had moved to their neighbourhood and had become friends with his late elder brother's wife.

'Then we became friends too. She loves to talk of politics. But we talk of all kinds of other issues as well. I've never expected anything other than friendship from her.'

He paused for a moment, pondering, then went on, 'To be honest, I'm not sure. I mean I started to like her from the very beginning. Then, I think I was about falling in love with her. Even when my brother and his wife moved out, she kept visiting us. But, you know, she was becoming part of the family. So, I was trying to put my feelings aside. Also I knew she was deeply involved in politics so wouldn't have any time for me.'

He then explained to his friend that the Neighbour-Girl used to be a member of an underground sub-organisation connected to the Patriots in the most dangerous years, before the uprising, and that she was now working in the party's youth department. 'There is also one other thing I have to admit,' said the Photographer, smiling, while looking away to avoid his friend's gaze. 'I was in love with another girl. One of my classmates at the art school. Although we never had a real relationship, she knew how much I was in love with her. You can't believe it, in the same week I had planned to tell her about my love, she married someone else.'

He went silent for some seconds, and then continued, looking at his friend, 'And I also got an invitation to her wedding. Can you imagine?'

The Friend said nothing; he only stared at him with empathy, seemingly surprised at how such a short life of a young person can hold such intense experiences. Then he said, 'I'd like to hear more.'

'That devastated me,' the Photographer continued. 'My whole world was upside down. It took me a couple of months to mourn before I realised that I actually liked my Neighbour-Girl much more, but that unfortunate, obsessive love for my classmate had made me blind.'

Suddenly, he put down the bread he was about to put into his mouth and fell into deep thought. His friend observed him silently.

'Do you know,' the Photographer started again. 'It is very strange. Now I feel I love this girl a lot. And you're right, the attention she bestows on me is not only because of our friendship. You know what? I'll try to understand her better this evening.' He thanked his Friend for making him realise that, and continued with his breakfast.

The Friend told him proudly that he should ask him about these subjects because he was an expert on love.

'Okay, next time you should tell me about your love life. Maybe your expertise can help me even more. For now don't be late for your work.'

'Ah, no, no, of course not... Mine is not as romantic as yours. I'm not an artist. I'm only a mechanic, you know.' He wanted to collect the dishes from the table, but the Photographer told him just to leave. He said that he had not so much to do in this huge house on his own. He even barely saw his friend's mother who would wake up early in the morning, pray, have some breakfast and then return to her room, where she stayed for most of the time. Sometimes the Photographer would see her sitting on a prayer mat in the living room, conducting *zikr* with her *tasbeh*, reciting Quran verses.

Just before he left for work, the Friend looked over his shoulder and winked at the Photographer. 'You should do something about it tonight,' he said of the Photographer's feelings. 'I'm going to help you. See you later.'

That evening the three of them were sitting in the room where the Photographer was staying; a small room behind the other five rooms at the back of the house. The Photographer and his friend sat on the mattress on the floor and the Neighbour-Girl on the only chair in the room. She talked about the events of the day, giving the Photographer an update about what people had said about the Tree and the Naked Young Man. The Neighbour-Girl said that she had heard that people had been spotting the Naked Young Man in the Sheikh Muheddin and Chwarbakh districts, and that in the Saholaka a group of men had almost caught him. Some others had said they saw him further away running towards Julakan, the Jewish quarter.

Suddenly, in the middle of her account, the Friend said he had to leave them alone because he had to take his mother to one of his sisters, whose child was sick.

The Neighbour-Girl and the Photographer both blushed. Immediately, the Neighbour-Girl made a reluctant move as to stand up. 'Oh, I actually have to leave too,' she said. 'I've got loads to do.'

The Friend nodded to the Neighbour-Girl and said, 'Stay a little bit longer. He needs you.' He opened the door, then added, 'We will be away only for a few hours.'

When the Friend was out and closed the door, the Photographer shouted, 'Ah, don't shut it. We're going to sit in the kitchen.' He jumped up from the floor, opened the door quickly, and asked the Neighbour-Girl to follow him to the kitchen.

'Your friend seems modern, having a lunch table!' the Neighbour-Girl said, dragging one of the chairs from under the kitchen table and sitting on it. She sensed his nervousness and tried to lighten the situation.

'It's much nicer to sit at a table than on the floor, don't you think?' said the Photographer, while pouring water into a kettle. He then lit the hob and put the kettle to boil. He came to the table, lighting a cigarette with the same half-burnt match. 'I mean, of course we also have a small table in the kitchen, but you know that's more because of my father's leg.'

'How come you never told me about him?' the Neighbour-Girl said, looking at him with a frown.

'Oh, we were school friends, but then fell out of touch for years. We just recently caught up,' the Photographer said, taking a deep puff from his cigarette and blowing out the smoke immediately. 'He's an amazing friend, taking good care of me. I mean, he's given me a shelter. And he—'

'It's great to have a good friend like him,' the Neighbour-Girl said, slouching in her chair.

'But I have more amazing friends,' he said, then put the cigarette between his lips. 'And the loveliest of them is sitting just across of me.'

'Are you flirting with me?' the Neighbour-Girl said with a questioning gaze.

The Photographer let a nervous laugh out, took a drag and pulled the cigarette out of his lips. He sat upright, clearly avoiding her gaze. 'Oh, my... God, no!' He blew out the smoke.

'It's not a bad thing, though! It's just the first time you've called me lovely.'

'Well, I mean... Isn't it lovely of you to do all this for me. And for my father? And you know, all the—'

'I was teasing you, silly boy. Of course I am your best friend. No one can take better care of you.'

'But there is also... Hold on a second,' the Photographer said, standing up quickly. He rushed to the sink cabinet and picked an ashtray from a cupboard over the sink. He flicked the cigarette in it, took it to the table, and sat again.

'Listen,' said the Neighbour-Girl. 'We should think of a good way to clear your name from this whole nuisance. I'm going to talk to this horrible man—'

'No, wait! I was going to say something about friendship,' the Photographer said, taking another deep drag. 'I've been discussing with some friends lately. You know, a few of my intellectual friends. There's this lad my age, a very open-minded man. He's got these somewhat extreme ideas about relationships and things. I mean, I agree with most of what he says. You know, he even held a symposium very recently about sexual revolutions... I mean, he's very extreme in his ideas. But I quite agree with him you know, he says we should accept free relationships and such—'

The kitchen door slowly opened, and the Friend stuck his head in. 'We're leaving.'

'Oh, my God!' Neighbour-Girl startled and turned. 'I thought you already had left.'

'We are now,' the Friend said, smiling to her. 'I hear you're having a nice conversation.'

'Why don't you join us,' she said, returning the smile.

'No, thanks! We have to leave now. See you later.' He shut the door.

The Neighbour-Girl turned to the Photographer, her smile still on her lips. She watched the Photographer slouching in his chair, blowing out smoke like a steam train. He looked relieved that the subject was interrupted. Maybe she should challenge him a bit more.

'But what do you exactly mean by free relationships?' she asked him with a tone more witty than curious.

'Ah, I think they should leave us youngsters to choose the way we live our lives,' he said, sitting upright. He took a deep drag and blew out the smoke over the table between them. 'They should leave us to have relationships without marrying first. I mean wouldn't it be too late to get to know your partner after you have already married? You know, when I—'

'I haven't seen any written law that forbids us from having a relationship outside marriage,' the Neighbou-Girl interrupted him with a sharp look, dispersing the smoke with her hand. She noticed that she had made him uncomfortable again. But too late. She should make her point now. 'It's all traditional bullshit,' she said. 'And we just obey these rules, follow them and revive them. We just go with the flow and that's not good. I know it's hard to break rules we have grown up with. And for sure, as a woman, I must cope with that in so many ways. For you guys, it's much easier, isn't it? All you need is some courage.'

'Not as easy as you think,' said the Photographer, shaking his head. 'I wouldn't dare to even—'

'That's exactly what I mean,' she interrupted him again, irritated.

They heard a slamming door. They both stopped talking and pricked their ears. They looked at each other. They were now alone in the house.

The Neighbour-Girl continued, to saving him from discomfort,

'You know, for me as a girl, it's even dangerous. Okay, maybe it's a bit different for me personally. I don't have a father or brothers, as lucky as I am. But a crazy cousin or just some honourable man could also feel that my behaviour would hurt his pride and shoot me down or throw some acid on my face.' She lifted her head a bit, put her fingers in her hair and continued, looking at the ceiling, 'Oh, I'm sorry, Dad! I wish I had known you. Maybe you were different.'

She looked back to the Photographer, pulled her hand out of her hair, clutched a salt cellar on the table and started to play with it. She then said, 'But you know, I don't remember my dad. Only very vaguely. I was five when he died. My mother says he used to be a nice, soft man.' She stopped for a few seconds, looking at the Photographer who was staring at her through the smoke, as if he was drowning in masses of clouds, a satisfying smile emerging gradually on his lips.

'I'm sorry to come out with all this all of a sudden,' she said. 'It's funny, we've never talked this way. But I feel—'

'Oh, no, no... Please... It's very interesting to me. Tell me about your father. How was he for a man?'

'Oh... Well, as I said—'

'I mean what does your mother say about him?' the Photographer said and took another deep puff of his cigarette, exhaling slowly. Wisps of smoke spread all over the table, curling through the empty *piyalas*, the ashtray, the salt and pepper cellars and the big sugar basin.

The Neighbour-Girl said, 'You know, I'm really lucky being raised by a single mother. I mean she wasn't less strict than any other person, but you know how it is. It's just different from the oppression we have to bear from you men.' She winked and started laughing.

The Photographer rose from the chair, laughing, and hurried to the hob. He quickly lowered the heat under the boiling kettle. He put some tea leaves in a teapot, poured the hot water in it and left it on the hob. Standing there, he looked over and said, 'Come on, you know I'm not like other men.'

'Oh, no, absolutely not. I'm just teasing. On the contrary, sometimes it's your softness that annoys me. I mean all this complaining about the community and blaming others for preventing us from doing what we want, but do you do anything active to change all that?' She stopped talking, looking at her friend, waiting for his response.

The Photographer turned off the hob and brought the teapot to the table, all while avoiding her gaze. Before he almost placed the teapot on the table, she said, 'Wait!' and ran to the sink to grab a rag. She folded it and put it on the table. 'Now you can put it down, silly.'

When they both sat down again, the Neighbour-Girl continued, 'You know all this complaining about the political parties and the politicians, that they are thieves and looters, that they have sold the whole country to foreigners, even if it is all true, these guys were guerrillas just coming back from the mountains and villages. That's all they know about governing. And honestly, they are not all so inexperienced and unlettered as people think. There are also many well-educated people among them. So let's give them some time. They can't make magic. We've only just got a parliament. And I can guarantee that this will be a real democracy.' She stopped and waited for his response, but the Photographer only stared at her and smiled.

'Is it not amazing that we, after almost a century of struggle, are finally ruling ourselves?' she said, ending her tirade.

'No doubt!' the Photographer said, leaning forward. 'I haven't denied that, have I? No one would claim such a thing.'

'You see?' she said with a wide grin. 'You can be challenged. That's a good sign. You're not as passive as you would like to believe. Come on, everyone is happy about what we have achieved, right?'

'I hope so!'

'So let's not forget the misery of the past so soon. Just be realistic.' She leant back in her chair and stared at her friend, frowning, waiting for his response.

No sooner had the Photographer opened his mouth to say something than she preceded him saying, 'Listen, I didn't mean to offend you. I'm maybe trying to challenge you, but you know I'm politically active and like practical action rather than sitting and complaining. Don't take it personally, but this is one of the sick attitudes of this community. We only sit whining and grumbling but don't take any steps to change things. Now's our chance to be part of all these changes. We're in an extremely important transition, so let's try to make something out of it, don't you think?'

The Photographer nodded.

Was that confirmation or he was losing interest? She stared at him and shrugged as to invite him for a response. When he didn't respond, she continued, 'Besides, I think my role in all this as a woman is crucial because I don't think men will let women be part of any kind of decision making for years to come. I'm not delusional about that.'

'Maybe you are right,' the Photographer finally said. 'I'm somehow passive and don't like any engagement. But I'm an artist and cannot... I mean, how can I change a society that... eh... I mean I'm just as powerless as... And they don't let us participate in anything if we don't belong to their parties. It makes me sick that you have to belong to a political group to be able to do anything at all. It's... I mean, it's so—'

'That's exactly what I mean,' she interrupted him. 'Listen darling, I don't mean you personally, but that's whining.' She lifted the teapot and poured them tea, first in his *piyala*, then in hers.

'Oh, sorry, I forgot about the tea,' said the Photographer, blushing.

'Ah, never mind...' she said with a smile. 'I know how gentle you are, dear.' Then she grabbed the sugar basin, just as the Photographer went to reach it. Their fingers touched. Both of them tried not to take notice. She shot him a quick gaze. He was blushing again. She lifted the lid and put a scoop of sugar into his tea. She then looked at him demonstratively. He looked up.

'Would you like another scoop?'

He nodded.

She put another scoop in his tea, then two in her own and put the sugar basin back on the table.

He started stirring his tea.

After stirring her own tea, she took a sip and then continued, 'Listen, what I want to say is this... Or, no, no... Let me first explain... You know if there is one good thing I've learned from being active in politics it is that if they stop you from doing something, you can do it anyway in secret.' She looked him in the eyes to see if he'd understood.

The Photographer smiled and lowered his gaze to his own hands, playing with the top of his fingers.

'As simple as that, my dear,' she said, still staring at him.

The Photographer lifted his head, looking at her shyly, trying to draw a smile to his lips.

She smiled back, blinking repeatedly, waiting for him to break the silence that made her comment more embarrassing than it needed to be. Realizing what her own statement implied, she was looking for another way to explain that she did not mean anything particularly but asked herself if she really did not mean what she said. Then she thought she could maybe change the subject or tell an anecdote from her experience in the politics.

She saw that suddenly something changed in the Photographer's face. Maybe he had noticed that her smile was gradually disappearing, changing to concern and some kind of disappointment. Maybe he was also concerned about losing the perfect opportunity to reveal his love to her?

At the very moment that he wanted to say something, she said, 'Have I said something wrong? I hope I haven't said something offensive, have I?'

'Oh, no, no… Definitely not. You know, I really appreciate your work in politics. It's me… I just don't like politics… I mean, I respect your engagement, but… I actually want to say that you do a great job.' He leant back. 'Yes, you can change a lot through politics, I assume.' He stopped, blinking rapidly as he gradually blushed, as if he was fighting through some kind of internal anger.

She decided to ease the situation and give him a helping hand, so said, 'Oh, I wish it was normal just to go for a walk. Then we could have some ice cream in Tooy Malik.'

The Photographer looked up, forcing a smile.

'But I don't think that's a good idea, is it?' she said, shifting in her seat. 'Maybe better for me to leave.'

The Photographer stared at her and started moving in his chair impatiently.

The Neighbour-Girl stood up, ready to leave.

He did the same, blushing and sweating.

Trying to save the moment, she said, 'Or, wait a second. If you're going out to search for the Tree tonight, I'd like to come with you.'

A wide smile appeared on the Photographer's face.

She smiled back triumphantly.

'You know what? Why not?' said the Photographer, taking a deep breath. He then darted to his room.

The Neighbour-Girl stood up and put both hands on the table, waiting.

In the blink of an eye, the Photographer came back to the kitchen, putting on his coat, and said, 'Let's go.'

13

The Neighbour-Girl sat behind the Photographer on the luggage carrier of his bicycle, both her legs dangling to one side, holding the carrier in her left hand and embracing his waist with her right arm. Though the wind in her face was refreshing, she was scared as hell.

'I can't believe I'm sitting on a bicycle,' she yelled, her hair blowing backwards in the breeze. 'But, it's so amazing,' she shouted as loud as she could.

'It's the happiest evening of my life,' the Photographer shouted back, pedalling at a fast pace through the alleys of the Ibrahim Pasha district where his friend's house was.

When they reached Ibrahim Pasha Street he pedalled right to the end, then turned right onto Sarkarez Street. Halfway the street, when it began to slope down, he pedalled firmly, then lifted his feet from the pedals with both legs up into the air. He yelled and let go of the handle-bars, spreading his arms in the air.

As soon as the Neighbour-Girl realised that her friend's only grip on the bike was his buttocks on the saddle, she screamed anxiously and hugged him, tightly. She closed her eyes and pressed her head against his back, shouting, 'Hold the handlebars, please, please, please!'

The bike lost balance and they almost fell, but the Photographer quickly brought it back by moving his arms and legs up and down in the air. He shouted back, 'Don't worry. Just trust me. I'm the best cyclist in this city. Didn't you know that?'

'Ah, don't show off. Hold the handlebars please. I believe in you. I know, I know. You are a real man.'

The Photographer laughed. 'That's true. But you know why I'm the best cyclist in town?' he shouted again. 'Because I'm the only cyclist!' He laughed now louder.

'You silly! Just slow down please!' she said, now seeing houses and shops zoom by. She turned her head to the other side. Her dizzying feeling toned down as the farther buildings on the other side of the road looked like moving slower.

When they reached the crossing with Chwarbakh Street, the Photographer put his feet back on the pedals and clutched the handle-bars, pressing the rear brake slowly with short grips until the bike slowed down. He then pressed both of the brakes firmly to stop, just at the junction, and put his right foot to the ground to steady the bike.

The Neighbour-Girl released him and jumped off the bike. She rubbed her buttocks and said, 'This thing is so hard. I've got cramps everywhere.'

The Photographer looked at her and smiled. 'Unfortunately I can't do anything about that.'

'But why did we stop here, in the middle of this empty place?'

'Look, if it's true that today the naked man was coming from Chwarbakh, which is over there and if he was heading towards Julakan, as you said people have claimed, that means... Look, that's Julakan in front of us. But if he had been here, I guess I know where he could have ended up spending the night as a tree. I know even you wouldn't believe me, but that guy and the Tree are the same creature.'

The Neighbour-Girl looked at him and shrugged. She didn't know what to think. She believed him. But how could she confirm his theory? She had seen neither the Naked Young Man nor the Tree with her own eyes.

'Anyway, let's go. I'll surprise you,' said the Photographer, while helping her back on the bicycle by holding her arm.

Once she was safe, she embraced him again from behind and said, 'I'm ready.'

The Photographer started pedalling, but instead of heading towards the Jewish quarter, he cycled left in the direction of Qarajawa.

Halfway along the road, he turned right down another street that continued in a curve with houses on either side. When they reached the end of the road, he turned right again and after hundred metres he stopped beside a high wall with a copse of trees behind it. The wall continued for another hundred metres.

The Neighbour-Girl jumped off the bike. She stared at the wall and the trees behind it, then looked at him, in surprise.

'This is the Sheikh Latif Garden. Have you ever heard of it?' the Photographer said.

'Of course, silly. I live in this city too. Didn't you know that?'

'But you have never been inside, I bet.'

'I wish I had. But I didn't know it was a public garden.'

'It's not,' the Photographer said with a smirk and put the bicycle against the wall. He grasped her by the wrist and dragged her gently along. 'Come on,' he said.

They walked beside the wall to the end, then turned left to the side of the garden. After fifty metres, the Photographer stopped and removed a huge door that was a wooden frame covered with pieces of flattened, rusted tins, unfixed to the wall, blocking an opening that was more of a hole in the wall than a gate. He grabbed her hand again and pulled her in.

The moonlight shone on most of the trees and the narrow paths between them, but darkness still overwhelmed the garden. The streaks of light that revealed glimpses of the paths gave a magical, mysterious feel to the garden. The Neighbour-Girl clenched her friend's hand and came closer to him, closing the gap between them.

'You needn't be afraid,' the Photographer said. 'This is perhaps the safest place in the city. Nobody would come here except a gardener in the daytime. And maybe the naked guy. So let's look for a very unusual tree, shall we? It doesn't look like any other tree you ever have seen.'

'Oh, come on, I wasn't so afraid, but now you are frightening me. I feel as if I'm in the middle of a horror movie!'

Suddenly, a rustling sound behind them made them both flinch. They squeezed each other's hands and turned swiftly.

'Is it the Tree, do you think?' the Neighbour-Girl whispered, hugging his arm.

The Photographer took his arm slowly from hers and replied, 'Wait here.' He walked quietly towards the place from which the sound seemed to come.

The Neighbour-Girl watched him bend near the trunk of a huge tree and then kneel on the narrow gravel path to inspect something in the nearby shrub.

She walked slowly and carefully towards him. 'What is it?'

'A puppy.'

The Neighbour-Girl sighed, relieved. She then looked around and knelt beside him.

The little dog had retreated under the shrub, looking at the Photographer who tried to offer reassurance by stroking its head.

'Let's leave him. I think he's afraid of us,' the Neighbour-Girl said as she stood up and dusted her skirt at her knees.

The Photographer stood up too and said, 'Come, let me show you something.' He walked towards the middle of the garden. She followed him, holding his hand, trying to keep up with his steps.

They arrived at an open space where there was a lawn with a little fountain in the middle. The water was not running. The Photographer pointed to a worn bench under a tree and asked her to sit down. He went to the fountain and turned on the tap. The water started to dribble with a soothing swoosh; its drops glistened in the moonlight. Then, he came back and sat beside her, looking at the fountain without saying anything.

Some moments of silence passed, which felt ages to the Neighbour-Girl, and maybe to him too, she thought. Suddenly, she broke the silence, looking at him, altering her position in order to turn a little towards him. 'Why do you want to find that tree?' she asked.

'Well, I'm not at all sure,' said the Photographer after a few seconds, still looking at the fountain. 'It's become a challenge for me now.' He bent forward, put both his elbows on his knees and placed his face between both his hands.

The Neighbour-Girl stared at him and wondered if his mind was really with the Tree or if he was thinking of her and how to drive the conversation towards a more romantic subject. What was the point of bringing her to this dreamy little paradise-like spot otherwise?

The Photographer leant back, then changed his sitting position to turn towards her just as she had done a moment earlier. He sat symmetrically face to face with her. 'You know, I feel somehow connected to this creature. I hope at least you believe me that that naked guy everyone is obsessed with is the same being as the Tree.'

The Neighbour-Girl turned her face to the fountain, looking in the dark empty space rather than at the water dripping into the small round basin.

The Photographer said, 'I know that you might now believe in the Tree, but do you also believe—'

'Honestly!' the Neighbour-Girl interrupted him and stood up abruptly. 'I don't care anymore.' She stared at him and said decisively, 'Let's leave here before I get scared. It's a bit weird sitting here and... Let's go.'

The Photographer looked at her in surprise, worry sparking in his eyes. He stood up, ran to the fountain, turned off the tap and quickly came back to her. He took her hand, and they left.

When they stepped out of the garden, the Photographer pushed back the door and followed the Neighbour-Girl, who had already gone almost to the end of the wall. She turned right and disappeared behind the wall.

When the Photographer turned the corner, she was already ten metres ahead. He let her walk alone until she reached the bicycle and waited for him.

As soon as he straddled the saddle, the Neighbour-Girl settled behind him on the luggage rack, with both her legs to the left, holding the carrier's iron bars with both hands.

The Photographer started peddling, first slowly, then gradually sped up. 'I'll take you home, shall I?'

'But I left my handbag behind at your friend's. I shall need it tomorrow morning.' She hugged him from behind.

They rode back the whole way in silence.

14

Once they arrived back at the Friend's house, the Neighbour-Girl walked straight to the Photographer's room. He watched her rearrange her cloths, stroke her skirt at the thighs, then put her handbag on her shoulder.

Ready to leave, she said, more cheerfully than moments ago, 'I think it's more appropriate if I took a taxi. Would you come with me to the main street? I might find a taxi on Ibrahim Pasha Street.'

Standing at the door opening, blocking the exit, the Photographer looked at her with a smile and said, 'Sure!'

The Neighbour-Girl looked at him with a smile, then rolled her eyes and made a would-you-then-let-me-pass? movement with her hands.

Encouraged by her smile, the Photographer grabbed her shoulders gently and kissed her lightly on the lips.

The Neighbour-Girl drew her head slowly back and looked at him, smiling shyly.

The Photographer, surprised by his own move, collected all his courage and hugged her firmly. He merged his face into her neck, under her bushy, curly hair, and started to kiss behind her ear. He knew that that was the right thing to do to arouse her senses as he had heard from experienced friends or had seen in movies and read in books. But he didn't know that it would also feel so amazing. He felt that he was dissolving in her warmth and submerging in a delicate tenderness that elevated all other kind of pleasure.

Suddenly, the Neighbour-Girl grabbed both his shoulders and pushed him softly back, while pulling herself tenderly out of his arms. She said in a low, sleepy, hesitating voice, 'I think we shouldn't...'

The Photographer stared at her flushed face and lustful glance, and felt confused.

They stood still for a few seconds in that position, looking each other in the eyes in disbelief; his shoulders crushed between her clutches, both of them shivering. Then he grasped her neck, put his fingers behind her ears and pulled her into his arms. The girl in turn clasped his neck with both hands and put her mouth on his. She then lowered her hands to his hips, then climbed them up again, softly stroking his back until she reached his shoulders. She pressed her right hand, wide open, between his shoulder blades and mounted her left hand to his neck and the back of his head, pushing him firmly into her bosom. That gave him more courage to stroke her neck and lower his hands over her back, down to her hips, squeezing her soft flesh. He waited there for a moment, then slipped both his hands onto her buttocks and grabbed them.

After a few minutes, they found themselves naked on the mattress on the floor in a corner of the room. Big boxes full of shoes, worn-out clothes, cutlery, as well as old fridge and freezer motors, equipment, screws and the odds and ends of various devices surrounded them. Several mattresses, blankets and pillows were piled up on a *Buraq* cupboard behind their heads with two glazed doors. One of them was painted with a miniature scene from the Persian mythology: Rostam, the son of Zal, mounted in the saddle of his horse, *Rakhsh,* thrusting a spear into the gut of a dragon that was leaning back on the ground with spread wings, wrapping its tail around the horse's legs, blood splashing from his wound. On the other glass door, a Quranic *Mi'iraj* scene was painted of the divine steed *Al-Buraq* flying with its white wings, hiding the face of prophet Mohammad, who was sitting in the saddle. The Photographer diverted his eyes, back to the heavenly, beautiful face of the Neighbour-Girl who, head bent down backwards on the pillow, was moaning between his arms – her eyes closed, her lips becoming thicker, glowing as burning coals, her cheeks blushing and little pearls of sweat rolling over her neck, dropping onto the pillow. The sight of a few scattered strands of hair sticking to her neck aroused him, so he pushed himself between her legs back and forth faster and faster, in a feverish movement, wishing that the moment would last forever.

It was midnight when the Friend came back home with his mother. He opened the door to the Photographer's room and saw his half-naked friend lying on his mattress on the floor with the blanket wrapped around his legs, hugging the pillow, deep in sleep. His glowing face, under the dim golden-yellow light of the bulb that hung from the centre of the ceiling, looked like that of a happy child who had just fallen asleep to his mother's lullaby.

15

The next evening the Photographer couldn't care less about who would or would not see him, and went out with his friend. They went to the Civil Servants Club. The bar had a huge garden with three sections, and a big hall for the colder seasons. It had originally been a club for government officials, but for years now any man with good manners had also been accepted.

Both young men passed through the first two sections of the garden and found a table in the corner of the third section. As soon as they sat down, the waiter came, and they each ordered a cold beer. The Friend's constant smile and the intriguing sparkle in his eyes revealed his longing to know about what had happened last night. Thus, before the Friend could ask him any question, the Photographer took the initiative and thanked him for making such an incredible night possible. 'It meant the world to me,' he said, then told his friend a story quite different from what had in fact happened. 'We finally admitted our love for each other. But we decided it was too early to think about getting married and having a family. So we thought it would be better for us to stay as two close, special friends, and who knows, we might change our minds one day.'

He watched his friend's face through the clouds of smoke coming from the cigarettes they were smoking, and could tell that he doubted his story. Nevertheless, he changed the subject and realised that his friend did not mind the change in topic. Deep in his gut, the Photographer felt that he wished that his friend had asked him for more, as it was obvious he knew something had happened between them.

Still living in the euphoria of what happened last night, the Photographer drank beer after beer and smoked cigarettes one after another, trying to listen to his friend but could grab only now and then a sentence or a word. He would also make an effort to take part in the conversation, but his mind was still on the last night. Since he had woken, he had done nothing except recall the previous night in detail: how the Neighbour-Girl had stood in front of him, ready to leave, and how he had blocked the door, burning from the inside. He wondered how red he must have looked. He envisioned himself in flames reflected in both her eyes, as she stood there in front of him, waiting for something to happen. All day long, he had done nothing but touch his own arms, his chest and his abdomen and remember how after that precious hug, their bodies had stuck together, pressed against each other, becoming as one. He then remembered how she, after some minutes of sucking on each other's lips, put her tongue into his mouth and turned it slowly around his. He still felt the warmth of the kiss; the taste of her lips; the softness of her breasts pressed against his chest; and the heat that came up between his legs, ascending gradually towards his groin, to his stomach.

He still couldn't imagine where he had gathered all that courage to suddenly grasp her, put his hands on her neck, behind her ears and to bite her lips, as if he would never get such a chance again. Now, as he thought about that moment, he blushed, embarrassed by the fact that he'd had no previous experience. But he had realised that it was not her first time.

That night, at the drinking table, watching his friend slouching in his seat, immersed in smoke, the Photographer decided never to return to this subject, neither with this friend nor with anybody else. Even with the Neighbour-Girl herself, he would never talk about that night. He knew that he will keep his feelings for her as intensely as always, and that in the depth of his heart he wanted to spend his entire life with her. But at the same time, he was also afraid of taking that responsibility. He knew that he, with this young woman, could be the happiest – a woman who combined both beauty and intelligence – but when the timing is not right, nothing good would come out of it.

They had both drunk six or seven bottles of beer each, when the Photographer and his friend left the club around midnight. The Photographer suggested taking a walk through the streets of the Aqari district before going to the Saholaka, where hundreds of youngsters were hanging around, many with a sandwich and a *piyala* of sweet tea from the vendors on the street. Even though the Friend was afraid that some malevolent people might see the Photographer, he accepted the offer. They took the street behind the public garden and walked, staggering and swaying, talking and laughing without caring where the road would take them.

16

The Tree had just passed the boulevard in front of *Amna Suraka,* the Red Security building, and had turned around the corner, heading towards the Aqari district. It was walking so slowly and calmly in the dark that no one could notice it moving. When it saw two young guys walking down the street, it halted and stayed silently.

As the two got closer, the Tree recognised the Photographer who was so drunk that he could hardly walk. His friend held his left arm firmly, begging him repeatedly to let him catch a taxi, but instead of agreeing to his request, the Photographer dragged the Friend down the road with ungainly wide steps. As they approached the Tree, the Photographer stumbled over the edge of the pavement. He was about to fall, but the Tree took a step forwards so that the Photographer could grasp its trunk while the Friend held his left arm.

When he regained his balance, the Photographer sat at the foot of the Tree, leaning back on its trunk. The Friend, obviously no less drunk, sat on the ground in front of him, cross-legged, with his back to the street.

The Photographer lay down on the pavement and said to the Friend that he felt as if the frightening Red Security building lay on its side too. He sounded as if he was talking more to himself than to his friend. He said that he wondered if fate had brought him to this place that he has so often passed only by bus or bike. He would never dare walk along this road when the building used to be the most terrifying prison of the security forces in the city during the time of the regime, he said. 'Just until over a year ago, can you imagine?'

He then turned to his friend and said that even on the bike, he could barely look at the place at that time as it was surrounded by gunmen.

'I know, dear. Of course I know,' the Friend said, staring at the building as well.

The Photographer continued his monologue and said he remembered that he had always been frightened that he might someday, for no reason, end up in there. 'And why do you think we called it the *Red* Security building, while it was pink?' he slurred, smirking. 'Was it because we were so afraid of it? Or maybe we never dared to look at it enough to know which colour it was really painted.'

'Maybe it was originally red but fainted through the years. And you don't need to tell me all that. I might even know more than you about this building. My cousin was incarcerated there for more than six months, until it fell into the hands of the people during the uprising. He still can't tell his story without shaking and tearing up, poor lad.'

The Photographer made effort to sit upright and leant on the Tree, staring at his friend.

'He was captured with a couple of other young men when they came back from Iran after having stayed there as refugees for two years. My cousin had left just at the end of the war with Iran. When he couldn't manage to travel on to Europe, he returned.'

'And how did he survive in the end?' asked the Photographer.

'Well, I told you, he got freed when people took over the building in the uprising.'

'Oh, yeah, right...' said the Photographer, lying again under the Tree on his back, his arms under his head.

'He says they were—'

'Who said—?' the Photographer interrupted him again.

'My cousin... Are you actually paying attention or am I talking to myself?'

'Oh, oh, I am—'

'No, let's leave. We are both tired.'

'Come on, I'm listening. But I'm drunk, remember?'

'Okay, that's what I mean. I feel like the alcohol gets to me too. Let's move on.'

As the Friend tried to stand up, the Photographer put his right hand on his knee and mumbled in a drunken tone, 'Tell me... I'm listening... I really want to know all about it. I haven't heard much about what happened inside this Bastille. Tell me, please!'

The Friend sat again, looked at the building and continued with the story, 'They had brought the guys in, and after a quick interrogation put them in solitary cells. They were five, including my cousin. In the next days they were taken, one by one, a couple of times a day for interrogation and torture. No matter what they said, they were beaten.'

He looked at the Photographer who was trying to show that he was listening, by forcing his eyes to remain open. He then continued, 'I think one of them had admitted to be an underground member of one of the political parties, I forgot which one. But they wanted him to confess that the others were also members of the party. My poor cousin knew nothing about politics and didn't even have any political affiliation. He was a young musician and just wanted to leave this gloomy country. You know how terrible it was during the couple of years before the uprising. I also would have liked to leave. Who wouldn't have? But my poor cousin came back exactly when the regime invaded Kuwait. So, it was war again.'

'Wait a second. I've lost you... Why did your cousin come back when we all wished to leave at that time?'

'I told you, man. He couldn't get through to Europe. He ran out of money. And I'm not sure why he couldn't work there. Maybe he was not allowed to... And you know, after the war, the Iranians didn't want the Iraqis in their refugee camps any longer, nor did the Europeans accept Kurds as refugees anymore. That's what my cousin says. So he was desperate. He came back and ended up in this building... Now stand up, man. Let's leave, I don't feel well.'

The Friend tried again to stand up, but the Photographer prevented him and said, 'You're supposed to tell me about the conditions inside the prison.'

'How do you think it was? Come on, you have been inside the building, haven't you? You've seen the cells in there, right? The ones downstairs.' He pointed to the building.

The Photographer rolled over to his left side and looked at the building again. He said he felt dizzy and rolled back, facing his friend again. 'Oh, my gosh, I feel even dizzier.' He then tried to straighten himself and said, 'I think I'm going to throw up.'

The Friend held his arm, helping him to sit uptight.

The Photographer closed his eyes and took deep, quick breaths.

Then, he opened his eyes and put his hand on his friend's shoulder. 'Tell me, my friend. I feel fine now.'

'Come on, let's go home. I'll ask my cousin to come over and tell you everything about it.'

'Is he still alive then? How did he survive?'

'That's what I mean. You are too drunk to pay attention. Come on.'

'No, no, I'm sorry, I really am listening to you. Tell me, please!'

'Look, those must be the windows he was talking about. You see those low windows over there? Or maybe not. Oh, no, no… The cells are behind this part of the building. Anyway, he says that there was one tiny window in the cell through which they could see a bit of the street. Every day, one by one, they would hop on one of the other prisoner's shoulders to see what was out there. Sometimes, they would see buses passing and hoped that they could recognise a relative or catch a glimpse of someone who dared to walk past the building on the other side of the street. But of course it was too far to recognise anyone or for the passers-by to see them at that tiny window.'

He looked at the Photographer, who was staring at the building, with his head leaning against the Tree's trunk.

'I still remember vividly,' said the Photographer in a far away tone, 'how on the second or third day of the uprising, here, on this street, at this exact spot where I'm now sitting, tens of burnt bodies and soulless torsos of the security agents were spread all over the street, torn apart.' He looked around for some seconds, his head swaying. 'Sorry, what was I talking about?'

'You were saying—'

'Oh, yes, I know. You see, I know. I am fine. The people… When the people and the *peshmerga* took over the building, I came here with some other friends and walked inside the building. I was wandering amongst the smoke, the smell of gunpowder and the ashes of burnt documents and furniture. In every corner dead bodies were piled up.' He closed his eyes and bent his head down.

'Come on, man, honestly,' the Friend grabbed his arm. 'We really should—'

'No, no, wait. I am fine. They, they… You know, those who had ran outside were killed by bullets and stones or cement bricks or they were stabbed by daggers and cut up in pieces, lain down at the edge of the streets and on the pavements.' Then, the tone of his voice slowed and he started slurring. 'The rain... the rain had washed off the blood... and the bodies... they looked like... you know... pale... like the plastic mannequins.'

He lay down again, put his hand under his head and stared at the sky. Then he told his friend how seeing one of the dead bodies across the street had made him no longer be able to look. He raised his arm slowly and pointed to the other side of the street. 'It laid there, look... Over there... Just on the edge of the pavement, in front of that shop. Exactly over there, my friend,' he slurred, without turning to where he was pointing to.

The Friend turned and looked to the other side of the street. 'You mean the shop that used to be on the corner? It's no longer there.'

The Photographer raised his hand sluggishly to his chin and closed his eyes for a few seconds to open them and look at his friend again. 'You know, my friend, I truly believe that if one of those people who are so rancorously searching for me and for that naked man, if one of them were to find us here right now, they would immediately bash in our heads with that brick over there.'

The Tree shivered by hearing what the Photographer had just said. Its leaves started to tremble, spreading a chill breeze. The rustling of the leaves made the Photographer and his friend look up. The Photographer managed to get on his knees and put his hand on his friend's shoulder, pressing his other hand against the Tree's trunk, trying to stand up. The Friend put his hands under the Photographer's armpits and hugged him to help him stand straight.

The Photographer pushed him back and stretched his arm towards the other side of the street and said, 'You see that brick over there, my friend? With that damn brick...'

The Friend hugged him again and said, 'Look there is a taxi coming...' He then turned to the street to signal to the driver to pull over.

The Photographer freed himself from his friend's arms. Both fell to their hands and knees.

The Photographer straightened himself and pointed to a place across the street where a concrete brick laid. 'Look... It was there, exactly there, on that corner... I still remember very well...'

The taxi got closer and slowed down to stop in front of them. When they both stood up, pulling on each other's shoulders, the Photographer fell to his knees again and instantly vomited before the Tree.

Again, the Friend put his hand under the Photographer's armpit. The Photographer pulled his arm away and tried to stand by himself, but was sick again, this time in four bursts.

The Taxi Driver jumped out of the car and helped the Friend to lift the Photographer into the back of the car. The Friend sat in the front. The car turned around and drove off up the street, in the direction where it came from.

When they were gone, silence overwhelmed the street. The Tree felt an unknown sadness spreading through all its parts, intensified by the sound of its own shaking leaves.

17

The next day, in the early morning, the Taxi Driver told a passenger about two drunken young guys he had taken home last night. 'But I wish I had left them to die where I found them. Oh, you know how filthy the youth of this city has become, sir!' He threw out his cigarette stub through the car window and looked at himself in the rear-view mirror to adjust his *jamane*, the traditional Kurdish turban, on his head. When his passenger wanted to say something, he preceded him and said, 'They think that freedom means, forgive me, drinking that shit and vomiting on the street. I hope you don't drink, sir, do you?'

The passenger, who sat next to him in a suit, turned to him and said, smiling, 'Well, sir, I sometimes drink that shit too...'

The deafening rumble of the old engine and the creaking sound of changing the gear overpowered both voices. The Taxi Driver put his hand under his *jamane*, scratched his bald head, then fixed the turban again. Embarrassed by his own comment and the answer of his passenger, he tried to buy time by looking through his side window, then in the rear-view mirror and after that, in the side mirror.

'But I don't think you would walk around drunken on the streets, talking about other people's daughters, would you, sir?' he asked apologetically. 'One of them kept wishing he had his camera with him to take a picture of the tree I had picked them up near. "It could have been *the* Tree", he was repeatedly saying all the time. I don't know what they were up to under that tree. And you know, the other asshole, excuse me, kept saying, "Tell me about your girlfriend, tell me... Why don't you just admit it? I swear you have done something with her." Oh God, save me, you know how these dirty lads have besmirched this town? Am I not right, sir, not to let my daughters go out, in fear for those jerks? I just withdrew my oldest one from school.'

He dropped the passenger off in front of the city's old cigarette factory, and gently said that he didn't need to pay.

The passenger threw a dinar coin on his lap and closed the door.

When the Taxi Driver put the money in the pocket of his *sharwal* and started the car, he saw the man through the rear-view mirror, scrutinising his taxi from over his shoulder. He then crossed the street towards the *Asayish*, the Security Agency's building, tidying his tie and straightening his jacket.

18

In his office, the Asaiysh Director apologised to the Neighbour-Girl for bothering her this early in the morning, but he had some good news for her. The Asayish Director's ambition was to link his building with the next door building, the Youth Culture Centre, where the Neighbour-Girl and other young men and women of her party, mainly artists, were working.

'Oh, of course not, sir. You're not a bother. I'd be delighted to hear some good news about our building,' the Neighbour-Girl said, clearly annoyed at the way he looked her over from head to toe. Nevertheless, he did it again.

'We've found you a nice building in Bakhtyari district. It's the building of the—'

'But we told you the other day, sir, we don't want to leave this building. We—'

'Listen, darling,' the Asayish Director interrupted her in turn. 'I know you like this place and of course there is nothing wrong with you staying there. I mean I would be happy to have you there next to me all the time.'

The Neighbour-Girl perched herself on the edge of the sofa while trying to pull down her skirt, whose hem was already far below her knees. She looked him in the eyes and said, 'Sir, I think it's better if you talk about this issue with the head of the youth department of my party. I don't know why you keep approaching me about it.'

'Well, I thought you were in charge,' the Asayish Director leant forwards over his desk, picked up a pen and started spinning it with his fingers. 'Those other youngsters listen to you, I know that. But wait. There is another thing I wanted to talk to you about. Your Photographer friend. He was seen with a girl the other night. I thought you might want to know—'

'No, why should I want to?'

'Well, come on. Do you think I don't know you two have...? I mean—'

'We are only neighbours. That's all, sir. I should go now.' She stood up and, as she seemed to wanting to say something, a man in a suit knocked on the door and came in. He wished the Asayish Director a good morning and, while walking towards him, stared at the Neighbour-Girl with a smirk.

The Asayish Director threw a reprimanding gaze at him.

The man immediately said that he had some information about the Photographer and thought that if they acted quickly, they might find his hiding place.

The Asayish Director blinked with one eye to warn him not to reveal any more details, but it was already too late. The man continued to say that if he could send some guards after the taxi that had just brought him here, the Taxi Driver might lead them to the Photographer.

The Asayish Director blinked again, and the man stopped talking.

The Neighbour-Girl smiled at the Asayish Director, excused herself and then rushed out of the room, closing the door behind her.

'Couldn't you hold it for a second, you idiot?' the Asayish Director reprimanded the man for having revealed all that information in front of a stranger.

'But I thought she wasn't a stranger anymore,' the man said with a nasty smirk.

'What the hell do you mean by that?' shouted the Asayish Director. 'Are you bastards gossiping about her already?'

The man wanted to say something, but the Asayish Director shouted louder, 'How dare you? She is not just *some* girl. You should damn well know that. Have you got his number plate?'

'Oh, yes, sir. Of course!'

'So get the fuck out of here and let them go get him.'

When the man hurried to the door, the Asayish Director called him back and shouted at him again, 'And tell everyone, I never want anyone to talk about her. She will soon be my wife, damn you.' Then he added after a breath, looking furious, 'Hopefully!'

The man ran out of the room apologising and reassuring

the Asayish Director that he was going to arrange a raid on the Photographer.

19

After he came out of the toilet at the Grand Mosque, the Taxi Driver washed his hands at the basin, in the heart of the Mosque's wide court-yard. He dried his hands on his *cummerbund* and tied it again around his waist. He then left the Mosque and went back to where he had parked his car, two hundred metres up the street, just across from the *Mahkama,* the city's Court. He saw two gunmen standing near his car. He gestured to them that it was his car and said, pointing to a hardware store, 'I just need to get something from the shop and will leave immediately.'

At the store, he asked the shopkeeper to give him a tin of sky-blue paint and some nails. When the shopkeeper went to the back of his store, the two armed men came forwards and asked the Taxi Driver whether he had picked up two young drunken guys at the Red Security building under a tree last night and, if so, where he had taken them to. The Taxi Driver confirmed all their questions, surprised.

'But are you sure they were under a tree?' one of the gunmen asked him sarcastically, adding, 'There is no tree in that place. You were not drunk yourself, right?'

The Taxi Driver stroked his grey bearded chin that had not been shaved for a week and said, 'Oh, God forgive me! Do I look like a drunken lad, for God's sake? I hope the Almighty wouldn't make me do such an awful thing! I'm not the man for these kinds of things, brother. Look at my grey beard!' Then when the other gunman asked him if the guys had a camera with them, he answered no but said that one of them kept saying that he wished he had brought his camera to take a photo of the Tree. 'I don't know why that tree was so important to him.'

The armed men looked at each other and asked him to take them immediately to the house where he had dropped off the two guys last night.

The Taxi Driver snatched the black plastic bag containing the paint and nails from the hand of the shopkeeper and paid him quickly before rushing into his taxi and driving away.

He saw through his rear-view-mirror the two gunmen also jump into the back of their car, which was parked in the middle of the street. Two other men sat in the front. The Taxi Driver drove down the street past the Grand Mosque and turned right. The armed men followed him.

The black moustached shopkeeper, who, the other day, after the Friday prayer locked his shop and went to search for the Naked Young Man, was outside of the shop next door and had heard the whole conversation between the Taxi Driver and the gunmen. When they left, he immediately locked up, tied his *cummerbund* and took a taxi right in front of his shop.

Just before the car made a move, he saw and heard his neighbouring shopkeeper, who sold the Taxi Driver the paint and nails, tell his other neighbour, 'Something is off with this man. He hasn't sold anything, yet he's closing! That's not like him, is it?'

20

The young Photographer woke up with a strong headache in his room at his friend's house. While he was rubbing his eyes, he saw the Friend at the door staring at him.

'Sorry, I woke you,' said the Friend. 'I hope you don't have a bad hangover. I've prepared some breakfast for us.'

'That's wonderful! I'll be there in a minute,' the Photographer said, looking around. He noticed that he had not undressed last night but had slept with his clothes and socks on, his shoes thrown beside the mattress. He lay back again, staring at the ceiling. He recalled last night's events and thought that the tree, under which he and his friend had collapsed drunk, must have been the very tree he was looking for!

He could not remember all the details of what precisely had happened or of what he had said, but he remembered very well that that tree was not just any tree. Above all, he was sure that there normally was no tree at that very spot in the street. And it was also unlikely that he and his friend were both hallucinating about the same thing at the same time. Despite his headache, he thought he had to gather himself together, so rolled out of his bed and put on his shoes.

At the breakfast table, he told his friend that he thought he had dreamt of the bodies they talk about last night. 'You know, those bodies have haunted me ever since. It was horrible. The one I told you about, you know how they had killed him? They smashed his head with a concrete brick. His head was flattened over the pathway and the rest of his half-naked body laid on the street.'

'Would you please spare me those details? We're eating, man!'

'I'm sorry. You're right. But, I saw the brick laid still beside his flattened head... Damn it!'

'Come on, man!' the Friend said with a sharp gaze, putting down a piece of bread he had just raised to his mouth.

'I'm sorry, I'm sorry,' said the Photographer, dipping his piece of bred in the yoghurt. But instead of taking a bite, he continued, 'After that, I immediately left my friends and walked back home. I stayed in bed with a fever all that night and whole of the day after. I didn't want anything and couldn't eat anything.'

The Friend shook his head and sighed. He wiped his hands with a tea towel and said that he too had seen three heads cut off and put on the ground, just under the old traffic-police post in the middle of Serah Square in the city centre. 'They had put a cigarette in the mouth of one of the decapitated heads,' he said with ridicule. 'I immediately vomited there, on the street.'

With a retch, the Photographer raised his hand to stop his friend from saying more. 'Oh, God, you're worse!'

'But you already ruined my breakfast,' the Friend said with a chuckle. 'Okay, no more those graphic details. I just want to say that I think that all that was a necessary evil that had to happen. Those people were cruel creatures that had lost all touch of humanity. They didn't deserve compassion, I think.'

The Photographer leant forwards and put his arms on the tabe. 'Violence is just violence, my friend. It's a brutal act, against whomsoever you may use it. I'm still shocked about the fact that I saw to what extent people could be violent.' He sighed and continued, 'You know what shocked me the most?'

The Friend was only nodding and staring at him.

'That both the executed guys and their executioners were as ruthless as each other and could both kill so easily, without pity. After that day, I lost my trust in the world. I started to mistrust every single person around me. I was sure that everyone in this country would lose all their kindness and could heartlessly harm anybody if they started to hate them.'

'I get you. But I have to leave now,' the Friend said, standing up. 'We can continue tonight. I like these kind of conversations.'

'Actually I'm coming out with you as well. Need to do something,' the Photographer said, also standing up.

'Are you sure you want to take the risk?'

'Don't worry, I'll be careful. Wait, I'm going to grab my camera,' the Photographer said and rushed to his room.

An hour after the Photographer and his friend had left, there was a knock on the door at the Friend's house. When the old, semi-blind Mother slowly walked through the front garden over the tiled pathway and opened the front door, three gunmen stormed in and ran past her into the house. Their Commander also stepped in and stood in the doorway. The Mother shouted what was going on and who they were. She trudged to the middle of the courtyard and stood there.

The Commander came closer and stood beside her. 'Did your son's friend stay here last night?'

The Mother flinched, turned to him and said, 'How should I know, sir! Oh, God I'm not complaining, but I can barely see. When my son came back late last night, I was already in bed. I have no idea whether someone was with him or not.'

The Commander took her arm and helped her to go inside. He heard one of his gunmen shouting for everyone to go to where he was, so he also darted out of the living room and ran through the house. He found all his three men in the back room searching some belongings. Books and clothes scattered on the floor, and an unzipped old bag laid at the foot of the bed that was not more than a mattress with a blanket on the floor. It was obvious that someone had slept in this bed who was not a member of the family.

One of the gunmen knelt beside the bag and rummaged through it. It was full of Agfa film rolls, dozens of developed negatives and a bunch of photos, many of them Polaroid. Most of the pictures were of trees.

'Bingo,' said the man, looking at some of the photographs quickly. He turned his head to the Commander, exchanged a knowing look with him and smiled.

Another one of the men bent down to pick up some of the pictures. Suddenly, he let a short shout, 'Oh yay!' He picked out one of the photos, brought it to the Commander and asked, 'Isn't this the girl our director is in love with?'

The other two gunmen sprinted to him, shoulder-fighting for a glimpse of the photo. One of them whistled and said, 'Oh my God! Is that her? I swear I have never seen such a beauty.'

The Commander shouted at his men, 'Grab the bag. Let's leave.'

One of the gunmen quickly put all the photos back into the bag and zipped it. He then left the room with the other two, passing the Commander who still stood at the door.

The Commander had one last quick look at the room, and left. In the living room, he told the old Mother, 'You didn't need to lie to us, *Daya*. That doesn't suit your age. We know that a friend of your son's has been hiding in this house for a while. We will find him.'

The woman replied with a weak voice, 'Sir, I swear to God, I'm not aware of anything. Sometimes my son brings his friends home and they stay for the night. The poor kid feels lonely. Also my nephews come over sometimes. Look! What a mess they have made here. I can't do anything about it, sir. And how should I know what you are looking for. Feel free my son, go and search my house yourselves...'

'Don't worry *Daya*. We've found what we were looking for,' the Commander said, patting her shoulder, then stepping out of the room and into the courtyard. He looked around the garden, then left the house to join his men in the car.

21

The Photographer sat on a Polish Nysa minibus with his camera around his neck. About three hundred metres before his stop, a vehicle in front of the bus slowed down and stopped in the middle of the street. The bus driver reduced speed too. As soon as he halted, a passenger opened the door and jumped out of the bus.

Immediately, a traffic policeman ran from his post on Salim Street and stood right in front of the bus. He registered the vehicle number on the ticket book, then came to the driver and asked to see his licence. The driver gave him his licence and apologised, saying it was not his fault. The passenger had jumped out without permission. The policeman insisted that it was impossible to ignore the incident and started to fill out a ticket. The driver tried to beg him to stop, saying he would never let a passenger step out of his bus again except at a bus stop. But the policeman tore the twenty-five dinar fine out of his book and handed it over through the window anyway, saying, 'Listen, give me just twenty dinars and off you go!'

The driver tried again, begging further, 'Could you please reduce it a bit more? Don't you know how hard it is to earn so much?'

The policeman ignored him, looking over his shoulder to his post on the opposite side of the street and putting his hand on the edge of the window, palm open. 'And what about us?' he said. 'The poor creatures who spend half of our lives standing in the sun, the wind and the rain? Believe me, my share of this bill is only five dinars. Come on, give me eighteen dinars and go. And don't break the law anymore.'

The driver realised that it made no sense to fight any longer. He counted eighteen dinars, put them into the policeman's hand and drove on. The old Polish-made bus started rumbling and roaring.

Throughout the clunk of the gear and the smoke, which was sneaking into the bus through all the gaps in the vehicle, the driver looked at the fine, spat on it, crumpled it and threw it out of the window. The wind forced the crunched paper back into the vehicle. The paper flew past the driver, over his shoulder, and into the body of the bus, where it landed in the lap of the Photographer who was sitting back to back with the driver.

The driver raised his voice and continued nagging, 'These people have no conscience. You all saw it, didn't you? Was it my fault for God's sake? I didn't even notice that damn man jump out of my bus, did I? I swear on the Quran, this is my third fine this month. For any small mistake they punch you with a fine. This is their newest trick. To stop the policemen accepting bribes and let the drivers go, the office now charges them for fifteen dinars out of any twenty-five-dinar fine they give to drivers. They are allowed to keep the rest. Before this measure, we used to slide five dinars into their hands and they released us. But now before you have said a single word, they start writing you the ticket.'

As the driver continued ranting, the Photographer unfolded the crumpled paper, wiped it on the seat and cleaned it of spit. Then, he spread it on his leg, straightened it and took a look at it.

The bust driver went on, 'I swear to God most of them have already filled in the papers and need only to register your name and vehicle number. Is this fair? You tell me. Damn this time we are now living in! Oh, let me not open my mouth. Believe me, I was better off before. Who would have dared during the regime to do such a thing? What should I do with freedom when I don't have enough to feed my children? Look... look at that truck full of gunmen. Did you see how they drove over the barrier and crossed over to the other side? Is this not unfair? Who the hell dares to talk to them? Oh, just leave it. Better not to say anything.'

The Photographer asked the other passengers if they would agree to share the fine with the driver. Some of the passengers took out their wallets immediately. The Photographer pulled one dinar out of his jeans' pocket, handed it over to the man beside him and asked him if he could take care of it because he himself had to get off at the next stop. The man accepted. A woman sitting opposite to them, who seemed to be a civil servant, also gave one dinar to the man beside the Photographer.

'For God's sake, sir,' she said to the driver loudly. 'Stop complaining. It's also your fault, you drivers. If they don't treat you like this, you guys are going to terrorise the streets. You also need to respect the law sometimes. Or at least think about your passengers. Look how your vehicle judders and fumes. We are going to suffocate here in the back.'

The driver turned and complained further, 'Oh, oh, you too want me to throw away my bus? Yes, you do, for sure! Who cares about us, the poor? Since all those new Japanese Coaster buses have invaded the town, no one wants to get in with us. I know it's not in fashion now to travel with a Polish bus, but what should I do? You want me to throw it away as everybody else has done? How do you expect me to feed my children then?'

'I haven't asked you that, sir,' the woman answered. 'But it's also our right, we passengers, to sit in a bit of comfort without getting choked. And, by the way, they invented this penalty system so that at least some money goes to the office itself. Besides, if fines are so high, you lot must also pay more attention. And not all the traffic officers behave like that, sir. Let me tell you, if you think you are not guilty, you can go to the office with your bill and sue them. If anyone has fined you unfairly, they will hang them.'

The driver looked through the rear-view mirror at the woman and shouted, 'Are you really living in this country ma'am? Who would listen to us! Believe me... I swear to God—'

'I'm getting off here, please!' the Photographer yelled.

The driver halted immediately with a jerk. The Photographer, who had already been standing near the door, fell into the woman's lap. Embarrassed, he stood up again apologizing and then rushed to the door.

The woman, her anger reduced by the accident, answered the driver smiling, pretending nothing had happened, 'Well, I'm living in this country and am aware of everything, yes, even more than you, sir. My brother is a traffic officer. He says...'

The Photographer got off the bus and closed the door. Because of the grinding of the bus, he couldn't hear the rest of the conversation. It took some seconds of clunking gear and roaring engine before the old bus drove away, wobbling as it went.

The bus stop was on the corner of the Red Security building. As soon as he stepped on the pavement, he looked around but couldn't find the tree he had seen the night before. He walked a few metres up the road to where he had laid last night and found a chunk of dirt on the footpath. It reminded him of his vomit. That was the place the Tree must have been last night. With disgust he approached the vomit to see if he could find any trace of the Tree. Nothing was evident from the Tree itself, but he saw some mud that seemed to have dropped from its roots.

He hurriedly crouched and took a few pictures of the mud patch. As he stood up, he stepped into the sick. The tips of his shoes got dirty. He stepped away and searched his pocket for a tissue, something he always used to carry, but he grabbed a piece of folded paper instead. He unfolded the paper and noticed that it was the fine the bus driver had received from the traffic police.

He crouched over his shoes, cleaned them up with the paper, crumpled it back up and threw it on the street. When he lifted his head again, he felt dizzy. While a wave of pain washed over his skull, he watched a man wearing Kurdish clothes and turban, search among scattered clutter in the front yard of the Red Security building; hundreds of pieces of abandoned clothes and other goods spread around the wrecks of a couple of tanks that were left from the regime, broken down in the uprising. The clothes and rugs must belong to the many displaced people from other parts of the country, who had fled from the atrocities during the uprising over a year ago and stayed for months in this building or in tents in the local courtyards.

The Photographer rushed towards the man and asked, swaying and panting, 'Are you the guard of this building?'

The man lifted his head from the clutter, looked at him, then said, 'Oh, yes, yeah, I am the guard.'

'Did you notice a tree around here last night or this morning? I mean it was right there last night. Now it's not. It must be somewhere around. It was some kind of a tree, which—'

'No, mate, I haven't seen any tree,' the man said, stroking his own black moustache, then continued his search.

As he looked up again, the man seemed to have noticed the camera slung round the Photographer's neck. He observed him eagerly, smiling, with a searching gaze and asked him in turn: 'Hey you, handsome boy, are you not the Photographer the whole city is looking for? What has brought you here?'

The Photographer felt a heat going through his head then his body and was sure he had blushed. He tried to say something but stuttered. He was looking for the right answer. At that same moment, they both heard a rustle in one of the wrecked tanks a couple of metres away.

They both hurried towards the source of the sound. The Photographer climbed onto the tank immediately, the man helping him by holding one of his legs and pushing him up. When he got on top he tried to look inside the tank through the hatch, but heard a vehicle draw up to the building and halt abruptly with a harsh screech.

The Photographer raised his head and saw a pickup full of gunmen at the gate. The armed men jumped out of the pickup and spread round the building. Another pickup, also full of gunmen, drove into the courtyard. When it halted in the middle of the courtyard, the gunmen jumped out of it and ran towards him and the man, shouting at them not to move but to stay where they were.

The Photographer clenched his camera, jumped from the tank and ran towards the brick fence. Just as he was climbing the fence, two of the gunmen reached him and grabbed at his feet. They ripped him from the wall and dragged him into the pickup, while he shouted and tried to free himself. Another man with a Kalashnikov rifle on his shoulder, climbed the tank and looked inside but apparently couldn't find anything, so jumped down.

Sitting in the back of the pickup, panting, the Photographer heard another one of the gunmen asked the man who he was and what he was doing there. The man said without any hesitation that he was the guard of the building.

In the course of just a couple of minutes, after they quickly searched the whole area, all the gunmen jumped back into the two vehicles and whizzed off, leaving dust clouds behind them.

The Shopkeeper with the dyed black moustache sighed, as he was released from the inquisitive Photographer. 'Are you the guard of this building?' he mumbled, imitating the Photographer's tone mockingly. 'No, I am not a fucking guard.'

He then climbed the tank, carefully, and looked through the round opening. He saw the two splendid hazel eyes of the Naked Young Man staring at him anxiously. The boy was wrapped only in a long, thick leaf. The sun, coming through dozens of holes in the tank, gave him an exotic look and accentuated his anxiety.

The Shopkeeper lent into the cavity of the tank and said in a soothing voice, 'Don't be afraid, young man, I'm not going to hurt you. Give me your hand, come on out, I'm taking you to a safe place, away from other people.'

The Naked Young Man hesitated, crawled back into the pile of dried leaves, twigs and old clothes inside the tank; his leaf curled around his body like a huge snake, rustling.

The Shopkeeper smiled to him, and said again, 'Don't be afraid. Come on, let's go.'

The Naked Young Man stood up slowly, gave his hand to the Shopkeeper, still with some hesitation. The Shopkeeper pulled him gently and helped him to climb out of the tank. As soon as he was on the top, the leaf stretched to wrap around his crotch, his abdomen and his chest.

The Shopkeeper couldn't believe the beauty of the creature who was suddenly and so easily before him. He barely could hide his happiness. When he noticed that fear and distrust were about to appear again on the Naked Young Man's face, he turned from him and looked around cautiously. Then, he untied his *cummerbund* and took off his *chogha,* the top part of his Kurdish clothes, in order to put it around the neck and shoulders of the Naked Young Man, and to hide the leaf. He then wrapped the lower part of his body down to his knees with the *cummerbund*. He climbed down from the tank carefully and opened his arms for the Naked Young Man.

Instead, the Naked Young Man jumped with a quick, astonishing movement, holding the *chogha* with both his hands, and stood in front of the Shopkeeper.

'Let's go,' the Shopkeeper said, grabbing his arm, staring at him amazed. 'You look very tired. You need to take a rest.'

On the street in front of the building, the Shopkeeper took a taxi. He opened the back door and helped the Naked Young Man to get in. He himself got in the front.

'He seems to be sick?' the driver commented, more surprised than curious.

The Shopkeeper let the driver know with a gesture of his hand that the boy was not right in his head. 'You know...' he tried to explain the situation, 'he sometimes leaves the house unnoticed, gets on the bus, jumps off somewhere and gets lost. Sometimes he even takes off his clothes and throws them away. I searched everywhere but couldn't find them.' He straightened the collar of his own shirt and looked at the street.

After twenty minutes, they reached Ibrahim Pasha Street then turned and drove down Sabunkaran Street. The Shopkeeper turned and saw the Naked Young Man look in childish admiration to both sides of the street. Moving his head quickly from one side to the other in excitement, he looked at the old buildings and the crowd. Women, men, the old and young were mingling with each other along the streets, hanging out at the shops, buying fruit, vegetables, cereals and dried food, walking from one shop to another, crossing from one side of the street to the other, ignoring loud car horns, hindering the traffic and making some drivers lose their minds and shout out of the window at them, 'Just walk away ma'am. You think they made the road only for you?' and 'Move on uncle. You're standing in the middle of the road as though you've just lost your donkey.'

After passing the *balakhanas*, the two-story old houses with balconies and balustrades, the taxi entered the Sabunkaran borough by the alley with the Mufty hammam, one of the oldest traditional women baths located on the corner of the street, and continued on through the narrow alleys. They passed a church and heard the bell tolling, along with the shrieks of football-playing children who as soon as the car appeared and honked, stopped their game, and stood, backs to the wall, until the car had gone. The Naked Young Man turned and looked at them through the rear window. When he turned back, the Shopkeeper saw a grin on his face.

The Shopkeeper imitated the sound of the church bell, vibrating his tongue between his teeth. He then said, 'Oh God! This is so annoying. These people disturb us every Sunday with all this ding-donging.'

The driver gazed at him and said, 'Ah, come on, leave them alone. They've only got this one church in the town. What could they say about us, shouting at them five times a day from a mosque on every corner?'

The Shopkeeper realised that he had made a silly comment, so said nothing more until they reached his house in the next alley. 'Just stop here please. We're getting off.'

At home, the Shopkeeper accompanied the half-Naked Young Man to his bedroom, showed him the bed and said, 'You should lie down and have a rest. I'm going back to work. Just feel as if you are at home, precious.'

He took off the *chogha* from the shoulders of the Naked Young Man, unwrapped the *cummerbund* from the rest of his body and helped him to sit on the bed. The Naked Young Man seemed to enjoy the comfort of the soft mattress.

The Shopkeeper said, while wearing back his *chogha* and tying his *cummerbund* around his waist, 'Look, that is the kitchen over there. Just grab anything you would like to eat. Can you actually cook? If not, wait for me. I'm going to come back early this evening. We will eat together.'

When he noticed that the Naked Young Man was not going to say anything, only staring at him in astonishment, the Shopkeeper continued speaking as if he was talking to himself: 'I live alone. I don't have children, so I have an easy life. No headache. No siblings, no parents. Alone, just as you are. You can stay here and you don't need to be worried. No one will be chasing you anymore.'

As soon as the Naked Young Man lay down, the Shopkeeper covered him with the duvet and left the room without closing the bedroom door. In the hall, he looked back at him. The boy's face shone under the yellowish light from a bulb that was suspended from the ceiling. The leaf stuck out from under the duvet, crept up his neck and over his chest.

The Shopkeeper returned to the bedroom, switched off the light, went out and closed the door. He went to the living room, sat on one of the sofas, put his hand under his chin and fell into thought. He felt himself to be wrapped in happiness – a strange feeling he didn't know how to deal with.

After half an hour of sitting and pondering, he stood up, went to the kitchen and drank a glass of water. Upon returning to the living room, he stood for some seconds before leaving his old Sabunkarani house through the front garden.

22

'Oh, great!' the Asayish Director said into his phone. 'I'll be with you in a minute. Right away!' He then hung up immediately and apologised to the three visitors in his office, informing them that he needed to leave for an urgent mission.

The guests said goodbye and hurried away.

The Asayish Director limped off behind them and, while the guests walked to the exit, he and two of his guards walked on to the courtyard in the middle of the complex. They crossed the courtyard and entered the part of the building which housed the cells. He walked down a long hall until he reached one of the cells at the end of the row. Two other armed men were already waiting for him, one of them held the Photographer's camera tight in his hand. When the other turned and went to open the door of the cell, the Asayish Director waved to him and said in a very low voice, almost whispering, 'Leave it. I don't want him to see me.' Instead, he looked into the cell through a small square hole in the upper part of the door. He saw how the Photographer sat on a narrow bed with a thin mattress and only one blanket. The prisoner's head was in both his hands, his elbows on his knees.

After a quick look at him, the Asayish Director stepped away from the door and walked back through the hallway with all of his men. He asked them, still in a low voice, to treat the Photographer very well, not to assault him physically or verbally, and to also put his camera somewhere safe. Finally, they must not permit any visit at all.

The guard with the camera said, 'I'm afraid the camera is damaged, sir. But it was not our fault. He ran and jumped on a wall.'

'Don't worry. We'll pay him for it,' said the Asayish Director before turning to another of the men, asking him to summon one of the interrogators. They then continued on to his office, through the courtyard, the Asayish Director limping the whole way. Just before entering, he asked the guard in front of his door not to admit the Neighbour-Girl if she were to show up, but to tell her that the Asayish Director would not be there again until tomorrow morning. 'Don't give her any information about the Photographer. Absolutely nothing!' he said, then looked at all his men and ordered, stressing each word, 'This applies to every one of you.'

23

Late in the afternoon, the Shopkeeper came home with two bags of food and went straight to the kitchen, where he put some of the goods in the fridge and left the rest on the kitchen table by the sink. He then went directly to the bedroom and quietly opened the door. The Naked Young Man was still asleep.

He drew back the curtains from the window that looked at the back garden. The dim light of the early evening fell on the Naked Young Man and made his flushed cheeks glow even more. The Shopkeeper stared at him for a few minutes, then closed the door quietly and went back to the kitchen to start cooking.

He lit one of the burners of the gas hob and put on a big pan. He put two large spoons of Persian ghee in it. While the oil was heating, he took a chicken out of one of the bags, which he had bought fresh from the market – killed and plucked in front of him. After cutting it up, he put all the pieces into the pan. The oil splashed out of the pan over his face and hands. He grabbed a towel from the top of an old wooden box full of cookware and wiped his face with it quickly. Then, he turned the chicken pieces, added some salt and curry powder and covered the pan with a large lid.

He took a traditional Iranian copper pot out the wooden box, put it on the hob and lit the burner. He put some ghee in this pot also, and left it on the heat. He chopped an onion and put some of it in the frying oil and stirred it with a skimmer. A good aroma began to spread through the house and increased his appetite. He then added some salt and took a small bowl full of Kurdish rice from a bag, put that in a plastic tub and poured cold water in it.

He went back to the copper pot to stir the onions until they were brown. He put a full bowl of water in the pot. The oil splashed all over again. But this time he had stood at a distance, stretching out his arm to avoid the drops of oil. Then, he took the lid off the frying pan and, while he held the lid with one hand over the pan for the steam to stay in the pan, he turned the pieces of chicken with a fork. After recovering the pan, he took a few tomatoes from another plastic bag and chopped them on the kitchen table.

When the water in the copper pot started to boil, he tested it for salt. He liked it. Then, he drained the rice, holding the fingers of his left hand in front of the plastic tub to prevent the rice grains from falling down the sink. When the rice was ready, he put it in the boiling water in the copper pot and started to stir it with a skimmer so that the grains did not stick together.

He quickly chopped another onion, put a small pan on another burner and lit it. Next, he put half a spoon of ghee in the pan. When the fat melted and began to hiss, he put in the chopped onions and stirred them with the skimmer. He then put a pinch of salt on the chopped tomatoes, put them in the pan and covered it. He took two other tomatoes out of the bag and a couple of cucumbers out of another bag and cut them for salad. The aroma of the frying chicken and the fat made him feel a mixture of pride and delight, giving him goose bumps.

Suddenly, he got overheated. He left the salad unfinished, unfastened his *cummerbund,* took off his *chogha* and threw them through the kitchen door into the living room. When he turned to the hob, he noticed that the rice's water had nearly evaporated. He grasped the skimmer and made some holes in the stuck rice so that the rest of the frothing water on the surface flowed down and vaporized. He then noticed that all the burners had slowed down and the one under the small pan with the tomatoes had gone out. He put the skimmer in the sink and shook the cylinder beside the hob a few times until the flames glowed again.

'That asshole must have put water in the gas cylinder,' he murmured, then lit a half-burnt matchstick from the fire under the copper pot and lit the extinguished burner under the tomatoes again. The fire flared all over the hob and under the pans and the pot.

'What a stupid plonker I am!' he mumbled, imagining what would have happened if the gas had exploded and he had been blown in pieces. His house would then have set on fire and the Naked Young Man with the leaf would have suffocated in the smoke while asleep. He could have been burnt before the neighbours could rescue him.

'Okay, let's focus now,' the Shopkeeper told himself. 'No rush!' But the excitement from the fact that the Naked Young Man was only a room away, laying under the duvet in his bed, was too great to handle.

The smell and sizzling of the burning chicken awakened him from his thoughts. He quickly turned off the burner, lifted the pan, took off the lid, put the pan under the cold tap and added water to its contents. At once, the sizzling sound of burning chicken pieces ceased, while steam and smoke rose to the ceiling. He also noticed that the rice was completely drained. He immediately put the pan in the sink, turned off the burner under the copper pot and stirred the rice with the skimmer. But it was too late. The rice had become thick at the bottom and had a smoky smell. He put half a cup of water in it, covered the pot again, then lit the smallest burner, turned down the fire to its lowest heat and put the pot back on.

Suddenly, his eyes fell on the pan with the tomatoes, and he hoped that those weren't burning as well. But when he took the lid off, he saw all the tomatoes and the onions were stuck to the bottom of the pan. He lowered the fire, added some water and covered it with the lid. He let out a sigh and grabbed the towel from the top of the wooden box, wiped the sweat from his face and neck and returned the towel. He then lifted the chicken pan from the sink, put it back on the burner, lit it and lowered the fire.

He waited for a couple of minutes, staring at the half-finished salad: the chopped tomatoes and cucumbers were waiting next to a few more of each that still needed chopping. He grabbed the towel again, wiped his sweat and tossed it on the wooden box where it belonged. He lifted the lid from the tomato pan, stirred what was inside and turned off the burner. He grabbed the knife and quickly chopped the rest of the tomatoes and cucumbers, put them in a plastic bowl, added salt and vinegar, tasted it and put the bowl on the wooden box beside the fridge. Then, he took the lid off from the rice, stirred it and ate a bit of it; it was not so bad, except for the smoky fragrance. He covered it again and turned off the fire. At last, he took a look at the chicken. The added water still needed to be drained. He turned the chicken pieces and stared in spite at the burnt sides for a few seconds. He shook his head, covered the chicken again and left it on the low fire.

He went to the bathroom and washed his face. He grabbed a towel, and while drying his face quickly, he went to the bedroom. The Naked Young Man was still asleep under the duvet; a dim orange light embellished his face. It was about getting dark outside.

The Shopkeeper threw the towel on the floor and closed the curtains. He turned on the light, then took off his clothes and crawled slowly under the duvet. He put his hand on the Naked Young Man's bare thigh, rubbing slowly towards his crotch. The leaf wrapped swiftly around his wrist and clutched it. The Naked Young Man startled awake and jumped out of the bed, dragging the leaf with him, which when unwrapped, its sharp edge scratched the Shopkeeper's wrist.

The Shopkeeper yelled in pain, and noticed a few drops of his blood on the white sheet. He jumped after the Naked Young Man, his balls and penis swinging from his crotch.

The Naked Young Man ran to the living room, the Shopkeeper right behind him.

The Naked Young Man tried to open the door to the courtyard, but it was locked. He jumped on the window sill and opened a window. But the windows were secured with grilles on the outside.

'Don't be afraid, precious. I'm not going to hurt you,' the Shopkeeper said, holding his bleeding wrist with his other hand. He stood still for a moment, in the middle of the room, staring at the frightened boy who leant back on the windows. It had become dark both outside and inside the room.

'Go and sit on that sofa. I'll bring you some clothes,' the Shopkeeper said, stepping back to the door, now covering his own groin with both hands.

The Naked Young Man jumped from the window sill and rushed to the door that led to the kitchen but bumped into the Shopkeeper in the dark. He tripped over the Shopkeeper's *cummerbund* and *chogha* on the floor, leading him to fall over, the Shopkeeper going down with him.

Flattened on the floor, the Shopkeeper hugged the body above him firmly. He started gasping for breath, as the Naked Young Man was becoming heavier and his waist thicker and thicker.

A pungent smell of fresh vegetation filled the air and the Shopkeeper heard chilling sounds of crackling tree branches and rustling leaves. In the dark, he was unable to see how the Tree became bigger and bigger, its branches and leaves filling the room. As though stuck in the middle of a nightmare, the Shopkeeper shouted breathlessly but his voice was smothered.

Minutes later, a tumult of shouting broke out. A few men jumped over the outside walls of the house into the courtyard. One of them opened the outside gate for other people, dozens of women, men and children, to enter the courtyard and garden. Some men began to pound on the door to the living room and call out for the owner of the house.

One of the men noticed the roots of a tree sticking out through the windows, amongst the broken glass and the window grilles. He held two of the iron bars, put his face between them, and stared in. He gasped when he saw that a huge tree was foisted on the room. It was caged in between the ceiling and the floor, its branches trapped in the sofas, chairs and coffee tables. The man noticed that the owner of the house was trapped under the tree. 'Guys, you should see this,' he shouted.

Some of the other men kicked the wooden door to the living room until the lock broke. But the tree's trunk still blocked it, preventing it from opening. So, then they broke down the door altogether and took it off its frame, that way everyone could lend a hand in removing the man from under the tree, but they pulled in vain. Two of the men ran back to their homes and brought a pick and a sledgehammer and started breaking down the doorframe and parts of the wall. But when another three men ran via the narrow side-path to the backyard, they found that the back door of the kitchen was unlocked.

They entered the house and ran through the smoke emanating from the pan of chicken. One of them rushed into the kitchen and turned the flame off from under the pan.

Other people entered the house through the same door. In no time the house was full of men, women and children. A few men entered the living room and helped from various sides to lift the tree, eventually freeing the naked Shopkeeper. They took him to the bedroom. Three women, who were opening the windows to enable the rest of the smoke in the house to disappear, turned their eyes away.

The men put the naked Shopkeeper on the bed and noticed that there were a few blood drops on the white sheet. They exchanged a glance and shook their heads. One of the men requested the women to leave the bedroom immediately. Another held the Shopkeeper's left wrist in his hand and put his own ear to his chest. Now and then he put a finger under his nose to check whether he was still breathing, but they all noticed that the insensitive body was turning pale and losing all signs of life. When they could no longer help him, they wrapped him with the sheet, lifted him on their shoulders and went out of the house to take him to the mosque.

In the living room children were yelling, jumping up and down on the tree, running along its trunk, swinging on its branches and picking its leaves. Now and then a woman would have a look at the tree or call her children to leave the house. Everyone who saw the strange tree for the first time, was astonished and wondered what had brought this tree into the house of this man, of whom the neighbours knew very little, except that he was handling paint and ironware near the Grand Mosque and that he lived alone. His mother had been the only other person living in the house for the last twenty years or so, for as long as any of them could remember, but she had died a few years ago. The neighbours had always been suspicious of him, especially because he was now aged over fifty but was still unmarried. When he walked through the alleys of Sabunkaran, children ran away and stuck their tongues out behind him or repeated the rumours their parents always hinted at when he was discussed at home. Sometimes they threw stones at him from the rooftops or shouted at him to leave the neighbourhood, but he always ignored this, which in turn made him more mysterious to them. Nonetheless, for him to have ended up like this no one could ever have imagined.

One of the neighbours asked everyone to leave the house, closed the kitchen door and told them to leave the courtyard and garden as well. He noticed that a man had brought an axe, apparently to cut up the tree. The neighbour told him politely that they had better leave it for now and think about what to do about it tomorrow. At last, they all left the house and the neighbour closed the outside gate behind him as he went.

24

When the people left the house and disappeared from the alley, an overwhelming silence dominated the house. The Tree heard only the soft rustling of its own leaves in the gentle breeze of the early evening coming in through the broken windows, and felt a pleasant chill in its roots. Suddenly, a couple of droplets hit its roots, then a few more, and more and more until a shower broke the silence.

Despite the stroking feeling in its roots and leaves from the late spring rain, a devastating grief seized the Tree from inside, as if a big amount of mud covered its heart and prevented it from pounding.

The rain stopped and the breeze became cooler. The Tree collected all its strength and moved slightly back and forth and side to side until it succeeded in pulling its roots out of the window bars and bringing them inside the room. Then, it made even more effort to free its branches from the furniture. With a bit more difficulty, it finally crawled backwards and out of the room. While in the garden, the Tree stood amongst the other trees and plants, stretching and breathing for some minutes. Then, it opened the high wooden gate, bent over and stepped into the alley. The pleasant savour of the mud that had emerged after the spring shower gave it even more strength. It took the same way back as the taxi brought them in the morning.

Walking through the narrow alleys of Sabunkaran, the moonlight and the clear sky eased the Tree and helped it overcome its grief. Furthermore, the Tree soothed itself by reasoning that the man's death was not its fault. It was just an accident and actually a result of the man's behaviour most of all.

When the Tree heard some men approaching, it went aside and hid beside a wall. The men were talking about the incident and of the mosque where the body of the Shopkeeper had been taken. The Tree followed them carefully.

As they passed the church, a small group of men and women accompanying a priest came out, greeted the passing men and stood in front of the church. The Tree immediately stopped beside a wall. The priest locked the door of the church with a big key and left with the men and women, in the opposite direction of the other men going to the mosque. When they passed the Tree, they didn't notice it, and because another shower had begun, they bent their heads and hurried up. As soon as they disappeared down another narrow side alley, the Tree rushed to catch up with the mosque-going men.

When it reached Sabunkaran Street, it stood in front of a closed shop, under the *balakhana,* a balcony with a wooden balustrade, found on an old Sabunkarani house. The Tree saw the men cross the street and took the alleyway beside the *Shaab* hamam, a men's public bath. When it made sure there weren't any cars and the few people on both sides of the street weren't aware of its presence, the Tree crossed the street swiftly and followed the men in the rain.

After a few minutes, as the rain had stopped, the Tree caught up with the men and entered the mosque. It stood beside some other trees in the small garden and saw how five men had gathered in a small door-less room beside the toilets, washing the pale naked body of the Shopkeeper. When they finished, three of them lifted him from the stone bench and two others wrapped the body with a clean white linen sheet. Then, they put him in a coffin, covered the coffin with a blanket, lifted it and took it inside the prayer hall.

Suddenly, a group of women accompanied by two children came into the mosque's courtyard, crying and beating their heads with both hands. They passed the Tree and went inside the prayer hall. The Tree heard a man in front of the row of toilets in the courtyard telling another man that those women were all cousins of the Shopkeeper. Watching this scene made the Tree sadder than it already was.

It noticed that there was another door at the other end of the big, long courtyard. It waited for a moment until nobody was left in the yard and then went through the door. On the other side was a narrow alleyway, which he took until reaching Goran Street. It stood there for a moment, waiting for the vehicles with flashing lights, splashing the rain puddles on pedestrians, to allow for a gap in the traffic. Then, it crossed the street and entered another narrow alley. It continued down the alleyways of Pirma Sur quarter until a window drew its attention. A golden dim light came out through the triangle opening between the half-drawn curtains.

The Tree halted in the shade, just beside the window, and looked inside. Two women – one looking a few years older – sat on a sofa behind the window, with each one leg resting on the sofa and their other leg hanging down on the floor. The younger woman talked about how she had spent her life's nicest night two days ago with a guy she's known for a long time. When the older woman asked her repeatedly, 'And? What have you done? Have you done anything?' she answered, shaking her head, 'Oh, no, no… that's actually not important. The most important thing for me was that I realised I wasn't wrong about his love for me. But what makes me sad is that we haven't been able to see each other since then. He didn't visit me or try to contact me in any way. I mean… But the fact is, he is now…'

Her friend tried to sooth her and say that she thought it was better that way and that normally it was the man who should take the next step. 'And come on girl, it's only been two days. Just wait until—'

'That's exactly the problem,' the younger girl said, clenching her friend's arm firmly. 'Why should it be like that? And besides, I think it was me who had to give him a sign that I also wanted him, poor guy. I mean we haven't done anything… But that's not the point. I'm just afraid he won't dare continue this any further.'

The girl stopped for a few seconds, staring at the ceiling before continuing in a regretful tone, 'It just took a long time before we told each other about our feelings for one another. I don't know why I revealed my love to him so late, when I fell in love with him the very first moment I saw him two years ago. I was sure it was the same from his side. The last two days I've had this feeling as if I've wasted the past two years of my life. Why did I wait so long? Why?'

The friend wanted to say something, but the girl had turned her face, looking to the wall opposite her and seemed that she was talking more to herself now than to her friend.

'Just as if those two years were of paper that got burnt with a spark,' the girl started again. 'Only ashes left… How can I not feel broken and battered? I wonder if he was right when he warned me all the time that I was wasting my time with politics. With something that not only makes me unhappy, it also doesn't do anything except for support those leaders and new senior officials who are striving for nothing other than to fill their own pockets and sell big words to us. Words they used to use for years to recruit the youth to fight in the mountains. They want us to stay rebels and their loyal *peshmerga*, while they themselves are looting the country's fortunes. I don't know why I always look at the world from another angle. He is right telling me I should have been a poet or musician. He is the only one who sees my poetical soul. But that's because he is a photographer and artist himself, you know?'

'Oh, so he's your neighbour, is he?' said the friend, surprised. 'Oh, God... You're in love with your neighbour-boy!'

'Shush! You shouldn't tell anyone. You promise?'

'Sure, sure...' said the friend, putting her hand on the girl's knee. 'But tell me more about him. Come on!'

The girl looked again at the wall opposite her and continued, 'Well, he tries to encourage me to write. But I would actually like to sing more than anything else. I always have such a desire to sing and express my sadness with singing. The grief of all that I'm experiencing as a woman in this society.'

'Oh, please sing for me. I'm curious to hear your singing voice,' the friend said, shifting in her place.

'Shush! Not now, darling,' the girl said, grabbing her friend's arm. 'You know what my problem is? I don't enjoy any Kurdish songs or music. I'm living in deep conflict because of this. Even though I spend all of my time and energy in politics, I'm sorry, I still hate all their nationalistic songs, anthems and patriotic odes.'

The other woman stared at her, frowning.

'And the most annoying thing is that I can't tell anybody about this,' the girl continued. Well, now I'm telling you. But I know you understand me, don't you?' She looked at her friend, putting her hand on her shoulder.

The friend nodded, still staring, lips pursed.

'In fact, I can't reveal to anyone that except a couple of songs,' the girl revealed, 'I really don't enjoy any of the songs people of this country are listening to collectively. I don't dare admit to anyone that most of the time, I secretly listen to western music on my small radio and cassette recorder without even understanding it.'

The friend looked at her with a questioning gaze.

The girl continued, 'Another problem is my shyness. You wouldn't believe it, but I'm really very shy.'

'I wouldn't say that,' the friend said with a smile.

'No, I mean it. The funny thing is that nobody sees it, but it has taken over my existence. It has influenced all my life. I think it's this sense of shame they give you with the mother's milk. They raise us up with it, don't you think? That's why whatever I do to hide this shyness, it emerges in the most crucial moments. It's so rooted inside me that it's become impossible to eradicate. I think my work in politics, and my seriousness is to hide it. But it's also unfair that in this society a girl like me cannot express her love for a boy.'

Her friend put a hand on her arm and said, 'Well, you're a real poet. He is right. And I'm happy you opened up to me this way. This is the first time you've talked to me like this. But I have to admit, I'm not sure if I understand you fully.'

The girl chuckled, looked down a bit, then raised her head again, looked into her friend's eyes. 'You promise this all remains between us, right?'

The friend nodded. 'Of course, girl. Whom should I tell? You're my only friend.'

'I mean I'm afraid it's already too late. I think this sensitive guy who hides his clumsy weakness and insecurity behind his camera doesn't see that this solid fort I've built around myself is just a gild. I'm afraid he will not dare to break it again. And I don't think I would—'

'Stop, girl! You know these intellectual talks of yours are a bit too vague for me. I don't get all what you say. You use so many difficult words, girl. But never mind! I think maybe it's just a bit too early. He's young, and of course he wouldn't dare to take such a step to marry—'

'It's not about marriage. I don't want him to come and ask for my hand now. I mean… And by the way, what I wanted to tell you was that he's been arrested, although I haven't been able to confirm it yet. But yes, they arrested him today.'

'Oh, dear! Why was he arrested? Poor guy! What did he do?'

'He didn't do anything. It's just this whole hassle with this tree-man. They are suspecting him of being this naked guy.'

'Oh, I didn't know that it was all about him,' the friend said with an expression on her face that the Tree did not understand. But by now, it had understood that they were talking about the Photographer.

'No, of course it's not him,' the younger girl said. 'I mean, how could it be him? I know what he's been doing almost every day and where he stays and—'

'But can you not help him through your connections?'

'Oh, yes, I think I can. I can for sure if I were to give in to this man.' She halted for a moment, looking at her friend's face that wore the same facial expression that she had had earlier, but this time the Tree could make out that it was maybe intended to show surprise.

'You know, there is this man... He is the Asayish Director, actually.'

'You're kidding me! Don't tell me the director of the *Asayish* is also in love with you! Oh dear, what a lucky girl!'

'Oh, no, you think so? That's a disaster. Have you seen him? I bet you don't even know who he is.'

'Not really.'

'By the way, he hasn't said anything yet. But I know what he wants. He always tries to create opportunities to see me and talk to me, to do something important for me. He is bullying me, actually. And he's done everything to put my friend in jail just to keep him away from me. Who knows, maybe he even created this whole commotion of some naked man and I don't know what, just to...'

An ambiguous feeling fluttered through the Tree; a feeling of relief about being thought of as a doubtful fable. At the same time, it felt sad not to be seen to exist in reality.

The girl was now staring at the ceiling. Her friend put her hand on her knee, looking straight at her, and said, 'Listen lovely. Don't lose your chance. It's really—'

'Oh, don't even think about it,' the girl raised her voice. 'You know how old he is?'

Suddenly, a door opened on the other side of the alley. An old man came out with crutches under his armpits, crossed slowly the alleyway and stood in front of the door beside the window where the two girls were talking warmly. While the old man pressed on the doorbell, he looked at the Tree, surprised.

Hearing the buzzer, the younger girl stood up briskly. Her friend stood up too and said, 'I should leave. It's late already and I think you have another visitor?'

Without answering her, the girl opened the door of the living room held it for her friend. Then, after her friend went out of the room, she turned off the light; the golden triangle of light disappeared abruptly, and the alley got darker.

In the dark, the Photographer's father wanted to press once more the buzzer, but the Neighbour-Girl opened the door. She greeted him, then asked for him to come in.

The old man shifted aside to avoid the dim light coming out through the gap in the door, and said it was too late to go in but that he wanted to inform her about his son who had apparently been arrested. 'Could you maybe go tomorrow morning to inquire what's happened, darling?'

'Oh, don't worry, sir! I know about it, and I've already made an attempt to help free him,' the Neighbour-Gril said, while looking back over her shoulder. She stepped aside and made way for her friend to come out. After the guest, Neighbour-Girl's mother came out. Both women greeted the old man and asked about his health. They also expressed concern for the arrest of his son.

The guest tightened her headscarf, said goodbye and walked away down the alleyway.

The Neighbour-Girl suggested to the Photographer's father that he go back home and sleep. He didn't need to be worried, she assured him. His son hadn't done anything wrong, there was just a misunderstanding that would soon be cleared up.

'I'm going to do my best, I promise. And now, I'm going to change immediately and go to this acquaintance who can help us get him released,' the Neighbour-Girl said. Before she returned inside, she added, 'I don't know why the people of this city have become so paranoid about him, poor guy! One moment they say he is roving through the city naked and another moment they say he's trying to horrify people by spreading a rumour about a tree that is supposedly wandering through the streets.'

The old man wanted to say something about the tree in front of their window, but when he turned round, the tree was no longer there. He frowned for a moment, wondering where the tree should be, but instead of saying anything about it, he thanked the Neighbour-Girl and said, 'Okay, darling! I hope you can get something done.'

'Have a good night, sir! Please don't worry!' the Neighbour-Girl said and went back inside.

Then, her mother said goodbye and went inside, closing the door.

The Photographer's father slowly crossed the alley back home in the dark, his crutches before him, his right trouser leg swinging from his half-amputated leg. When he entered his house and shut the door, he leant back on the door and stayed there for a moment. He heard a swish and rustling leaves. He opened the door but saw nothing in the dark.

25

The Neighbour-Girl felt more upset than happy when the Asayish Director told her that he would let her see the Photographer through a hole in his cell door. She pouted, as she sat on the sofa in his office, with legs crossed. He also warned that she was not allowed to talk to him, as he was under investigation. He said he hoped she wouldn't expect him to behave like a corrupt man and use his authority to permit her meet the Photographer. 'What would people gossip about, do you think, if I were to do that?' he said staring at her.

His remark made her nervous. She lowered her eyes and looked at her own shoes, swaying slightly. Suddenly, she realised she had red high-heels on. She immediately uncrossed her knees, placed them neatly together, and dragged both feet under the sofa. Her left foot hit the plastic bag she'd brought for the Photographer. She quickly bent and straightened it so it didn't fall and reveal its contents: food, clothes and a book.

The Asayish Director threw a glance at the bag, then lifted his eyes again to her and continued, 'They would say, of course, I did it for a woman because I wanted something from her and you know I am not such a man, don't you?'

'Of course, I know that. But it's not a big deal. I just wanted to check if you had him and everything was fine with him,' she said, trying to get herself out of his conspiracy.

'Oh, no, don't worry about him. He is fine. I'm actually not even officially allowed to let you watch him or go any close to his cell. But I'll do this for you. So you'll be sure he is okay.'

'Thank you, sir!' she said, adding, while she stood up, preparing to leave, 'No need actually. I am reassured already.'

'Oh, no, no… That's just a small favour. Wait. I'll take you there.' He stood up and hurried, limping, passing her, towards the door. Before he opened it, he turned and gestured to the plastic bag that was still under the sofa. 'Is that food and stuff for him?'

'Oh, I almost forgot it. Yes. But if it's not allowed, I'll take it back with me,' she said, turning to fetch the bag.

The Asayish Director said, holding the door for her, 'Leave it there. We will give it to him.'

When she was out, the Asayish Director followed her out of the room.

In the hallway, he overtook her by a step and led her through the courtyard. When they reached the cell, he shifted up a flap from the rectangle hole high at the top part of the iron door.

The Neighbour-Girl hurried to the door and stood on her toes to reach the hole. She saw the Photographer laying on his back on a simple, narrow bed. When he caught a glimpse of her, he jumped off the bed and ran to the door. The Neighbour-Girl lost her balance and leant backwards on her high heels but before she fell, the Asayish Director caught her by her waist and helped her to stand on her feet again.

The Photographer's eyes and nose appeared in the hole. He shouted her name.

As the Neighbour-Girl wanted to step forwards again, the Asayish Director closed down the flap on the hole.

'Are you all right darling? You didn't hurt your ankle, did you?' the Asayish Director asked her with evident concern. He turned immediately and said, 'Let's go. That was it.'

The Neighbour-Girl said, while following him, 'I wish I could talk to him for a second.'

'I can't allow that, dear. I may do soon.' He started limping faster.

When he said goodbye at the exit, he looked at her shoes and said, 'They are beautiful, but almost made you break your ankle.'

'Oh, I'm wearing them because I have an interview with the Minister of Culture in an hour.'

The Asayish Director lifted his eyes and stared right into hers. 'You didn't need to involve him in this matter,' he said surprised. 'I promised you everything would be all right. Or do you want him to intervene in the building issue? You don't need him for that, darling. It's all yours. You just keep it. Tell your mates you can all stay there.'

'Oh, no, no. I'm meeting him for something else,' she said. 'We want to organise an art event and want the ministry to finance it.'

'So you want to impress him with these beautiful shoes and smart shirt? What a lucky man!' the Asayish Director said, looking at her cleavage.

She immediately stuck both lapels of her shirt together and closed her chest completely. She then thanked him quickly for letting her see the Photographer and said goodbye. She hurried out of the building, going to her own building, next door.

Although she felt a kind of triumphant pleasure in hurting the Asayish Director's feelings or at least making him jealous, she thought her clothes might cause her some more trouble. She had heard of the womanising activities of the minister and his flirtatious character. He happened to be one of the most well-known poets of the last two decades. Despite him being in his early fifties, she would not mind being flirted with or pursued by him. Who wouldn't want that, she thought. Everyone, especially in the artistic world, agreed it was a pleasure to have a minister who was a poet himself.

At the entrance of the Youth Culture Centre, the Neighbour-Girl stepped back onto the street, took a taxi and went home to change before going to the ministry.

26

The Naked Young Man was spotted even during the four days the Photographer was in prison. Also, more and more people were now said to have seen a tree that disappeared as quickly as it appeared in different places. Some people thought that it was not possible for one specific tree to be in all those places; there must be someone or a group of people who intended to terrorise the city by planting this tree or several trees by the side of the streets. Others suspected that the governing political parties were responsible, planting and replanting trees in order to draw the attention of the people away from their inefficiency and the unbelievably vast amount of corruption that was growing more and more each day into all classes, all institutions and organisations; into all businesses and governmental and even non-governmental affairs.

For his part, the Asayish Director didn't pay attention to the bigger issue. He had held the Photographer for his own reasons and had got the most out of it. The problem was that it was already in the papers and on radio and television that a young Photographer had been arrested for suspicion of running around the city without clothes, terrifying people with the rumour that there was an exotic tree arising here and there with supernatural powers.

This most recent rumour had made the Photographer stare at his interrogators with his mouth wide-open, in total disbelief. 'Come on guys, you can't be serious. You know how people of this city are with rumours. It's unbelievable. How can I be in all those places so quickly in such a short time? I mean, I can prove where I was at all those times in which people claim that they saw me naked. Ask my friends. Go and ask—'

'That's exactly the problem: rumours,' shouted the *Asayish* officer who interrogated him. 'You are the one who is spreading the rumours. You are the very one who is claiming to have seen this tree and that naked guy. Okay, I would like to believe you might have seen some naked man, but you're confusing everyone with this tree hassle. And that is why you are here.'

The Photographer shook his head and tried to explain that he hadn't spread any rumour but had only told some friends what he had seen on that particular evening. 'And you know how gossipy people of this city are, sir. I don't know how this story was spread so quickly. And by the way, what made it all worse is the very fact that it's true, there is a naked gay roaming around in the city. When it comes to the Tree, I'm not so sure but honestly—'

'Is he still talking about this tree?' The Asayish Director came into the interrogation room and went straight to the Photographer, put a hand on his shoulder and said, 'Listen, brother. We can help each other get out of this nuisance. This is the last thing we want in these tough times.' He nodded to the interrogating officer to leave and took his place opposite the Photographer.

As soon as the officer had shut the door behind him, the Asayish Director turned off the recorder on the table between him and the Photographer, then stared at him and said, 'We can also help each other on another issue.'

The Photographer looked at him with questioning eyes, but also intrigued.

'I bet you want to get out of the country just like all other young men, right?'

'I might wish that, but I've got to look after my father who only has one leg. I mean I wish if—'

'Don't worry, brother,' the Asayish Director said. 'Your father will be fine. I can help you with all that. I mean I can help you to leave. I'll arrange a fake passport and you could—'

'But why do you want me out of the country?' the Photographer asked surprised, although he already had his suspicions of what the answer might be.

'I don't want you out. I'm only offering it if that's what you want.'

'But as I said, I can't even consider it.'

'So maybe I can help you with something else. I mean, you tell me, what can I do for you?'

'Thanks a lot for that! But I don't need anything if you just let me go. I don't know why I am here.'

'You're beginning to act a bit more courageous. No one dares to talk to me like this!'

'I'm sorry, I don't want to sound disrespectful. But I think there's been a lot of misunderstanding.'

'It's true,' said the Asayish Director, standing up, turning his back on him and limping towards the wall. 'Maybe there was a mistake in arresting you. But as you are here, we can still make a deal.'

'I don't understand how I can help with anything,' the Photographer said with fear of what suggestion might be made. He put his handcuffed hands on the table.

'Oh, it's actually very easy. You just stay away from that girl. You know whom I mean,' the Asayish Director said, turning to him.

The Photographer took a deep breath and then said, 'She to whom you didn't let me talk the other day. I saw her looking at me through the spyhole.' He closed his eyes and lowered his head to his chest. He didn't know what he should say more.

'Not so very difficult, is it?' said the Asayish Director, returning to his seat.

The Photographer raised his head, opened his eyes, and said, staring at the Asayish Director, 'I can't avoid her. We are friends and neighbours. We are very close. Both our families. I mean... And if you think we have something together, I can assure you we do not.'

The Asayish Director stared back at him for a few seconds, then stood up and hobbled towards the door. His hand on the doorhandle, he turned back towards the Photographer and said, 'So I assume we understand each other. I'll let you go home today. I promised her. She was so worried about you. You, lucky guy! But leave that tree hassle for us. I actually don't give a fuck about what that guy does and what magic he is going to put on the city. I've left all that to the police. We have more important things to do here at the *Asayish*.'

27

'Don't worry, my son,' said the Photographer's father, after listening to him talk about his time in prison, happy to see him back as he had not trusted the authorities to treat his son well. 'I'm sure no one will bother you any longer.'

'Is there something you're not telling me, Dad?'

'Actually, I wanted to tell you that it was our neighbour who saved you from this scourge of a man. But let's hope it didn't cost her too much.'

'What do you mean, Dad, please?' the Photographer pleaded. He looked his father right in the eyes, realising that a bad feeling he had earlier in the day was not misplaced. He told his father, 'I went to her place next to the *Asayish* building right after they released me, but no one would tell me anything clear about where she was. And just before coming home I knocked on their door, her mother was kind of vague about it too. She said "let's see", when I asked her to tell her to come and see me when she gets home. Dad, do you know anything?'

'Listen, love,' the Father said, putting a hand over his son's across the small table between them, seemingly trying to find the right words. 'This girl loves you. I'm sure about that. But you've been so careless to her. I know you love her too. I can see how she means almost everything to you. But lately, this whole tree drama and I don't know what has taken all your attention. I mean look at what all this has led to. They almost took you away from me. I really—'

'What's happened, Dad? Tell me,' the Photographer said, pulling his hand from under his father's.

'Two days ago, this *Asayish* man sent his old mother and sister to ask for her hand.'

'What?' the Photographer shouted, standing up.

'Sit down, Son. Nothing happened,' the Father ensured him. 'Yet.'

'Yet?' the Photographer asked with a mixture of surprise and relief, sitting down again, waiting impatiently for more.

'If you are careful, you could still win her back.'

'What do you mean win her back, Dad? What are you talking about? I mean… Are you saying she has agreed?'

'No, no, I think she is just trying to keep him in line. Maybe the man comes to his senses. This is what I've understood from her mother.'

The Photographer put his hand under his chin, with his elbow on the table, pondering. After a minute, he stood up, went to the sink, poured a glass of water, drank it, then turned to his father, asking him with a gesture if he too would like some water.

The Father shook his head, then stood up with the help of his crutches and suggested that his son should go with him to sit in the garden. The Photographer followed him, leaving the kitchen.

'By the way,' said the Father while sitting on the outside bench beside him, putting his crutches between his legs. 'Now, I believe you about this Tree. I also saw it… Oh, but shush! Don't tell anyone. They would think it's in the family.'

The Photographer laughed loudly, happy to see his father after so many days of being away from home and to hear his amusing pessimism. 'You are kidding me, Dad! Are you just saying that you have seen the Tree to stop me from thinking that I'm the only crazy one here?'

'Oh, no, no, Son. I'm bloody serious. I saw it across the street, right in front of our neighbours' window. But then it disappeared quickly.'

'But what do you think of it?'

'It was wonderful. I mean I saw it only fleeting, but it was so extraordinary. I also heard him behind the door, walking down the alley. But I think we're all deluded, my son. It's just an apparition. There's some kind of hope personified in this gorgeous Tree that appears only to people like you and me who are wishing for real change.'

'I love your attitude, Dad! Now you also have some hope.'

'My only hope is you, my son! I'm done! I really wouldn't care who is going to do what if it wasn't for your future. I'm more a burden now than anything else.'

'What burden? Please don't say that, Dad!' the Photographer said with a sad tone in his voice.

'Ah, of course! Now leave it. let's make dinner together. Or, you know what? Go and have some rest. I'll make it for us.'

'You see, it's still you who is looking after me. It should be the other way around. But okay, I'll accept it for tonight,' the Photographer said with a wink and went to his room, smiling at the sudden change in his father's mood. Maybe his release had given his father some hope after the gloomy days of thinking he might have lost his last son. Or maybe it was simply the tree's effect. It might even be by helping the tree-man to return to his natural environment.

28

It had been on the radio that a tree, very likely the same tree people were talking about, had squashed a man to death in his own living room. What had made people angrier was that even after the arrest of a photographer and the death of a shopkeeper, the Naked Young Man had still been seen in various places throughout the city. Some people even swore that they had observed the silhouette of a wandering tree.

The *Khatib* complained to the Governor that, in his view, the police and *Asayish* were wasting their time on this myth of a tree and had forgotten the main issue, which was this scandalous naked boy who was threatening the dignity of the community. 'A city full of armed men couldn't have arrested this crazy lad yet?' he said to the Governor before standing up and leaving his office furiously. At the door, he said reluctantly goodbye to the Governor.

The Governor, who during their conversation had left his desk to sit on a sofa opposite the *Khatib*, rose to his feet and offered his hand at the door. 'I promise I'll do my best to end this disturbance as soon as possible,' he said while shaking hands, and holding the door for his guest. 'But there are so many problems in the city that we simply can't cope with them all at the same time,' he added. 'And you know, sir, how impatient people are! They want us to become a state in the course of two nights and solve all their problems in a country as devastated as this.'

The *Khatib* gazed at him and dashed out of his office with a swoosh of his cloak. In the courtyard, he saw a group of men and women gathered on the other side of the street opposite the *Parezga*, the Governorate Council, holding a banner that he could not read. They were shouting slogans and demands, which were also inaudible. The policeman who accompanied him to his car told him, 'Those are teaches from the villages around the city, sir. They are threatening to strike until they get higher salaries and paid on time.'

While his driver was holding the front passenger door for him, the *Khatib* shook his head and got into the car. He turned to another imam who was sitting in the back, and said, 'It's all a desperate situation. Desperate!'

The driver jumped in the car and pressed the gas immediately. They drove into the street amongst the teachers who at that moment were crossing, blocking the town hall gate. The *Khatib* and his companions heard one of the teachers shouting, 'You are humiliating us by reducing us to second-hand clothes and expired rice and wheat.' A group of other teachers followed, 'We don't need your rubbish. Take it back, take it back!'

The imam in the back seat said to the *Khatib*, 'They are totally right, sir. I swear it's true. In the old days teachers had such a reputable image. They were respected and had a high position in the community. But now even their students earn more money than them smuggling goods and all kind of lucrative jobs after school. Can you imagine? Kids!'

While the car moved slowly through the teachers, the *Khatib* said, 'I know, *mamosta*. I know how miserable their lives have become. Indeed!'

The imam said, 'Oh, that's for sure. My son is a teacher in Arbat. He says that now and then some NGO guys come to his school and bring a couple of sacks full of old clothes. The pupils swatch their teachers put their heads in those sacks searching for a shirt and empty them on the desk of the school director to divide the clothes between them. He says that when they leave the school in the afternoon, the pupils laugh at them and… Is this not scandalous?'

When their car reached the end of the street, the *Khatib* turned his head and saw through the rear window that the Governor had come outside and was talking to the demonstrating teachers.

29

In the four days that the Photographer had spent in prison, the Tree had been wandering through the city's many streets and alleys; it had seen and heard countless things, though it had not understood everything. It observed people's life but failed to comprehend much of their behaviour. It could not understand all what they did or what they meant when expressing themselves. It missed the simple life it had left behind. And as a man, his biggest worry at the start of each day was to find a place to hide for the rest of the day from the people who couldn't stand somebody walking around half-naked as he was. His fear of getting arrested and being cut to pieces as the Photographer had described that night near the Red Security building or as the men had planned to do after the accident with the Shopkeeper, had made him more cautious. He was looking for a place where he could settle, but found himself every morning in another unknown location. He had desperately given up the search for Qilyasan as it seemed almost impossible for him to find his way back to his old life amongst the trees around the creek, the place where he had grown up.

Recently, a middle-aged woman had been looking for the Photographer to ask him where exactly in Qilyasan he had seen the Tree for the first time. She had read an interview with the Photographer in a newspaper for a small political party, in which he had revealed the story of the Naked Young Man. Although most people found it to be nonsense and thought that he truly had lost his mind, the woman had discovered a purpose in the story worthy of pursuit. Therefore, she had found the office of the newspaper and come in early in the morning to ask for the Photographer. The caretaker had asked her to wait in the small waiting room until the editor-in-chief came.

When the Editor arrived, the caretaker stuck his neck out of the waiting room, where he also had his place and small kitchenette, and said that there was a woman who claimed she had new information about the Naked Young Man.

'Amazing! Thank you! Can you tell her to wait ten minutes or so because I'm expecting a visitor who might show up any moment,' the Editor said, while opening the door to his office. He hadn't even finished his sentence when the guest came in and said hello to him and the caretaker.

'Oh, you're here already!' said the Editor, turning to the guest. 'Great! Come in.'

The guest was a writer who now and then wrote for the paper. The Editor shook hands with him and held the door for him to enter his office first.

'Have you got the cassette with you?' the Editor asked.

The Writer took a small cassette recorder out of a plastic bag, put it on the Editor's desk and switched it on. A young male voice begged a man to leave him alone and never to come to their house again. The man repeated through the boy's tears, 'Think about your mother and sister. If I don't support you, who do you think will?'

The Writer turned off the recorder, put it back in the plastic bag and put the bag on the sofa opposite the Editor's desk. He hesitated in the middle of the room for few moments, then sat on the sofa.

'You recognised his voice, didn't you?'

The Editor nodded, puckering his lips, while standing behind his desk. He observed the Writer fidgeting, utterly nervous.

The Writer grabbed the sack, took out the recorder again, put it on his lap, pushed the eject button, pulled out the cassette and put it in the pocket of his coat. He looked at the Editor, who was still standing behind the desk. They stared at each other for a short while, then the Writer broke the silence: 'But you recognise his voice, don't you?'

The Editor sat on his armchair, reached out his hand for some papers at the back of his desk, played his fingers through them, and then grabbed a pen. He played with the pen, rolling it between his fingers, before tossing it back on the desk. 'Listen,' he said. 'We are journalists, and it's true that we have to report any corruption and injustice. That's the reason I chose to work on this party's paper. They have promised not to pressure me and let me decide what I want to publish or not. If they hadn't, I would have chosen another job. But you know how dangerous this job is right now... Eh... I mean...'

While he was searching for better words to make his case, the Writer crossed his legs and asked again, 'But you agree that it's him?'

The Editor put his right hand under his chin and his elbow on the desk. He stared at the Writer and continued, 'Listen... We are friends and we understand each other, right? There is a difference between you and me. You use your journalistic work to fight against the political parties in power, while I... I do my best to remain neutral and keep this paper going. If there was an independent paper, I'd have worked for them. Maybe one day I'll establish one myself. For now, I try to bring up the changes from inside the political parties themselves. But of course, at the end of the day this newspaper belongs to a political party that will be held accountable for anything we publish. So I'm not the only one responsible for the content. I mean I am, but other people are also involved.'

He paused, waiting for are response. But the Writer was looking at the ceiling.

'This party is now in alliance with the Patriots and the Democrats. After all, we can't beat them. Oh, come on, let's give it a break! We could do without a civil war. We are no longer in the mountains!'

The Writer closed his eyes for a few seconds, pressed his lips together and then all of a sudden repeated his question: 'Just tell me whether you recognise this jerk's voice or not? Is there any easier question than this? Just answer this question and no more, do me a favour!'

At that same moment there was a power cut, and the room went dark. The Editor stood up, went to the window behind him and drew the curtains back. The room became a bit lighter. Standing there by the window, looking outside, he said, 'You know what, my friend? It doesn't make any difference if I recognise him or not. I've never met this guy personally and have never talked to him. But I've heard him enough on the radio and on TV to say yes, it's him. But you know that it is—'

'But I know him very well. In the mountains, I used to fight right beside him, shoulder to shoulder, for the same party, in the same trench. I know what kind of man he is. He has always done this.'

The Editor turned to him and said, 'Listen, for me right now—'

'And besides,' the Writer interrupted him again. 'And besides, this kid is a relative of mine. How do you think I got this cassette?'

The Editor frowned.

'I had to fix it under one of the sofas in their living room,' the Writer explained. 'This thug was visiting my relatives for a year on a regular basis. He would send the boy's mother and sister away, saying that he had a secret meeting with their son about some kind of underground political group, and some other nonsense like that. You know how old this boy is? Do you? He is only thirteen... Thirteen!'

He stood up and came to the Editor, who still stood beside the window. He put his hand on the Editor's shoulder and continued, 'Listen... I know you have reasons to hesitate. you have been sued twice in the last couple of months. I know you already have two court cases ongoing. We can't fight this new weapon the politicians use. I mean of course they have the right to defend themselves as citizens. But who could sue them and drag them to court? I consider all these things and understand you very well. But this issue has to get into the media. And the only newspaper to which I have access is yours, you know that.'

'Why don't you try the Socialist party's media?' the Editor said, removing the Writer's hand from his shoulder.

'Socia... what?' shouted the Writer, staring at the Editor. He then faked laughter. 'What big names you all have chosen! You Toilers, them Socialists, and the Patriots and Democrats... But, shush... Don't also tell me go to the Communists, please! You lot with your Fronts and Alliances. You know what the result of this Front will be? Your small parties give those monsters the chance to divide the country's resources between them. They mock you. They—'

'Wait, don't get so angry so quickly,' the Editor interrupted him, returning to sit at his desk. 'They have a paper, and they have this new radio too. I think you might know the Director... What I mean to say is that at least that guy, the Socialists' leader, he's got power. Not like ours. No one can touch him. He's got men and guns. He—'

'You mean...? Oh, dear...!' the Writer shouted again. He put both hands on the Editor's desk and said, looking into his eyes, 'Do you think he would care about who fucks whom and who rapes our children? He is infatuated with smuggling and selling shovels and bulldozers to the Iranians. Do you know he has also begun to smuggle copper? The thieves now steal the copper electricity cables at night and deliver them to him. And you're now telling me—'

'Listen, I know all this—'

'No... Why don't you publish that, then? Why don't you try to send a—'

'This is a different story. I want for your story to be heard. I'm trying to help, man. What I meant was that the Socialist radio station would most likely broadcast your cassette and no one would accuse them of anything. And if they did, he would be able to buy them off.'

At that moment, the concierge knocked on the door and came in with a tray of two *piyalas* of tea. He put one on the Editor's desk and the other for the guest on a small table in front of the sofa and went out. The Editor asked the Writer to sit and drink his tea so that he could calm down a bit. He leant back in his swivel chair, then immediately leant forwards again and stirred his own tea and lifted the *piyala* to his lips. After a sip he said, 'Of course we must do something on this. But now that I think about it, I think it's better not to take it to the media. Doing so would simply put the boy and his family in danger.'

The Writer, who was back on the sofa and had taken a sip of his tea, put the *piyala* swiftly back on the coffee table and stood up again. He calmly said, 'Listen my friend... I understand you very well. But I just don't agree with you.' He stood in the middle of the room, paused, rubbed his chin, then said abruptly, 'Thank you so much for your time, anyway! I know what I'm going to do with this story. And let me tell you, I have already taken this boy and his mother and sister away to another city. I've rented a house for them somewhere nobody could find.'

The Editor stared at him, eyes wide open. 'Well, that's—'

'And by the way,' the Writer interrupted him, 'I have threatened this jerk indirectly and sent him a message that I've got his voice recorded while he was raping a thirteen-year-old boy. If he harms them or even tries to find them, I'll make the cassette public.' He grabbed the plastic bag containing the cassette recorder from the sofa and stepped to the door but stood there and turned to the Editor again. 'Don't forget, I've been in this dirty politics business for a long time.' He smirked, then opened the door. 'I wish you a good day, comrade!'

The Editor rushed to him, stretching his hand for a goodbye shake. 'I hope you understand my position.'

The Writer walked out and shut the door, leaving the Editor to shake his head as he returned to his desk.

As he sat down, he heard a rustling and shuffling sound outside in the backyard. He stood up again and went to the window but saw nobody outside. At this time the concierge opened the door and let in the woman who had been waiting. The Editor offered her a seat and asked the concierge if he would remove those cardboard boxes behind the window.

The concierge took away the Writer's unfinished tea and went out. Before he closed the door, the Editor asked if he would get hold of the journalist who had interviewed the Photographer.

'Lady Journalist, you mean, sir?'

'That's correct! And would you please get us three of your delicious teas, dear friend?'

The journalist who had interviewed the Photographer was a young girl. She came in with a notebook and pen in her hand and greeted the woman before sitting beside her on the sofa. The Editor asked the woman how they could help. She said that she would be grateful if they could possibly arrange for her to meet the Photographer. She suggested that she might be the only person who believed in his story and wanted to ask him where exactly he had seen the Naked Young Man and from under which tree had he appeared.

Lady Journalist gazed at the Editor with a vague smile. She then turned to the woman and asked, 'Can I know why you have such a specific interest in this subject?'

'I should first see this photographer,' the woman said, staring at her own hands in her lap.

'But it would be great if you also related your side of the story, wouldn't it?' Lady Journalist said, putting her hand on her arm.

'Let me first see this young man, then I'll think about it. Deal, Lady Journalist?'

The Editor leant forwards over his desk and said, 'Look, ma'am, we can promise to hide your identity, if that's what concerns you. We'll respect your privacy, I promise.'

'Sir, I don't have any story to tell if I don't talk to this photographer guy.'

'I'm sorry to insist, ma'am,' Lady Journalist said, looking at her with her head askew. 'But if we first hear your side of the story, then we can connect you with the Photographer.'

The woman lifted her head and looked at her. 'Darling, I said—

'I promise, I'll do my best to put together a good story about the whole issue,' Lady Journalist insisted. 'You seem to know something. And I assure you, we will use a pseudonym for you.'

The woman sighed, then, looking into the void, started telling her story. Nineteen years ago, in the heat of the Kurdish revolt against the central government in the mid-seventies, just a couple of months before the failure of the revolution, she had been fired from her government job due to her husband being a member of the guerrillas, the *peshmerga*. She had decided to join him in the mountains.

'So I was with this man, a partisan, who was sent by my husband to help me escape and cross the mountains. On the way, because of heavy snow, we were stuck in the village of Sitak, you know, just behind the Goyzha mountain.'

'Sure, we know where it is, ma'am,' said the Editor, nodding.

'We were delayed there for a few days. It was a weird situation, and you know, I was young... And this man was... ehh... I mean it happened that we...'

Suddenly, she stopped talking as if something got stuck in her throat. Both her eyes and nostrils opened wide. She looked with a fixed gaze at the window.

The Journalist turned towards the window and gasped.

The Editor turned as well. His eyes caught that of a young man who had his chin on the windowsill.

Shocked, the young man slipped and fell with a faint thud.

Lady Journalist and the Editor quickly ran to the window and watched the Naked Young Man jump on a kerosene barrel and from there onto the fence, dragging a long, broad leaf behind him. When he disappeared over the fence, the Editor and Lady Journalist both ran towards the door. They saw that the woman had fallen and lay on the floor. So they stepped back, picked her up and replaced her on the sofa. She was quite breathless.

30

The next day, Lady Journalist was looking for the place in Qilyasan where the Photographer supposedly discovered the Naked Young Man. She found that all the roads leading to the creek and the orchards around it were fenced with barbed wire.

As she was busy digging a hole under the fence, an old man surprised her.

'If you are looking for that woman, they say she passed away yesterday, my dear,' the man said in a calm, hoarse voice.

Lady Journalist startled, stood up abruptly and leant against the fence, looking surprisingly at the old man. She swallowed and said, 'I'm a journalist, sir. I would like to know what the connection was of this woman to that... You know, that Naked Young Man who was seen here for the first... So you saw that woman, sir?'

The old man shook his head and said, 'I don't know why nobody ever cared about us and now every other day someone comes here to ask about this fag! Just leave us alone darling. Only God knows what the hell that woman was up to! Look how they have defiled this whole area. Oh, if I go crazy, I'll finally set all the trees here on fire. Then we will be released. Look, look at all those *arak* bottles thrown around here. Would God accept this? They have made a pub of this place, those pigs.'

Lady Journalist sighed and told the man that she understood his anger, then changed the subject and asked him again if he had seen that woman he spoke of. The old man confirmed and said she was wandering around there some days ago. 'But you know, this baby she was talking about, I had seen it years ago over there, between the trees on the other side of the creek. I saw a dog carrying a baby in its snout. But I couldn't free the baby. Oh God, I will never forget that. I don't know what the dog did with it. Did it eat it? Did it take it to hide it somewhere? I never found out.' He stepped forward, closer to the barbed wire fence, and looked at the other side. 'I swear to God this dog had held the baby in its muzzle just like it would carry its puppies by the scruff of their neck without hurting them. It was in its muzzle with a bunch of leaves and grass. You might think it had hunted a duck.'

At that time, two other men came and told the old man, 'Let's head off to the mosque, *haji*, before we miss the evening prayer.'

'Please listen to me, lovely uncle. It's really important for me to find out about this young man and the Tree. I'm sure you've seen the Tree as well. And now you seem to know even more. You just told me—'

'My dear, I don't have more to tell you. That's all I know,' the old man said, starting to step away with the other men.

'No, but I think you can help to bring that Tree back here. That's at least something we could do to save the Tree and the man,' she shouted. 'Can I please at least visit you at home?'

'Come and find me in the village,' the old man shouted back. 'But I don't think I can be of any help.'

When the men left, Lady Journalist turned her head to the orchards behind the barbwire mesh and stood still for a few minutes thinking about the words of the old man. She realised that the woman who died in front of her and the chief editor of her paper, was actually an essential link in the chain of this story. But what about the Naked Young Man himself? She should find him and try to talk to him, as she was sure that was now the best and maybe only option left. That way, she could also help him come back here to his place, which might even be his birthplace. She found the whole issue a crazy, dazzling puzzle, but thought the more complicated, the more interesting. Maybe a breakthrough for her if she could establish this story. She left the place hastily and went back to the newspaper's office.

31

One early evening, when it had just turned dark, the Tree watched as people, mostly young girls and guys, gathered in the garden of the city's archaeological museum, just in front of an exhibition hall for modern art. They went in and out, standing in groups under the light of a lamppost, talking loudly, and laughing. Sometimes, when a person left one of the groups to go to another or to enter the hall, the rest of the group started talking about them. Now and then someone would join another group and ask, 'What's the gossip here?'

They talked about art and asked each other about their recent work; things for the Tree not so much comprehensible. It saw through the entrance of the hall some pictures hanging on the walls and sculptures put on pedestals or just on the floor, and it understood that those must be the objects they were talking about. Apart from that, their main subjects were about which girl was in love with which boy, causing them lots of grief and long nights of sleeplessness and which guy had been masturbating to which girl. 'And if you want to know which girls at the dormitory are masturbating to which boy, you come to me,' one of the girls would say. 'Oh, my gosh, they do?' one of the boys would say. 'What do you think, thickhead?' another girl would say, to which the boy would beat his own head with both hands and run into the hall.

It appeared that many of the youngsters were students of art, and more than their art, they liked speaking of rumours about their fellow students or teachers who had affairs with their students. The Tree noticed that it was more the men who dared to talk about these subjects. The girls were mostly laughing, covering their mouths with their hands or plugging both ears with their fingers. Some of the girls walked away irritated, only to come back and yell, 'Wait, wait… Say it again, but please don't go into so much detail. And you bastard, stop using all those dirty words.'

Suddenly, the Photographer appeared, coming out of the hall biting on a sweet. He approached one of the groups, but as soon as he saw the Tree, he changed his direction, coming closer.

The Tree stuck its roots firmly in the ground and tried to look like the other trees in the garden and behave like them, as if it was not aware of the strange world around it. A breeze swirled through its leaves.

The Photographer took a leaf out of his pocket. It was one of its own leaves, the Tree noticed. The Photographer went to put it closer to the tree's other leaves, but a strong wind came and blew the dust off the other trees towards the Photographer and a group of girls and boys close to him.

The Photographer rubbed his eyes, wiped his curly hair with the top of his fingers and dusted his clothes off. He suddenly noticed that he had lost the leaf and started searching for it in the dark but couldn't find it. Some of the students asked him what he was looking for, but he did not answer. Another one said, 'Leave him, it's his tree-madness period.' All the others laughed, while a guy asked what he meant. 'Oh, you don't know about it? He has been looking for a tree he has fallen in love with.' The group laughed again. 'Haven't you heard he even got jailed for his madness?' the guy continued, while the others still laughed. 'Let him come and tell us himself how many bottles they stuck in his arse.' Now the group and some others who had heard parts of the comments laughed as loud as they could.

One of the guys said, giggling, 'Oh, no, no, no… You know why they really arrested him?'

The group stopped laughing, stared at him curiously.

'He was walking drunk through the streets with a bare arse,' he said, tittering, obviously trying to fake a passionate laugh.

Most of the guys and girls laughed even harder, while the Tree could tell some had not apparently got the joke.

A girl asked curiously, 'Wait, what does that mean? What did he do?'

Another girl shouted furiously, 'Hey… Don't you ever read the newspapers? Or watch TV? Where are you getting all of these rumours from? Poor guy!'

The group gradually quieted, looking at her, waiting for her side of the story. A guy who was, until that moment, talking to another group some steps away and had apparently heard their conversation, came to them and said, 'Hey guys, this beauty is right, if you don't know the story, why invent rumours? I know him very well. He's told me everything himself. It's the other way around. They respected him a lot. One of the *Asayish* guys has become a friend of his. He has promised to help him if he ever decided to leave the country. What a lucky guy! Isn't he?'

The Photographer ignored them and ran inside. In that very moment, the Neighbour-Girl arrived and when she saw him entering the exhibition hall, followed him without greeting anybody. Some of the people shrugged, but nobody said anything. Some of them looked curiously at the nearby trees but soon went back to their conversations.

The Tree took this opportunity and crept out through the main exit of the courtyard, which had been opened by some of the visitors. It took the road up the street, over the pavement, close to the walls and main entrances of the buildings and shops. It heard the Photographer shouting in the distance, 'Where did that tree go? The one that was just right here? Hey, you bunch of idiots! What is wrong with you all? Are you blind? How can you not have seen it disappearing?'

The Tree was already a few hundred metres away, running harder and harder until it reached a seven-story building at the end of the street. All the windows of the building were broken and covered with blankets, sheets or plastic linoleum; a dim light came out most of them. It was about to enter the building when it noticed the park across the street. While it waited for traffic to slow down, it stood beside another tree and looked to see if it had been followed. No sign of anyone.

When it was calm, and no cars were in sight, the Tree found the chance to cross the street swiftly and enter the park through its iron gate, which was ajar.

32

The next day, in the early morning when a thick mist had covered everything, the gardener of *Bakhi Gishti,* the public garden, opened the iron door and entered the park. He noticed the sunflower seeds vendor already standing half-visible, a metre from the gate, behind his tray of roasted seeds which he had put on a rickety wooden trestle.

'Hey, Son, how are you? Not too early?' the Gardener said, stepping back outside the garden. He went to the boy.

'Thank you, uncle! What can I do over there?' the boy said, nodding to the Hasib Salih, the seven-story building on the other side of the street, which was now hidden in the mist. The thirteen-year-old boy lived there with his family and dozens of others. The building, once the fanciest hotel in the city, was plundered during the uprising and since then, it had been used as a shelter for displaced people.

The Gardener gave him a quarter dinar and said, while stretching open the pocket of his *sharwal,* 'Give me my daily portion, buddy! And keep the change.'

The boy cauciously poured two *piyalas* of the sunflower seeds in the Gardener's pocket. 'Thank you, uncle, for your generosity!'

When the Gardener re-entered the park, he took the same route as every morning but today he could hardly see so much as the trees' trunks. Although he had spent a large portion of his life in this park, he felt confused and took some minutes to orientate himself. The idea of getting lost in a garden he knew as good as the back of his hand made him stressed and somehow, ashamed.

Soon, he found himself on a path that he knew to lead southwards, not northwards where his office was. When he turned, he stumbled over the tools of a sculptor who was working on busts of some old Kurdish poets. He then slipped over the pavement and almost fell into the mud but supported himself with one of his knees and could stand up immediately, cursing the sculptor who hadn't cleaned up his tools last evening again, despite the Gardener asking him to every evening.

Walking away, he regretted cursing the sculptor. It was thanks to him, and to his half-finished sculptures on both sides of the passageway, that he found his way.

A few steps before he reached the office, he took a bunch of keys out of his pocket and looked for the right one with the tops of his fingers. As he did, he noticed an exotic tree emerge from the fog. He stood still for a moment, calculating the situation. He rubbed his eyes and looked more carefully. Why would anyone plant a tree here, just like that?

He quickly opened the door, then turned to see that in the place of the tree was the silhouette of a naked man, wrapped in a long leaf, grovelling in the mud, trying to stand up, shaking from the cold.

The gardener was sure that what he saw was real. Was this what he thought it was? Despite the fear he still felt, he hurried towards the Naked Young Man, caught his arm and helped him to stand up. The Naked Young Man took two steps and then leant on the wall of the office. The Gardener led him inside, saying with a soothing voice, 'Come in, dear. I'm going to turn on this heater and you will be warm.' He closed the door and let the boy stand at the simple single bed in the corner of the room. He took a towel and wiped him clean of the mud and dried him. He then grabbed the blanket from the bed, covered the Naked Young Man with it and said, 'Sit down, Son. You'll be warm in a minute.'

The Naked Young Man sat slowly with hesitation, looking at all the corners of the room, examining the rough concrete walls and the minimum furniture in the room. Apart from the bed, there were only some other simple furniture in the room: a white plastic chair opposite the bed and between them, a small tea table with dozens of brown circles imprinted on its wooden surface; blueprints of the *piyalas* and saucers. A few steps from the door, in front of the only small window in the room, was a bigger, old table with a few plates, a teapot, a kettle, and a tray with *piyalas*, saucers and spoons on it. The boy stared at a *piyala*, half full of tea, on the small table in front oh him, with a teaspoon beside it, sugar hardened on its top. He looked fascinated at the brown circles on the table's surface.

'I'm going to light this Aladdin,' the Gardener said, startling him, putting down the device in the middle of the room.

The Naked Young Man stared at the grey-green object excitedly, observing its details: a round trunk, raising above a semi-round tank, held together with four thin bars and three rings surrounding the trunk and the tank. The vertical bars held the top of the Aladdin and formed four thin feet at the bottom of it. The boy looked even more excited when the Gardener took a matchbox out of his pocket and knelt down in front of the Aladdin, releasing the clip at the bottom and letting the trunk lay down with its top on the floor. Then, he lit the round, hard wick. A small flame ran around the wick, forming a fire circle that soon turned from red to blue. The Gardener put back the trunk with a click. He stood up, lifted the Aladdin with its handgrip and put it in front of the Naked Young Man.

'You stare so fascinated at the Aladdin. Have you never seen one? This is a traditional kerosine heater,' the Gardener said. As he did not receive an answer, he asked, 'Where are you from, Son? I heard Qilyasan.'

The Naked Young Man kept staring at the blue circle of the fire through the Aladdin's round, transparent window made of mica.

The Gardener gazed at him for some seconds, then stared bewildered at the shiny green leaf, which had jutted out from under the blanket, behind the Naked Young Man's neck, and crawled over the blanket above his chest. The other end of the leaf curled around his calf and snuggled between his toes. The Gardener did not ask about it. Instead, he acted as if it was the most normal thing. When his eyes caught those of the concerned Naked Young Man, he looked away, towards the table at the window, then walked immediately towards it. He grabbed the kettle, walked to the door, but before going out, turned to the Naked Young Man and assured him, 'I won't be late. I'm going to get some water to make tea for you. That will truly warm you up.'

Outside, the Gardener looked around. Though the mist was about to lift completely, and glimpses of sunlight were breaking through the top tree branches, the park was still desolate. The kettle in his hand, he squatted near the dirt and mud where the Naked Young Man had been earlier. He kneaded the soil with the tops of his fingers and was sure that this dirt was from a recently rooted plant. He knew the soil enough to judge it by hand. He stood up and went to the tap beside his office, then squatted again and filled up the kettle.

When inside, he put the kettle on the Aladdin. The wet bottom of the kettle started to fizz and hiss, making the water drops spring around. This made a cautious smile appear on the lips of the Naked Young Man, who was gradually becoming tranquil. The Gardener felt happy that the boy was beginning to trust him, but he also felt discomfort, standing awkwardly in the middle of the room, not knowing what to do.

Since his childhood, the Gardener had been dreaming about growing leaves on his body. Now he saw the personification of his dream in front of him, just like that. He thought if he was not child-less and had a son, his son could have looked exactly the same as this angle-like young man. That he was not talkative was not a problem; the boy could speak with his eyes. The Gardener couldn't remember ever seeing such honest eyes. The sad thing, however, was that they revealed a deep grief and distrust in the world around him.

The Gardener was tempted to hug him and give him all the affec-tion he wished to give to a baby child, but instead he took a step back so as not to frighten the boy. When he began to see his own unhappiness and frustration reflected in the Naked Young Man's eyes, he looked away. Again, the room became uneasy, and he didn't know what to do.

He sat for a few seconds on the chair beside the door, then stood up again and walked to the table, then from there again to the chair. Instead of sitting, he opened the door and stepped outside. He closed the door and leant against it for some seconds. Then, he went to the toilet a few metres from his office.

When he came out of the toilet, the Gardener felt that peeing had made him relaxed. He washed his hands under the tap beside the office, dried them with his *cummerbund* and tied it again around his waist before opening the door carefully. He saw that the Naked Young Man had laid down on the bed, covered himself with the blanket, looking at the concrete ceiling that was not plastered.

The Gardener entered the room and lifted the lid from the kettle, noticing that it needed longer for the water to boil. He said to the Naked Young Man, 'My son, I know you must be very hungry. Until the water boils, I will go and grab something for us to eat. I also haven't had my breakfast yet.'

When he exited the park, dawn was breaking over the city and the street was already becoming busy. A few other young boys stood with the sunflower boy, eating the seeds and joking around. He smiled at them, and crossed the side street, passing the Governorate Council building and encountering Mawlawi Street. After two hundred metres, he crossed over and entered the Sa'a Takoyee alley. He saw his favourite vendor's cart surrounded by a few workers who were slurping their chickpea soup delightedly. He hoped that there was some left for him – most of the mornings the soup was sold out earlier.

Arriving at the cart, he greeted the old vendor, asked him about his family, to which he was asked about his, and requested two portions of soup with chicken feet, as a real traditional chickpea soup is meant to be. He paid quickly and headed back to the park.

Opening the door of his office, the Gardener saw that the Naked Young Man was asleep; the kettle was steaming and whistling like a steam train's locomotive, and the window had completely fogged up. He left the door ajar, put the bag with the chickpea soup quickly on the table and removed the kettle from the Aladdin. When he grabbed the teapot, he realised that the rest of the tea from yesterday was still in it. He went outside and washed the teapot under the tap.

When he entered the room again, the vapour had dispersed and the window was clear. He closed the door, put some tea in the pot, poured the boiled water in it, put the kettle back on the Aladdin and put the teapot on top of it. Then, he untied the plastic bag and poured the chickpea soup in two bowls with a spoon in each. He wanted to wake up the Naked Young Man but thought it was better to let him rest and warm up his soup whenever he woke up by himself. He sat on the chair opposite the bed and started eating the chickpeas, and slurping his soup, all while staring at the long, green leaf that jutted out from under the blanket and covered the Naked Young Man's chest, down to his hips. The fragrance of the tea, mingled with the aroma of the chickpeas, made the Gardener feel as though he was the happiest man in the city.

Whilst the Gardener worked throughout the day – most of the time around his office, though he did go inside for the occasional rest break and to make tea – the Naked Young Man slept. For that reason, the Gardener had not gone home for lunch. Instead, he bought some cookies from a vendor in front of the park and ate them with sweet tea.

In the beginning of the evening, as it was just about to get dark, sparrows were nestling and swarms of starlings were moving in different shapes high in the sky over the garden, rippling into each other and landing in groups in the trees, chanting and chirping over each other.

The Gardener was still busy with planting flowers when he saw the Naked Young Man come out the office slowly, the leaf around his legs. He walked with heavy, steady steps into the garden amongst the trees, while bark started to cover his legs and arms, branches shooting out his limbs and leaves growing gradually all over the branches, quivering in the breeze of the evening twilight.

33

The Tree had spent about a week in the park when a late-spring heat started. In the daytime he slept in the Gardener's office, which stayed unlocked. Although no communication occurred between them, the Gardener was happy to see that the Naked Young Man felt safe in his presence, and that as a tree, it also had found a home amongst its kind in the garden during the night. In the evenings, before he went home, the Gardener poured a bowl of water under the Tree, looked up and smiled at it, knowing that the Tree would do the same. In the mornings, when he came to the park and opened the door of his office, the first thing he did was kiss the forehead of the Naked Young Man, observing traces of peace and serenity in his face while he slept.

At night, when he was home, sitting on the sofa in his living room, sipping his strong, sweet tea right after he had supper, watching the news or chatting programmes in which people were saying that nobody had seen the tree-man for a while, the Gardener would feel proud and happy that he was the one who had saved this creature from a dreadful situation and that his fellow citizens of the city were no longer worried about a naked man whom they said was threatening to bring down the community. This secret – that even his own wife did not know about – gave him a feeling of power and dignity. Gardening had already given him a great amount of self-respect, for he felt that he was doing one of the most important jobs on this planet: planting the seeds of life and creating new creatures. But the honourable position that this newest creature had now given to him had made him the most important person in society, though his salary was so meagre that it was barely enough for him and his wife to lead a comfortabe life. And when his wife put a second tea on the small table in front of him, they would look at each other, both knowing that recently, happiness had filled their house.

34

The Photographer would have felt happy and proud had he found the Tree and could have returned it to Qilyasan. Or at least if he had made that one photo. A single picture would be enough to satisfy him and make him feel he was the luckiest man, he told the Neighbour-Girl one afternoon while he was watering his father's beloved trees and flowers on an early-summer day. His father sat on the bench, drinking tea with some cookies the Neighbour-Girl had just baked at home. He called them to come sit beside him.

'Your teas have become cold, dears. Come and have some rest. It's fine, just leave the hose in that small trench, it will spread the water to all the trees. Come and have your tea.'

The Photographer and the Neighbour-Girl went and sat on the bench, each on one side of the Father. They stirred their teas, sipped and said simultaneously that it was indeed cold. The Photographer ate a piece of cookie and said, 'Mmmm… Delicious! You really have become skilled in these cookies. I think your time has arrived.'

They all laughed, and the Neighbour-Girl reached her arm behind the Father's back and gave the Photographer a slap on his neck. 'Don't embarrass me in front of your dad, silly!' she said while bending her head down and to the other side, avoiding the Father's eyes.

'Ah, don't worry darling. You don't need to be shy. He's just doing his best to be funny,' said the Father, putting his hand on the girl's shoulder.

'It's a fact. I'm not joking,' said the Photographer, bending to the side, raising his hand in front of his own face to avoid another slap. Then, he straightened himself to look at the Neighbour-Girl from behind his father's neck and asked her, 'By the way, has your suitor got over your rejection?'

Swiftly, the Neighbour-Girl gave him another slap and shouted softly, with a shy tone, 'Cut it off! You're embarrassing me, dude.'

'It's fine, lovely! My dad knows about it. I'm asking a serious question. Is it all over? Did he get it?'

'Well, I haven't heard from him for a week now. So hopefully he did. But it's now you who should be worried. I'm sure he'll try to make your life difficult, mind you,' she said looking at the Photographer behind the Father's back and saw that he bit on his lower lip quickly to warn her not to say anything more of this subject in front of his father.

The Father was staring at the trees, listening to them. He suddenly looked at his son and said, 'Anyway... Tell me, my son, why are you so obsessed with this Tree? What can such a photo do for you? I mean you can't sell it, can you? Take some pictures of these gorgeous trees otherwise.'

'It's no longer only about the picture, Dad,' the Photographer interrupted his father.

'What's it about then?'

'It's about the Tree itself. About...' The Photographer closed his eyes and bent his head backwards over the back of the bench for few seconds, then leant forwards and opened his eyes again. He continued, 'It's also about a human being. This Tree is, in essence, a human being. People just don't want to understand it.'

'Listen, Son! I believe you. I know that you've seen a tree and a naked man—'

'Half-naked, Dad!'

'Okay, whatever... I mean it's possible that they are two different things, right?'

'No, Dad! They are the same. They... I mean he is a human being that becomes a tree. So simple!'

The Father smiled and said, 'Well, that's not so simple, is it?'

'Anyway, here is the thing...' the Photographer said, putting his hand on his father's shoulder. 'This human being is in danger, as a man as well as a tree. And I think I can do something about it.' He looked at the Neighbour-Girl and added, 'Actually we... *We* can do something to rescue him.'

'Tell him the truth,' said the Neighbour-Girl, staring at the Photographer, biting on her lip, as she must have realised she probably shouldn't have said that.

'What truth?' asked the Father, surprised, looking at them in turn.

The Photographer looked at her, frowning, wondering if that was a good idea. Then, he looked at his father and said, 'Look, Dad... I don't want to hide it from you. I was arrested again, a week ago. I mean not arrested, but the *Asayish* called me for an hour interrogation. I made a fuss again a few weeks ago. I didn't mean to, but it happened. I'm sure this artist guy told the *Asayish* about it.'

'Ah, come on, that's not ture. I don't think it was this poor guy!' said the Neighbour-Girl. 'Do you think the *Asayish* themselves wouldn't have known it? All hell broke out that evening. And you thought that nobody would notice?' she asked, irritated.

'Wait, wait... What guy, what artist? What are you talking about?' said the Father, moving his head back and forth between them.

The Neighbour-Girl tried to explain, 'Well, we were in this guy's exhibition at the museum's gallery, you know. Then all of a sudden this Mr Photographer, your son—'

'Dad, the Tree was there, in the garden...' the Photographer interrupted Neighbour-Girl. 'Everyone saw it. I mean they didn't notice it until it disappeared. Just at the point I wanted to photograph it. I think it can see and hear us or at least sense us. You know what I mean? That's what I'm trying to make clear. It's a human being, even when it is a tree it feels or maybe even sees the world around it. It avoids me all the time, I can tell. It recognises me and every time I approach it, something happens, and it disappears. I'm also confused. I don't know how to help.'

'Help whom? What did the *Asayish* say? You promised me not to get in trouble with them again.'

'Dad, I'm not in trouble or anything. I told you, it was this guy who made a case of it. Somebody stole one of his small sculptures when everyone ran out of the gallery.' The Photographer laughed and turned to the Neighbour-Girl. 'Did you hear what someone said?'

'Oh, yes. He said maybe the Tree lifted it.' She burst into laughter too. 'But listen, I'm sure it really wasn't him. He hates this bloody Asayish Director. I know this sculptor. He's a Patriot too and his studio is in the building where our youth union is.'

The Father was still moving his head sluggishly from his son to the Neighbour-Girl and back and forth again and again, trying to make some sense out of the disrupted fragments of their story. 'Guys, what are you talking about? I'm getting dizzy between you two. What happened, tell me.'

'Dad, when I saw the Tree in the courtyard I went inside the gallery to get my camera, but when I came back, the Tree had disappeared.'

'I thought your camera had broken,' said the Father.

'I bought a new one. I mean a second-hand one. I borrowed some money. But anyway, I shouted at the people out there—'

'Oh, oh, this camera business of yours!' the Father said, standing up with the support of his crutches. 'Wasn't it better for you just go back to your job at the studio?'

'Dad, do you want to hear this story or not?'

'Tell me, I'm listening,' the Father said and hobbled on his crutches to the hose, which he then bent over and picked up.

The Neighbour-Girl sprinted over to take the hose from him, but he hobbled further away and placed the hose under another tree.

'Leave him, darling! He likes to do it himself,' the Photographer said and continued his story, 'So as I was shouting at the people, asking how it was possible for them not to have noticed a tree walking away, they realised that a tree had in fact disappeared. So, they got scared and started to yell and run around. Some followed me to search in the streets and alleys around the museum. But we didn't find it. That's what happened.'

'So, the *Asayish* let you go without trouble?'

'Yes, Dad! Don't worry. The problem now is that they are seriously looking for the Tree… Well, let's say for the guy. And they will find him soon, I'm sure. That's why I'm afraid something bad will happen to him.'

'And there is this girl, a journalist who knows so much about the tree and the naked guy. I mean the half-naked guy,' the Neighbour-Girl said sarcastically, looking at the Photographer through the corner of her eyes, then looking back to the Father. 'I spoke to her. She said that the police and the whole city are also looking for him. They might hurt him if they find him, she thinks.'

'Who thinks?' the Father said without looking at them, picking up the hose again.

'This journalist, her colleagues call her Lady Journalist. You actually know who she is. The one who interviewed your son for the paper, you know? She has talked to many sides about the whole matter and knows a lot. She thinks someone could stop him from roving so aimlessly around the city. It would be better if someone could take him back to Qilyasan. I think we could do that, indeed.'

'That would be great! But how can you do that if the whole city and police and *Asayish* can't find him?' the Father asked, now looking at them, waiting for suggestions. He tossed the hose under another tree. The water splashed around, the droplets shining in the sun.

'That's what we're also trying to figure out, Dad. I think I know where he might be. Just thought about it when I was watering the trees.'

'Where? Why don't you tell me then?' the Neighbour-Girl asked him in a reprimanding tone.

'You know that evening, the Tree could have gone towards the public garden. We were stupid we didn't follow him in that direction. This Tree can run very fast and unnoticed. He could have gone to the park that night.'

'Wait!' said the Neighbour-Girl. 'Now that you say that... This same sculptor told me that the gardener of the park has been behaving strangely over the last few weeks. He said the gardener no longer let anyone going into his office, even though he used to invite people in for tea all the time. The sculptor thinks he may be hiding something.'

'I think it makes sense,' said the Photographer. 'Let's go to look for it tonight. I mean we could go now, but it's much more difficult to find him as the man than as a tree. Are you busy tonight?'

'I've got nothing to do tonight. We can go,' said the Neighbour-Girl, standing up. 'Let me leave now. I need to help *Daya* make some food for dinner. You know what? You don't need to cook. I'll cook for all of us.'

'Hmmmmm. What a great idea!' said the Photographer, looking at his father.

The Father confirmed, while creating with one of his crutches a little groove in the mud for the water to flow towards the other plants. 'I can't think of anything better. Oh, I love your cooking, darling! Thank you! Really lovely of you.'

35

The Tree had spent a peaceful, comfortable time in the park, but it also felt bored. Living in a fenced garden was different from life in the orchards around the creek of Qilyasan. It wished it had never left its trusted familiar environment.

In the daytime, when he was the man, he saw through the only window in the office that people were visiting the park for a walk. Students sat alone or in small groups on a bench or on the grass, studying, joking and laughing or now and then, arguing. Young street vendors, mostly children, came along selling sunflower or pumpkin seeds, sweets and *chorak*, sesame-covered small cookies in different shapes, which the Gardener seemed to love exceptionally. He saw him every day buying a couple of them from different sellers in different times of the day. He would bring them inside and eat them with his sweet tea. If the Naked Young Man was awake, he would tell him stories and explain the ways of life in the city. He would offer him some of his cookies too, to which the Naked Young Man would only respond with a smile and an appreciative glance towards the *choraks*. But that was not appropriate food for him. After three or four days, the Gardener had understood that he didn't need to eat anything as he was absorbing enough from the water and the soil he received as a tree. Nevertheless, the Gardener would still ask him.

The Gardener had even brought him a small television set. He had apologised that it was only a black-and-white one and not in colour. He had bought it, he said, from the *Mazadkhana*, the bargain market for second-hand furniture and electronic goods. He had also fixed a small aerial on the office roof and had explained the function of it, all so that the Naked Young Man could have some entertainment and learn about the society. Once, he brought another device, which he said was a video player that would give the Naked Young Man the opportunity to choose what he liked to see on the large tapes. But no matter what the Gardener tried, the old thing didn't work. Anyway, the Naked Young Man preferred watching the people from the window.

In the afternoons, families came to the park with their children to enjoy the city's only proper garden. They would leave behind kilos of shells from their cracked sunflower and pumpkin seeds on the grass, which workers would sweep away in the early mornings with long brooms. He enjoyed watching the people and admired how skilled they were at cracking the seeds. Some people were slower than others, but some were extremely fast and could crack two or even three seeds per second. Some put a couple of seeds at a time in their mouth, cracking them, spitting out the shells and chewing the seeds all together. He saw that children even ate the seeds in the shell; some of them spat all of it out. He would watch that scene for hours through the window.

The most spectacular time was the evening, as it got dark and the Tree stood there among the other trees observing young people, mostly newly engaged couples, coming into the park holding each other's hands shyly in the dusk, looking for a darker spot to sit on a bench or under a tree and talk while stroking each other's hands or cheeks. Some boys would dare to steal a kiss from their lover's cheek. And if the girl was daring, she might move closer to her boyfriend so that they could hug and kiss each other on the lips.

Some evenings the Tree would walk through the garden with stealthy steps to the park entrance, standing behind the fence to watch the street. It saw every evening how the last customers of the white-headed street bookseller in front of the park browsed among the books, magazines and newspapers. They were leafing through the magazines under the gloomy light of the street lanterns while the tall, slim bookseller was packing up and putting the books and magazines back into cardboard boxes to take them home by a taxi. Some of the costumers would buy a book or newspaper and walk away quickly, while some would try a chat with the bookseller, who always, the Tree had noticed, replied with complaint, as if annoyed, even when he occasionally laughed. Nevertheless, he would make a short affirming comment about any book that was bought. The Tree could sense bitterness in his voice and in the expressions on his face but could not place them in any of the experiences he had with other people during his trip through the city, either as the Naked Young Man by day or as the Tree by night.

None of his experiences inside the garden satisfied him very much. Nothing could disturb the silence inside him. He missed his adventurous wanderings about town. One evening, after the Gardener had completed his ritual performance of washing off his gardening tools, then pouring a big bowl of water under the Tree, looking up at him smiling, taking the bowl back to the office, leaving the door unlocked and leaving the park via the main exit, the Tree walked slowly along the same path as the Gardener, and sneaked out of the park. It stood still on the corner of the wide pavement in front of the park and saw the Gardener further down talking to the tall white-headed bookseller who was standing beside four boxes. A Coaster, a twenty-one-passenger bus, arrived and stopped about ten metres down from where the men were standing. The Gardener ran after it and got on the bus just as it started to move; the folding door closed after him. Then, the bookseller waved to a taxi that halted abruptly in front of him. The driver jumped out and helped the bookseller to put two of the boxes on the back seat and the other two in the boot. When they both got in, the car drove away swiftly.

On the other side of the street, in front of the Hasib Salih building, some children were playing on the pavement, under the dim light of a street lamp post. A few young men stood round, talking and laughing, while waiving with their *tasbehs*, chaplets, around their fingers or moving the beads repeatedly between two fingers. The Tree stayed for a short while enjoying the atmosphere before crossing over Parezga Street to the left of the park, passing the Governorate Council building and encountering Mawlawi Street.

36

That evening, after dinner, when the Photographer knocked at the Neighbour-Girl's door and she came out, ready to rush down the alley with him to the park, they saw the Asayish Director's mother coming towards them with two gunmen – her son's guards. The Photographer and Neighbour-Girl immediately ran into the Photographer's house and hid behind the large wooden gate in the front courtyard. His father sat on the bench in the garden, illuminated by a *fanos* laid beside him on the bench. Just before he could say anything, the Photographer shushed him. Neighbour-Girl left a split in the door through which they could watch the half-dark alley. There was an electricity blackout.

When the Neighbour-Girl's mother opened the door on the other side of the alleyway with a candle in her hand, and the Asayish Director's mother went inside, the two guards stayed at the door.

After five minutes, the Photographer whispered that they should find a way to get out of the house before it was too late. 'Or let me go via the roof and you come later if you want.'

'No way,' said the Neighbour-Girl, grabbing at the Photographer's hand, dragging him behind her through the courtyard, walking into the house. She said she had a better idea. 'Let's just find two *abbas*. I bet you still have old ones of your mother somewhere?'

'Let me ask my dad,' said the Photographer, running back to the garden. His father gave him the *fanos* as well.

Ten minutes later, they both rushed out of the house covered from head to toe with black *abbas*, a traditional women's all-covering cloak, and walked down the dim alley. The two guards were staring at them.

The Neighbour-Girl and the Photographer entered the park from the back entrance. They looked almost everywhere in the garden; in every corner; between the trees; staring at all the trees one by one, each with a torch in hand, scanning the trees from top to root. They looked again, twice and then for a third time, everywhere, but there was no sign of *their* Tree. They were now sure that it was not in the park. When they left the garden through the main exit, the Neighbour-Girl stopped abruptly and said, 'Wait a second… I just realise I saw the remains of an uprooted tree over there.'

'I saw it too. Leave it. I checked, there was no sign of the Tree there,' said the Photographer, confidently.

'Which one? There were a couple. But I don't think you saw that one. It was when your torch stopped working. I just don't know why I didn't take it seriously. Let's go back.'

The Neighbour-Girl ran into the park again, the Photographer right behind her. When they were close to the Gardener's office, she turned on her torch and looked for the site. They found it between two trees and immediately bent to kneel beside it, examining the soil. The Neighbour-Girl found a small leaf, held it under the torch, showing it to the Photographer.

The Photographer grabbed the leaf, turned it around few times, then took the torch out of the Neighbour-Girl's hand, shed the light on the leaf and looked closer. 'Holy shi…' He jumped from the ground and stood up with a jerk. Neighbour-Girl stood up quickly too and came closer to him. The Photographer started shouting, 'It's him… It's him!'

'Shush…' the Neighbour-Girl reprimanded him, grabbing his arm, and looking around to see if anyone had heard them. A boy ran to them and asked, panting, 'What have you found? It's my money. Is it a five-dinar bill? I just lost it around here.'

'Ah, walk away man, what five-dinar bill?' said the Photographer irritated, putting the leaf in the pocket of his jeans.

The boy shook his head, surprised by so much excitement about a simple leaf.

'Let's go. Hurry up,' said the Neighbour-Girl. But just at the moment they wanted to leave, Lady Journalist appeared from behind a tree.

'Hi,' she said and asked the Photographer, giggling, 'Did you find new evidence?'

'What are you doing here?' the Photographer asked her.

'Ah, I was just wandering around.'

'No, seriously,' said the Neighbour-Girl. 'Tell us. I think you know something. Did you know that he was here? Why didn't you let us know?'

'I was going to. But I wasn't sure. I assumed that the Gardener knew, and I actually suspected him to be holding the boy somewhere in his office. He didn't let me in. He really was very tight with his information. And he was so cautious when he answered my questions about the Tree. I didn't even tell him I am a journalist.'

'Come on. Let's go and find him,' said the Photographer and walked away quickly, both girls following him.

'If it wasn't for this bloody woman, we could make it on time here,' the Neighbour-Girl said, while walking beside Lady Journalist, hurrying to catch up with the Photographer.

'Which bloody woman?' Lady Journalist asked.

'Ah, it's a long story,' the Neighbour-Girl answered, panting.

'Oh, I am interested in long stories. The longer a story the better for me,' Lady Journalist said, laughing, while catching up with them, trying to make the Neighbour-Girl reveal more.

37

When the Tree reached Sa'a Takoyee alley – the first side road to the right of Mawlawi Street about two hundred metres from the public garden – it wanted to go in but noticed a beam of light coming from under the roller shutter of a shop on the corner. It was obvious from the signboard that it was a workshop for making paintings and sculptures, framing pictures and stuffing birds and animals, though the Tree could not understand all the images. It changed its mind and instead of going into Sa'a Takoyee alley, it walked towards the shop and stood in front of the shutter. It noticed a small hole in the roller shutter glistening like a diamond in the dark. It looked through the hole and saw two young men sitting on old wooden chairs on each side of a big table watching a television opposite them. Both had put their right hands inside their pyjama trousers. The Tree recognised them; they were among the people in the courtyard of the city's main museum the evening the Photographer made a commotion, weeks ago. The Tree smiled, remembering how it had sabotaged the Photographer's effort to take a picture of it.

Suddenly, it heard a hubbub of talk and laughter approaching the shop. It looked up and saw a group of armed men, mainly young, carrying Kalashnikovs or pistols, and walking in a hurry down the street, towards the shop. They wore Kurdish clothing, with the top designed as military fatigues; their waists wrapped with ammunition clips. While their voices echoed in the silence of the empty street, they walked carefully, looking around and up at the buildings on both sides of the street.

The Tree stood still beside the shop, just like all the other trees on both sides of the street, lined up on the edge of the road, one every few metres.

When the men reached the shop, three of them noticed the beam of light and halted abruptly, signalling behind their backs for the others to stop.

'Hold on! What is that light?' one of the three hissed.

The Tree felt an anxiety that it had never felt before.

One of the gunmen bent over, looked under the shop's shutter and stood up again. He turned to his fellows and said, 'The light's coming from under the shutter. It looks as if there are people inside.'

Another one, who looked much older than the rest, evidently their commander, spread his arms and moved them backwards as a sign for his group to spread. 'Keep quiet. Maybe there are thieves inside,' he whispered.

The group spread immediately to both sides of the shop, aiming their guns at the shutter. One of them bumped into the Tree and got angry. He kicked its trunk and said, 'Look where some motherfucker planted this tree...'

The commander waved and beckoned him forward, whispering, 'Shut up, sucker, and take your position! It's not planted.'

The man took his position behind the Tree, leaning his Kalashnikov on its trunk.

While it tried to hold itself and soothe the pain in its trunk, the Tree could see through the hole in the shutter that the two young men inside were becoming greatly disturbed hearing people talk outside the shop. One of them stood up and turned the television off quickly. Then, he took a cassette from the video player under the television and hid it in a box in the corner of the office.

Outside, one of the gunmen noticed that the shutter was not locked, as shopkeepers usually lock up with one or two strong iron padlocks that unite the shutter to the ground. The man bent down and tried to pull the shutter up from one side but noticed that it was locked from the inside. He looked at his commander and whispered, 'Maybe it's the owner himself inside.'

The commander pointed to him to be quiet, then banged on the shutter, shouting, 'Who's there? Raise the shutter. Open up!'

The two young men were panicking, running around from one side of the office to the other, not knowing what to do. One of them, a tall guy with a large black moustache, gestured silently to his companion to go upstairs. The companion, who was shorter and had a much thinner moustache, looked at the shutter then back to his friend before running up the stairs. After three steps, he hesitated, then ran down again to take the videocassette from the box and ran back up the stairs.

Once more the commander banged on the shutter and shouted, warning the inhabitants that if they would not open, he would break in. 'Open up! We are the *Asayish*. We'll not hurt you if you are the owner.'

The tall guy came to the shutter and said in a dull voice that he was going to open up, but when he grabbed the big padlock, he found that he did not have the key. Through the thunder of banging and kicking, he shouted that he was going to get the key.

The commander stopped hitting the shutter and shouted back, 'Hurry up then.'

After only twenty seconds, as soon as the tall black-moustached guy pulled up the shutter, the gunmen stormed into the shop, pushing the guy aside. They spread out quickly and carefully inside the shop, pointing their guns at every corner.

The Tree saw hundreds of paintings and photographs of landscapes, flowers, birds and other animals framed in gold-coloured aluminium frames, and huge portraits of gorgeous women, some half-naked in odd positions, and of crying children with exaggerated tears on their cheeks, hung on the walls in different sizes, one above the other up to the ceiling. On the floor, beside the walls, under the photographs, there were tens of small, coloured models of dancing couples, some in wedding clothes, put on plinths. On other stands, there were acrobatic elephants, happy playing cats and dogs, lines of walking camels, and stuffed birds and animals, many owls and squirrels among them, fixed to wooden pedestals.

Two of the gunmen ran immediately up the stairs and the others started, each in a corner, to search in the many boxes that were full of strange materials and equipment unknown to the Tree, and apparently to the gunmen too who took them out, stared at them, examined them and put them back in the boxes. They looked under the tables and behind some glass display cupboards, which were also full of small sculptures.

The commander asked the tall young man, 'What are you doing

here buddy? Are you alone?'

The young black-moustached man stuttered, 'I, I'm an artist and… I'm… My friend and I are staying here to finish some work.' He pointed to the staircase.

One of the two gunmen who had run upstairs came back to the top of the stairs and shouted, 'Everyone, come upstairs. There are so many rooms up here.'

The commander and the rest of his men ran immediately up the stairs.

Also the tall artist walked up hesitatingly, looking at the open shutter, not knowing whether he should go to close it or not.

When the artist was upstairs and could no longer see outside, the Tree came in and followed them carefully up the stairs. It saw the commander and his gunmen standing at the doorway of a room. The Tree stood behind them. There they saw the shorter, younger-looking guy wearing a tracksuit smeared with a thousand old spots of paint, a brush in his right hand and a bunch of other brushes and a rag smeared with paint in his left hand. He looked in astonishment at the gunmen, while beside him was an unfinished portrait of an armed *peshmerga*, a Kurdish guerrilla fighter looking like the gunmen themselves, painted in still wet oil. Clearly, it looked like the young artist was working on the painting all along. What a clever move, the Tree thought.

The other gunman, who had gone upstairs first, was now searching a couple of boxes full of paint tubes, brushes and other painting materials in a corner. At that moment the tall artist arrived and said, pointing to his friend, 'So this is my friend.'

The commander nodded and looked around in the room. The room was crammed everywhere with paintings on canvas and hardboard, hung on the walls or stacked up on the floor in the corners or beside the walls. A big easel in the middle of the room carried another unfinished painting and a small table in front held a big palette of coloured paints and a tin full of used brushes. Against one of the walls a narrow, long panel on two trestles was used as a table: on it stood two more undried paintings and lots of paint tubes and brushes, some with paint at the tips. In a corner of the room were piled two thin, folded mattresses and some blankets and pillows.

The commander went to the window, opened it, stuck his head outside and looked to both sides of the street. He pulled his head back inside, closed the window and was about to ask a question when his eyes opened wide at the sight of the Tree. He frowned at the tall artist, then looked round the room again.

The gunmen looked at each other, asking with their eyes whether they should leave these men alone, as it was obvious that they were not intruders but worked there and appeared to be doing nothing wrong. Just as the commander was about to speak, one of the men came in and said that there was another room that was locked. They all hurried out of the studio and walked through the wide long landing that also was full of strange objects and materials: wooden bars, big pieces of glass, piles of gold aluminium framing sticks, and a huge barrel-like metal cylindrical container connected with a hose and a pistol-like head.

'What's this?' one of the gunmen asked the tall guy.

'Oh, this is a compressor, a paint sprayer machine. For painting the sculptures, you know?'

When they passed another room that was already open, the commander stepped back and stuck his head through the door. There were workspaces alongside the walls, all dirty with plaster dust and two long wooden tables in the middle, on which stood hundreds of small statues made of gypsum. The commander withdrew from the room and walked towards his men who were standing by the locked room. He asked the tall guy, 'Where is the key? What have you got here?'

The tall guy said that other colleagues stuffed birds and animals in there. 'They're taxidermists,' he explained. 'Let me see if I can find the key,' he said, walking towards the stairs.

One of the men kicked the door firmly and broke it open.

The artist ran back, entered the room and switched on the lights.

Everyone was surprised when they saw so many stuffed animals and birds on two huge tables, while in a corner, two live squirrels had started jumping and spinning in a small narrow cage, clinging anxiously to the metal mesh. Some of the animals and birds were slit down the middle and stuffed with cotton; some were wholly stuffed, but their heads had not yet been fixed, so lay beside the carcases. In place of the heads, a thin iron bar and cotton tufts jutted out of the necks. Some of the fully stuffed and finished birds were attached to branches of trees.

In the middle of the room, in front of the two tables, were stools. On the floor lay a huge tree trunk with only a few branches left. An electric saw lay by the trunk. Everywhere – on the tables, the window ledges and the floor – were scattered bloody cotton tufts, dozens of cutting implements and razor blades, small and large pieces of metal sticks and wire, scissors, needles and thread, thin nylon gloves, used, bloody, torn or unused. There were bottles of Dettol and other hygienic material, tubes and tins of paint, brushes, hammers, screwdrivers, saws, and wood chisels, all lay haphazard on the tables in a horrific chaos that looked like a psychedelic torture chamber – which the Tree had seen as man in a movie during his stay at the park. The strong smell of ammonia suffused the air in the room and strengthened the alarming atmosphere.

All of a sudden, an owl came from out of nowhere and started flying towards the door. All the men, even the two artists, jumped back, while three of the gunmen pointed their Kalashnikovs to the ceiling. The bird landed on a tree trunk in the corner by the door. The two young artists looked at each other and then to the commander. The shorter one said, 'I think it's better to close the door again. Look, there are another couple of owls over there.'

The men, and the Tree, saw two other owls sitting on a branch of a tree trunk looking out through slitted eyes. The commander nodded, then the shorter guy returned inside and switched off the lights. The eyes of the owls opened wide, shiny golden marbles glistening in the dark. The men giggled.

The commander looked at the taller guy and said, 'What the hell is all this craziness here? Is this a madhouse or what?'

All the men laughed, but when the tall artist wanted to explain, the commander continued, 'It's like we're in the middle of a horror movie. Who the hell are those people who work here?'

Everyone again burst out laughing, except for the two artists.

Without waiting for an answer, the commander walked away towards the stairs. The men followed him. One of them bumped into the Tree and shouted angrily, 'They've fucking got trees in every damned corner. It looks like a jungle here.' He laughed at his own joke, but nobody else did.

The shorter artist closed the broken door and wanted to run after them but halted at the Tree. He stroked its trunk and looked at his friend with an enquiring gaze of "what-is-this-damn-tree-doing-here-after-all?"

The tall guy shrugged and followed the men. His shorter friend patted the trunk again and ran after them. The Tree followed cauciously.

When they were all at the stairs, the commander noticed a rusty iron door at the other end of the landing. He pointed to it and asked the guys where it went. The two artists said simultaneously that it led to the roof of the back shops. All the gunmen ran immediately to the door. One of them slid the bolt and opened the door. They all walked outside onto the roof and looked carefully at all sides with their guns pointed to the walls of the neighbouring buildings and into the Sa'a Takoyee alley behind the shop. The Tree looked at them from the landing. Moonlight illuminated the area. The commander sniffed, looked around and asked the two artists disgustedly, 'Are you fucking peeing up here on the roof, guys?'

The two young artists blushed.

Again, without waiting for an answer, the commander turned to the door, returned to the house and ran through all the clutter down the stairs, his men after him.

When downstairs, and all the men left the shop, the commander returned inside and shouted, addressing the artists that it would be better to turn off the lights in the office when they worked upstairs. 'And actually, better not to stay for the night. You know it's not allowed to sleep overnight in a shop? So let this be the last time, understood?'

The two artists shouted back, 'Sure, sir! We do.' The tall one went to turn off the lights in the studio, and the other went to lock the roof door.

The Tree slowly went down the stairs.

When the Tree came out of the shop and stood still by another tree at the edge of the curb, it saw the gunmen walking down Mawlawi

Street. Suddenly, one of them halted, turned his head back to the shop and asked surprisingly, 'Wait, where is that tree that was in front of the shop?' He looked at his mate and said, 'You bumped into it, you remember?'

The commander said, 'I think that tall guy with the black moustache had brought it inside.'

'Oh, these motherfuckers have even mummified the trees. Let's go,' said the one who had bumped into the Tree upstairs.

The Tree heard the tall painter with the thick black moustache come down the stairs. It then saw him roll down the rattling shutter and heard him lock it from inside. The light on the sidewalk dimmed, only a strip left under the shutter. And the little diamond light appeared through the hole once more. After a moment, the light inside the shop went out, the little diamond in the shutter ceased to sparkle, and the beam of light under the shutter disappeared. The steps of the painter on the stairs inside the shop became quieter, then total silence overwhelmed the street with all the shops and empty buildings on both sides.

38

Just at the start of Mawlawi Street, at the corner with Parezga Street, across from the public garden, the Photographer and his two companions, the Neighbour-Girl and Lady Journalist, saw gunmen on the other side of the street.

The gunmen immediately crossed towards them.

The group's commander greeted them and asked if they would not mind halting for a second.

The three stopped and waited for his questions.

'Don't worry, nothing's wrong. But I wonder what you are doing at this time of the night here!' the commander said.

'Ah, we're just walking home,' said the Photographer.

'I wouldn't walk through Mawlawi Street and the town centre with these two beauties at this time, man! Take a taxi and go home. Don't bring people's girls into trouble.'

'Don't worry, sir,' said the Neighbour-Girl. 'We are adults. We wish you a good night.' She continued walking, with Lady Journalist behind her.

The Photographer followed them, looking over his shoulder at the gunmen.

The commander must have felt ignored, as he shouted, 'Halt! I am not finished with you.'

The three stopped immediately and turned to him.

'Come back here, guys,' the commander beckoned. 'I didn't say you could go, did I?'

At that same moment, one of his men whispered something in his ear. The commander looked at him surprisingly and asked, 'Are you sure?'

'One hundred per cent,' the gunman replayed.

When the three stood in front of him, waiting to hear what he had to say, the commander looked at the Neighbour-Girl and asked her,

'Are you not the Asayish director's fiancé-to-be?'

'What?' the Neighbour-Girl shouted surprisingly.

The Photographer pulled at her arm and told the commander, 'Sir, this is all a misunderstanding. We are just—'

'I'm not talking to you,' the commander interrupted him, still looking at the Neighbour-Girl. He then looked at Lady Journalist and asked, 'What are you girls doing with this guy at this time of the night?'

'I thought we were in a different time now and no longer in the Baathist era,' the Neighbour-Girl said, looking at the commander challengingly.

'I am an *Asayish* commander, my dear. I'm just doing my job, making sure you are safe.' His walkie-talkie beeped, and he pulled it out of his *cummerbund,* while a garbled voice asked through the static sound, 'Are you on a patrol shift?'

'Yes, sir, we are,' the commander answered while pressing on a button.

The Neighbour-Girl looked at the Photographer with a gaze of do-you-recognize-this-voice? The Photographer shrugged enquiringly with a gaze of who-the-hell-do-you-think-he-could-be?

When the commander released the button and the static noise started again, the garbled sound asked, 'I heard you're on Mawlawi Street?'

'Yes, sir. In front of the *Parezga* right now,' the commander answered and released the button again. The noise started again: Shhhhhhh… beep… tut…

'I'm looking for a girl with this photographer guy. You know him? They must be in your area now.' Shhhhhhh… beep… tut…

'We'll see, sir. I'll let you know.' Shhhhhhh… beep… tut… He then put the walkie-talkie back in his *cummerbund* and told the Neighbour-Girl, 'He's looking for you, darling. Better if you go home. Hurry up. I'll not tell him I saw you.'

'This is just bizarre. I am not his daughter!' the Neighbour-Girl said angrily, looking at the commander then at the Photographer and Lady Journalist. The Photographer seemed to know now who the caller on the other side of the line was.

'And sure not his fiancé,' she added, this time walking away immediately, then turning her head over her shoulder to tell the commander, 'Don't worry, sir. We will be fine.'

The Photographer looked at the commander and shrugged. He said goodbye and walked away, pulling at Lady Journalist's arm. She followed him, looking to be still stunned at the whole conversation.

The commander shouted, 'And you must be the Photographer. Better he doesn't see you, my friend.'

Just as the gunmen crossed the street again and walked down towards the square, a Land Cruiser turned very fast around the roundabout, passing the gunmen and braking noisily at the curb on the wrong side of the road. The car pulled over to the three pedestrians and forced them to a halt. The front door on the right opened immediately and the Asayish Director stepped out. One of his armed men also came out from the left rear door, while the driver opened his door and put his left leg out of the car, with his foot on the curb, yet remained half sitting, holding the steering wheel with one hand.

The Asayish Director limped from the street towards the three on the sidewalk, holding a huge heap of black clothes under his arm. When he reached them on the pavement, he tossed the heap at the Photographer and said, 'Take your *abbas* back, old chap. Next time you disguise yourself as a woman, make sure you hide your *abba* somewhere better. We found them at the *Serah*. Such a shame!'

The Photographer picked up the two *abbas* from the ground, piled them into his arms, but said nothing.

'What are you doing out at this time of night, girls?' the Asayish Director asked both girls, while looking only at the Neighbour-Girl.

Lady Journalist stepped forwards and said, 'We wanted—'

'We are just having a nice walk. Is that not allowed?' Neighbour-Girl said, staring at the Asayish Director challengingly.

'You are allowed, darling. But it's not so safe around here at this time of night,' the Asayish Director replied, looking at them one by one, embarrassed. He then said, 'Let's take you home. Get in the car.'

'Oh, no, I don't think so. We'll walk. That's what we've come out for,' the Neighbour-Girl said and started walking again.

'Don't worry, sir. We'll be fine. Have a good night,' the Photographer said, waving to the Asayish Director, while walking away. Lady

Journalist followed after them.

'Okay, as you like. Just be careful,' the Asayish Director said, shaking his head, disappointed. He then limped back to the car and got in.

When the other gunman got in the back and shut the door, the driver shut his door too and started the car. The Asayish Director put his hand on the driver's hand on the steering wheel. He remained silent for a few moments, watching the three walking slowly, for obviously they knew they were being observed.

'I'm getting tired of this fucking dude. But what shall I do to him, huh? I don't want to upset my girl. So, let's leave them for now. Take me to the fucking club.'

The driver made a U-turn, squealed off, and drove back through the square, then turned onto Parezga Street.

39

When they reached the first side road on the left side of Mawlawi Street, opposite to Sa'a Takoyee alley, the Photographer and the two girls stopped, just in front of the Post and Communications Office, right on the corner. The Photographer asked the girls which way they thought they should take.

'Which way do you think the Tree could have gone?' the two girls asked.

'Let me think,' the Photographer said, looking to all sides.

'I think if it had taken this street, those gunmen could have bumped into it. Don't you think?' said Lady Journalist. 'And look there are people in the Sa'a Takoyee,' she added, nodding towards the alley.

'So?' asked the Neighbour-Girl.

'So, it might have taken this alley,' said the Photographer. 'Is that what you're suggesting?' he asked Lady Journalist, pointing to the short side street to their left, where the Post Office was.

'That's most likely, isn't it?' Lady Journalist said, looking at them both.

'Hey, what are those men doing over there?' the Neighbour-Girl asked. 'What are they eating?'

'Oh, they're eating chickpeas. That stall has the most delicious chickpea soup. He's very well-known by all the workers around here,' said the Photographer. 'I didn't know he would still be there at this time.'

'Let's go and have some. I can smell it from here,' said Lady Journalist.

'Ah, let's move on. It's late. We'll never find the Tree this way,' said the Neighbour-Girl, irritated.

'Come on, let's do it. Why not? It's really delicious,' said the Photographer.

Lady Journalist had already crossed the street.

'Leave her. We don't need her. Let's go,' the Neighbour-Girl whispered, grabbing the Photographer's arm.

The Photographer freed his arm gently from her clutch and said quietly in disbelief, 'Ah, come on, we can't leave her here at this time of night.'

'And now you play the *Asayish* guy? Come on, leave her. She is an adult.'

'Are you jealous or what?'

'What? Where did this come from?' She turned towards the alleyway on the left and added, 'You know what? You go with her. Go and have your chickpeas you two. I'm going after the Tree by myself.' She walked away.

The Photographer shrugged and crossed the street towards Sa'a Takoyee, almost shouting, 'As you like. You are an adult too, aren't you?' He heard the Neighbour-Girl let out a deep sigh and saw her shaking her head, before turning around and walking back to Mawlawi Street. She also crossed towards the chickpea stall, joined the Photographer and Lady Journalist again, clearly trying to hide her anger.

40

The Tree walked slowly along the road at the top end of Mawlawi Street. Looking at both sides through the silence, it imagined how crowded this street must be in the daytime. The thought of not being able to walk around in the street during the day made him sad. At the end of the road, not so far above the grey-purple mountain behind the city, the almost-full, round moon shone in the sky, shedding an outlandish light on the buildings and the trees on both sides of the street. Its reflection on the asphalt revealed the hundreds of potholes and water puddles. The Tree also noticed the moon's blue silvery shimmer on its own leaves, intensified the heavy grief that spread through all its branches, its bark and the cellulose fibre cells inside its trunk.

Arriving at Mawlawi Bridge, it stopped to try to cheer up and reflect on what it had encountered moments ago and found that it was, in fact, quite amusing, though not entirely comprehensible to him, to discover what had been revealed to him. While trying to make some sense out of it, the Tree looked at the street down by the bridge. It was full of rubbish, thrown away cardboard boxes and discarded fruit and vegetables, bird poo, paper, tins and plastic bottles.

The Tree descended the stairs and walked under the bridge. It passed dozens of empty cages in different sizes and colours, bound together with chains. It was walking slowly through the puddles over the many bits of cardboard and crumpled packing paper under the bridge, when it suddenly heard a man panting. It stopped there immediately, and noticed that right at its feet a man with a big black moustache, wearing Kurdish turban, knelt on the ground between a couple of cardboard boxes, holding the ends of his fallen down *sharwal* with both his hands, while a young boy squatted in front of him with his head in the crotch of the man. The Tree bent over to see what the child was doing.

Frightened by the rustling sound of the leaves and the sudden appearance of a tree beside him, the man shivered and hopped away. The boy fell over and his face hit the ground hard.

Pulling up his *sharwal*, tightening it with its string, the man ran from under the bridge towards the square of the Grand Mosque.

The boy jumped up quickly, got to his feet and ran after the man, wiping the blood from his mouth with the back of his hand.

The Tree followed them with its rustling leaves.

In the middle of the square, in front of the Grand Mosque, the boy caught up with the man and grabbed his *sharwal*. The man pushed him so that he fell into a puddle at the feet of the Tree.

The man quickly pulled a five-dinar bill out of his *sharwal's* pocket, threw it to the boy and walked hurriedly towards the high fence of the mosque.

The Tree saw that on the other side of the square, diagonally opposite the mosque, in front of an old two-story building, some men of various ages sat around a small fire made from cardboard boxes and wastepaper. They were enshrouded in white smoke.

At the same time, a police car drove down the street opposite the mosque and halted in front of the man. A policeman opened the rear door and jumped out, stopped the man and started to question him. The Tree could not hear what they were saying but saw that the man was pointing to the boy angrily. It also saw that at the same time, the men by the fire scattered, running in all directions.

The police car drove slowly to the spot where the Tree stood.

The boy leant on the Tree, rose up from the muddy puddle and ran towards the street under the bridge, from where he had come.

The car stopped. A police officer opened the front door and stepped out with the shiny stars on his shoulder. While he approached the Tree, the car accelerated towards the street under the bridge, chasing the boy.

The other policeman left the man in front of the mosque and ran towards the Tree and stood behind the officer who was stroking the Tree's trunk, looking at its muddy roots.

The ranking officer looked astonished at the policeman, who held his beret folded in his hand and put his other hand on his pistol in the holster at his waist.

'What's this bloody tree doing here?' the officer said, then looked at the abandoned fire in front of the two-story building.

'Sir, I wonder where that kid got it from,' said the policeman. 'And what did he want to do with it, anyway? Oh, these damn beggars tend to do anything, sir. Anything bad that comes into their minds.'

The officer looked again at the Tree, then at the policeman and said, 'This tree doesn't belong to the kid. Why did you let that man walk away, sergeant?'

The policeman felt that he had done something stupid. He seemed to regret that he had believed the man and let him go. Embarrassed by this, he became clumsy and seemed not to know what to say or to do. He hugged the Tree and tried to carry it but it turned out to be much heavier than he had thought.

'Oh, sir, you know what the man said? Oh, my God, why did I let him go!' He ran, without saying what the man had said, in the direction in which the man had headed.

The officer called him back, 'Stop sergeant. There is our car coming back.'

The sergeant stepped back. The car arrived. Another policeman put his head out of the rear window and said to the officer, 'We got the kid, sir.'

The officer and the sergeant jumped into the car, the officer at the front and the sergeant at the back. The other policeman at the back continued, 'So this boy says that he had done nothing. He had only asked that man to show him the road, but the man had thought that he was a beggar and had pushed him away, but threw him some money. He says he is a plastic-bag vendor and had fallen asleep among the cardboard boxes under the bridge. Now it's late and he cannot find his way back home. He's living in Haji Awa, outside the city.'

'But what is this damn tree doing here then?' the officer interrupted him, turning his head to the back of the car.

'Sir, maybe it doesn't have anything to do with them, sir,' the sergeant said with a cunning tone, obvious that he was trying to compensate for his earlier blunder. But the boy, who sat between the policeman and the sergeant in the back, shouted, 'Oh, yes, it was that man's, for sure!'

'But I still don't get it,' shouted the officer. 'What would that man

181

want to do with this huge tree at this time of the night?'

'Oh, dear! I now know… It's the Tree… It's that fucking Tree,' the sergeant shouted.

They all turned to where the Tree was outside the vehicle. But it wasn't there.

'Where did it go?' the driver shouted and at once opened the door and jumped out of the car, after him all the other men, leaving only the boy inside.

The four policemen looked around a couple of times, then looked at each other and jumped back into the car, except for the sergeant who grabbed the boy's arm and tried to pull him out of the car.

'Leave him,' the officer shouted at the sergeant. 'We will take him to interrogate.'

The boy started to cry, saying, 'Sir, I really haven't done anything. Believe me I just…'

The policeman on his other side said, while shutting the rear door with one hand and grabbing the boy's arm with his other hand, 'Shut up you little shit… We'll take you home later, you fucking troublemakers.'

The driver accelerated towards Mahkama Street, in the same direction the man had taken, passing the Grand Mosque as they went.

After having observed the scene from a corner, standing beside another tree at the beginning of Kaneskan Street, the Tree walked away, back towards the street that passed under the bridge. When it had just passed the bridge, it turned left and walked amid muddy puddles and piles of fruit and vegetables, blood, chicken heads and feathers. It arrived at the marketplace with its many empty stands in front of the shops around a large, open space full of rubbish left from vendors and customers.

The Tree looked at an old empty building located above a row of shops; its balcony – with wooden ornamented pillars, from which most of the pale sky-blue paint had fallen – formed a canopy over a few stalls in front of the shops. The pale blue paint of the building and the shiny green of the grass on its roof under the moonlight, amazed the Tree. It wished that it could stay in there when the sun rose at dawn.

After staring at the building for a while, the Tree turned right and entered the large covered market with its maze of entangled alleyways. It passed the old town hall and walked down the covered passage of the Grossers. When it reached the passage of the Butchers, it took a right, and then a left towards Naqib passage, which was the oldest part of the covered bazaar in the city. When it passed the huge iron gate of the bazaar, it walked down the alley of the Tailors.

41

After the Photographer and the girls had slurped their chickpea soup very quickly – all the time being looked up and down by the men around the vendor's cart – they hurried to cross over Mawlawi Street again and enter the side street with the Post office. From there, they went right into the street that took them to the Grand Mosque.

'Let's hope Iago understands now,' said the Photographer, without looking at the Neighbour-Girl.

'I really don't care anymore. He's being very childish now. I don't have any respect for him, even if he is the most powerful man of the city,' the Neighbour-Girl said, also without looking at the Photographer.

'What's the story of you and this man, anyway?' Lady Journalist asked the Neighbour-Girl. 'He seems to be fixated on you. I don't think he will ever get it that you're just simply not interested in him. Most men don't. I've also had an experience like this.'

'Ah, leave it. It's only annoying, because he's started harassing me,' the Neighbour-Girl said, making it obvious that she no longer wanted to talk about it.

'And, by the way...' Lady Journalist grabbed the Neighbour-Girl's arm, slowing her down to keep some distance between them and the Photographer. 'What's making you do all this? I mean, looking for the Tree and—'

'Ah, I actually don't know. I'm not even sure if I really believe it exists or... I mean, I even haven't seen it.'

'Oh, it exists for sure. I've seen him... I mean I saw him as a man.'

'What? You really did?'

'For a couple of seconds. But, girl, I fell in love with him. Oh, God, the expression in his eyes! He looked right into mine.'

'Where? Where did you see him?'

'At our office. He's so unbelievably gorgeous. Maybe I'm disillu-

sioned, but he really... Okay, I wasn't the only one in the room, but...
Anyway, he's stolen my heart. I don't know... I absolutely have to see
him again.'

'Oh dear, you really sound in love!'

They both laughed.

The Photographer turned his head and shouted, 'Hurry up, will
you? No time for girly talks. Come on...'

When they reached the Grand Mosque square, they saw a group of
men around a fire in front of the *Maarif* building, the old education
department office. They halted a few metres from them to listen, soon
noticing that the me were speaking Arabic. The Photographer knew
a little Arabic, but the Neighbour-Girl could barely understand what
they were saying. However, Lady Journalist said that her Arabic was
perfect, as she had grown up in Baghdad until she was twelve when her
family had moved back here, so she had attended an Arabic-language
school. She said that the men seemed to be talking about the Tree,
as one of them swore he had seen a tree in the middle of the square
running down the street towards the bridge, while the others laughed
at him and said he was hallucinating. 'I didn't know that you could
get high just from the smoke of burning cardboard,' one of them said
while the others burst out laughing.

The three came closer to the group and greeted them, still from two
metres distance. Lady Journalist asked them whether they had seen
a tree around. The guy who claimed to have seen the Tree running,
answered immediately, 'Oh, yes, yes. That's what I'm saying but nobody
believes me. Come on guys, you see? They are also looking for it. I told
you, this is a strange city. Now do you believe me? They even have
running trees here.'

The other guys started to laugh again and one of them said, 'Oh,
yeah, so strange that you could become high without paying for it.' The
group laughed again.

Lady Journalist asked them what they were doing there. A couple
of them started speaking at once, saying that they were construction
workers, coming from the central and southern provinces for work.
They were waiting for the contractors who usually came in the early

mornings to collect workers. One of them said, 'Can you believe that I haven't had a job for the last six days and I can't even pay for a place to stay?'

Lady Journalist said she was sorry. 'But guys, seriously, what happened? Where did you see that tree? What—?'

'I don't know. The police came,' said the guy who claimed he had seen the Tree. 'We thought they were coming for us because that's what they usually do. But they arrested a kid and I also think a man. When we saw the police, we tried to scatter and get out, so we missed the ending. I think they were arguing about that tree. When the police went away, we came back to the fire. I saw the tree suddenly running! But these guys still don't—'

'I saw that tree too,' another young man shouted from behind the others. 'But running?'

Another one came forwards and said, 'Actually, I saw it too. But it disappeared suddenly. I think the police took it away, or maybe that man. I mean I didn't see the man. But—'

Lady Journalist thanked them and turned to see that the Photographer and Neighbour-Girl had already moved away towards the street to which the Tree was supposed to have run down. She rushed towards them, but one of the guys ran after her and asked, 'Hey, how come you speak such perfect Arabic? Are you a Baghdadi?'

'Oh, no, I'm a Kurd, but I was born in Baghdad and grew up there.'

'So you *are* a Baghdadi, like me!'

'Sorry, mate, I have to catch up with my friends.'

'Would you please translate this for me?' The young Baghdadi pulled a piece of paper out of his pocket and gave it to her.

She read it quickly and said, giving back the piece of paper to him, 'It says: "Come in the early morning," but it doesn't mention a date.'

'I know,' the guy said. 'Doesn't matter which day, but where is the address?'

'Wait, that's what I'm about to tell you,' said Lady Journalist, amused.

'Ok, *habibti,* that's so kind of you,' said the guy in an accent that proved that he also came from near Baghdad.

'There is of course no address. Who has an address here?' said

Lady Journalist sarcastically. 'But they have explained how to get there. It is—'

'Yes, I know, darling. That's what I need to know,' the guy interrupted her again.

'I'm telling you, man. Just wait. Have some patience, man!'

'Okay, okay, darling. I'm all ears'.

Lady Journalist looked at him with a charming gaze and a subtle smile and continued, 'It says across from the clothing factory, enter the street, then take the first side road on your right. After a couple of hundred metres, there is a huge construction site.'

'I already went there, darling, but there was no construction site,' the guy said.

'Oooooh, poor guy. What a pity!' Lady Journalist laughed at him slightly to hide her own flirtatious attempt at seduction.

'Come on, hurry up! What are you talking about?' the Photographer shouted from the corner of the street, waiting with the Neighbour-Girl.

'Okay, okay, I'm coming,' said Lady Journalist, hurriedly. She then turned back again to the guy and asked him, 'So you have already been there?'

'I went there yesterday but didn't find any construction site. There is only one clothing factory, right? It's down there,' he said, pointing towards south of the city. 'Is there another one?'

'No, no... There is only that one. Actually, it's over there, on the Sixty-Metre Street.' She pointed more towards southwest.

'Come on. Hurry up. We won't find it this way,' the Photographer shouted again, as he started rushing into the street, holding Neighbour-Girl's hand.

Lady Journalist ran after them.

'Thanks a lot, *habibti*. I'm grateful!' shouted the guy.

'You're most welcome!' Lady Journalist shouted back, lifting an arm in the air.

Another one of the guys yelled, 'And the kiss? Where is the kiss? Muah...' After him some others also started kissing loudly in the air. One shouted, *'Bussa, bussa!'*

Lady Journalist ran down the street after the Photographer and the

Neighbour-Girl, while laughing, but didn't turn towards the excited young workers.

When they reached the passage under the bridge, the Neighbour-Girl stopped running and pulled at the Photographer's hand. He almost fell over backwards but balanced himself and held the Neighbour-Girl's arm.

'I can't run anymore. Let's walk slowly,' she pleaded.

Lady Journalist also halted, looking at them, waiting to see what would happen.

'I don't know why I'm doing this,' said the Neighbour-Girl. 'Let's go home, please! This's just crazy.'

'Come on, we can try the passages in the bazaar. Then we will go home. I mean, we are almost on the way back home already. We won't run, okay?' said the Photographer, putting his arm in her arm, starting to walk slowly.

'But how do you think we can find it? Who knows which side he's taken? And he can run much faster than us. You said he would feel us coming, remember?'

The Photographer pulled her gently and took the way through the Baladiya Market, where the old town hall was, trying to avoid the many muddy puddles but failing again and again.

Lady Journalist followed them, managing on her turn to avoid the puddles. She kept a few steps from them, trying not to get involved with their argument.

42

The Tree reached the beginning of the *Mazadkhana,* with its maze of small streets and alleyways. All the shops were now closed. Suddenly, it noticed that a group of gunmen had taken positions on all corners of a crossing and were silently creeping along the walls towards a shop. The Tree stood still by the wall, behind a pillar, and saw in the dark a young boy of about thirteen or fourteen years old in front of the shop, trying to break the lock with a crowbar.

With a gesture from their commander, the gunmen loaded their guns, with a thunder-like, iron sound, and shouted, 'Don't move!'

The boy was not the only one to hop anxiously away from the shop's roller shutter, with his arms in the air, for the Tree also shivered so heavily that its leaves started to rustle, making a dust cloud around itself.

All the gunmen turned to the Tree, pointing their guns in its direction; three of them released shots that hit the wall and shop shutters behind the Tree.

The commander shouted, 'Hey, who is out there behind that tree? Come forward.'

The Tree remained still, trying to tame its panicked movements.

Two of the gunmen attacked the boy who was crying and yelling to be let go as he had not intended doing anything wrong. However, they took his *cummerbund* from his waist and used it to tie both his hands behind his back. At the same time, another two of the men came, running towards the Tree and when they did not find anybody behind it, they returned to their companions.

The commander grabbed the tied arms of the boy, kicked him in the bum and shouted, 'How many were you? Did anyone run away?'

The boy said, panting and grunting in pain, 'No one... Believe me, no one... I swear by God I'm on my own.'

The commander released the boy's arm and walked down the alley.

Some of his men followed him. Another one started to kick the boy and beat him with the butt of his Kalashnikovs until the boy collapsed and fell on the ground. Then he and one of his companions carried the unconscious boy down the alleyway, following the rest of the men.

After the last gunman had checked the area around the Tree again, he went to catch up with his fellow gunmen.

The Tree waited for a short while, then left its place behind the pillar and followed the men. It saw the gunmen enter a side passageway and reach a main street, where a covered pick-up carrying gunmen in Kurdish khaki fatigues was waiting for them. They threw the boy into the covered back of the pick up, followed by the rest of the men, except for the commander, who went to sit at the front beside the driver. The car drove swiftly away.

43

When the Photographer and the girls heard gunshots and shouts, they were near the Naqib passage. They quickly walked back through the covered bazaar to Mawlawi Street. On the corner of Asri Bazaar, at the northern part of the covered market, they saw three men hurrying out of one of the bazaar's passageways into Mawlawi Street. They were coming towards them. But after two steps, they turned and changed direction to the other side. They turned right round the corner, crossed the street and when they reached the *Shaab* teahouse, they hesitated at first, deciding which direction they should take, then headed hurriedly down towards Ashaba Spee and disappeared.

'Let's just go home, please. It's getting eerie,' said the Neighbour-Girl desperately.

'We are. We are going home now, darling,' the Photographer assured her, emphasising each word.

'I mean really now,' the Neighbour-Girl stressed. 'I'm so tired and have to wake up early tomorrow. I have to take my neighbour to the hospital. She will come and wake me early in the morning.'

The Photographer repeated that they would go right away and told Lady Journalist that they lived close by, in the Pirma Sur quarter, just past the Serah Square. He said it would be better if she went home with them, as it was far too late for her to go home alone. 'Where do you live by the way?' he asked her.

'In Rizgary. So I can just take a taxi,' said Lady Journalist.

The Neighbour-Girl said it would be a long time before a taxi would appear, so she suggested she stay with her. She lived alone with her mother, she said, so they had lots of space. Lady Journalist agreed and asked if they had a phone so that she could tell her parents she would not go home. The Neighbour-Girl said they did, but she shouldn't say anything in detail, as she was sure her phone was being tapped.

44

The Tree walked back by the same passage to the *Mazadkhana* quarter. In one of the alleys, with a row of closed shops on each side, it heard men approaching. It took a position as a planted tree between two shops until the men had passed. It was another group of six gunmen in their khaki fatigues, walking while joking and laughing together. It seemed that they were also security guards on a night surveillance mission. When they passed the Tree, one of them was talking about the previous night, when he had been on patrol with another group in the Sabunkaran district. He told how they had caught three youngsters on Sabunkaran Street and had asked them what they were doing at that time of night, lingering there. The boys had said that they were about to finish speaking and then go home. But during the interrogation, when he had put the barrel of his Kalashnikov to one of the guys' forehead, the boy had peed himself. The gunmen all burst out laughing at this.

The Tree felt so sorry for the boy, for it had just itself had a similarly dreadful experience.

A few metres away from the Tree, the men noticed a thread of light squeezing through a slit in a thick curtain of a narrow window above one of the shops on the other side of the alley. Suddenly, they all halted and kept silent. A rhythmic grunting of a man and a woman invaded the silence and was becoming steadily overwhelming. The men looked at each other, their open mouths becoming nasty grins.

Without exchanging a word, as if they knew what to do in a situation such as this and had trained rigorously for it, they all slowly stepped aside, two of them moving backwards and the other four forwards, each to a corner. They pointed their guns to the window, taking position beside the walls; two of them at the two sides of the shop's rolled-down shutter. One of the two, who seemed to be their commander, gestured with his head for the other to examine the shutter, which he did, shifting it with care.

The grunting stopped abruptly.

The gunman noticed that the shutter was unlocked, and rolled it up with one quick push. While the rumbling thunder-like sound filled the alley, all the men stormed into the shop.

The Tree saw a glimpse of a man appear behind the slit in the curtain, to disappear again immediately.

Just as the men ran up the shop stairs to the second floor, where the source of the light and the grunting of people came from, the Tree sneaked in.

The shop was full of old radios, televisions, recorders and other electric devices, through which the Tree shuffled its way towards the narrow wooden stairs. It stealthily went up and stood halfway the stairs, observing how a naked young woman and a middle-aged man were trying, panting, to dress in a hurry, in front of the twelve dilated eyes of the armed gunmen.

One of them approached the woman, whose blue tattoo of three dots on her chin matched her blue eyes. Just as she put a flowery Kurdish dress over her head, trying to roll it down over her body, and while the dress had only half covered her breasts and one of her reddened nipples was about to disappear under the fabric, the gunman put the barrel of his Kalashnikov between her breasts to prevent the dress from going further. The rest of her bare pale body was shining under the dim light.

Another of the gunmen grabbed the man by his neck and prevented him from putting on more clothes as he had only got into his *sharwal* so far; his half-erect penis still visible under the thick fabric of his baggy trousers.

The commander stepped in, grabbed the barrel of the Kalashnikov with a quick movement and removed the gun from the woman's cleavage, permitting the dress to roll down and cover the rest of her body. The commander also nodded to the other gunman, who immediately released his grip on the shop owner's neck, allowing him to dress fast.

When the woman stooped down to pick her knickers up from the floor, the gunman who had put his gun on her chest, bent faster, stole the knickers and put them in the pocket of his *sharwal*. 'This is a souvenir,' he said, raising his eyebrows. Then, he took another step towards her, stroked her rosy cheek with the back of his fingers and tweaked it softly. The woman said nothing, looking fixedly at the floor.

Another gunman pushed his mate away and stood in front of the woman, his Kalashnikov in his left hand. He stroked her hair with his right hand and asked her, 'And where is your bra?'

The woman said, with a choked voice and lowered head, 'I haven't got one.'

The gunman moved his gun from his left to his right hand, put his left hand under her chin, raised her head and said, 'You are not from here, are you?'

The young woman shook her head slightly, looking away towards the ceiling, as if trying to avoid the eyes of the gunman who was so close to her that the Tree thought she might have felt the warmth of his breath on her face.

'Let's go, mates. Bring them down,' the commander said.

The Tree descended the stairs quickly, shuffled back through the shop and went out to stand in its place again. It saw from there the commander running down the stairs, followed by his gunmen who pushed the man and the woman in front of them.

In front of the shop, the commander asked the pair for their names, enquiring where the woman came from and why she slept with that man. He then gave the man a couple of slaps and kicks and ordered him to close his shop. It seemed that the information they had gathered from them had changed their attitude towards them. They were now more aggressive towards the man, while some of them had become kinder to the woman. The Tree heard through the rumble of the descending shutter that the gunman who had asked the woman for her bra, now told her to put on her *abba* and disappear quickly from the area. The woman raised her head and, for the first time, looked the man in his eyes and said, 'I don't have a home.'

The Tree heard the man who had put the knickers in his pocket arguing with one of his mates over the woman; should they take her with them or let her go? The Knickers Man ran towards the woman, pushed his mate aside and told the woman, 'Come with me. I'll take you home. You won't find transport now. And, anyway, it's not safe for you at this time of the night.'

His mate shouted at the woman, 'Just go away!' He then jumped at the Knickers Man and grabbed his arm, trying to pull him from the woman.

The gunman who, upstairs, had asked for her bra, came forward, between them, and shouted, 'Where? She doesn't have anyone nor anywhere to go. Don't you get it? She is one of...'

The mate who told the woman to disappear, succeeded in pushing away the Knickers Man and said, now calmly, 'I know... I know who she is... No one with a bit of conscience or honour would treat these women like this fucking bastard has done.' He raised his voice, pointing to the shop where the shop owner was supposed to be, but was no longer.

'Where is he?' the angry gunman shouted. 'What did you do to him? You haven't let him go, have you? I want to go and cut off that motherfucker's dick.' He looked around and saw the shop owner a few metres away, begging another pair of gunmen to let him free, swearing he would never do such a thing again. The two gunmen were shaking their heads and slapping and kicking him.

The angry gunman walked towards them, but halfway there, he stepped back towards the Knickers Man and told him in a hoarse, tearful voice, 'I also have some relatives who have undergone the same as this woman and I know how...' He could not finish his sentence and came to sit under the Tree before bursting into tears.

The commander and another of the gunmen hurried to the woman and the Knickers Man, while the other two dragged the shop owner towards them. The commander instructed the Knickers Man to stop making such a fuss. Another of the men asked after reflection, 'Is it really not a shame, guys, that you are fighting over a whore? Seriously!'

The Knickers Man shouted, 'Me, making a fuss? It's him.' He pointed to his mate under the Tree. Then, he looked furiously at the shop owner and continued, 'She is fucking with this bastard and my mate blames me!' He kicked the shop owner heavily in the crotch, which made the man cry out so loudly that his voice echoed all down the alley. He crumpled to the ground, holding his testicles in both his hands and lay groaning at the feet of the men. The Tree could imagine his pain and felt a chill pass through its trunk and up to its branches. It shivered, and the rustle of its leaves made the gunmen turn their heads towards it, but no one said anything. The crying one under it looked up, then leant back on it.

The Knickers Man clutched the woman's arm and said, 'You are coming with me, and nobody's allowed to say shit about it.'

The *abba* slipped from the woman's head and fell to the ground. When she bent to pick it up, one of her breasts fell out of her dress. Because one of her arms was held by the gunman, she couldn't pick up the *abba* and remained for a moment exposed and in an ungainly position.

One of the men saw her rosy nipple under the dim light of an alley lantern. He swallowed and began to gasp. Suddenly, his eyes caught that of the woman, who was about to stand up again. He blushed and started blinking madly, looking between the woman's eyes and her nipple. The woman used her free hand to slowly replace her breast modestly under her dress. The man hurried towards them, came in between the woman and the Knickers Man, and said, 'You are absolutely right. This angel is irresistible. But...' He calmly grabbed his mate's hand and released the woman's arm so she could pick up her *abba*. 'Let her go,' he said. 'Now is not the time for that. This woman is a victim, and we are supposed to help her, not to—'

'You're such a fucking whore fucker yourself, but you're now preaching to me?' the Nickers Man shouted, freeing his hand again from the rival's. He clutched once more the arm of the woman, who now had put back the *abba* over her head and shoulders. 'Hey, why have you all become such noblemen so suddenly? You bloody bastards!' Nickers Man shouted again, now looking at his mates one by one.

His mate tried once more to calm him down: 'But dude, this one is different. She... And now... Listen, it's really not the time for this, now.'

Another of the gunmen, the one who earlier had joked about how he had so scared a boy in Sabunkaran so that he peed himself, came between them, stared at them both and said, 'Guys it's not the time for this nonsense. We have wasted the night. Don't forget what we came for. Let's sort this out quickly.' He grabbed the Nickers Man's arm, took him aside, dragging the woman after him, as her arm was still in the knickers' firm grip.

The mate said, 'Leave this guy,' pointing to the one who had reacted strongly to the sight of the exposed breast. 'Don't listen to him,' he warned. 'He used to be a musician. He is a sensitive artist, you know? He shags them and then plays violin to them. By doing this, he imagines he is not a whore fucker.'

All the gunmen burst into laughter, except for the one under the Tree, who had stopped crying and was now leaning back on the Tree, observing his mates. The Tree wanted to give him a shove, but didn't want to attract the attention of the gunmen.

While one of the men walked over to his pal under the Tree and sat beside him, the commander grabbed the arms of both the woman and the Nickers Man and pushed them to the shop. He shouted at the shop owner to raise the shutter.

The shop owner went in pain towards his shop, holding his testicles in one hand, unlocked the shutter with the other, and rolled it up.

The Nickers Man, with his Kalashnikov in his right hand and the arm of the woman in his left, entered the shop, and as the shop owner was about to let down the shutter, the commander shouted, 'Don't take too long, Knickers. And don't forget to give them back to her!'

The Nickers Man shouted back, 'I won't,' though his voice got lost in the sound of the down-rolling shutter.

The commander beckoned to the shop owner and led him down the alley, whispering to him. The joking gunman looked at his musician mate who was standing next to him, watching the scene in disappointment, and said, 'You see? That's a good commander. It's not the time for all this nonsense. Leave poetry and preaching aside. It's soon going to be light and we haven't had any loot yet.'

The Tree saw the shop owner down the alleyway pull a bunch of banknotes from his *sharwal's* pocket and give it to the commander before walking away.

'Except that bit of money, though,' the joking man continued, pointing to his commander and the shop owner. He then shouted to the commander, who was coming back to them, counting the money, 'How much is it? Worth anything?'

'Ah, not bad. It's two hundred dinars,' the commander said, putting the money in his pocket. Then, he put both his hands on the shoulders of his two men, the musician and the joker, pushed them forward, and said, 'Let's go to work guys, it's late. It will be light soon.'

'Is it going to be the Naqib Bazaar tonight?' said the gunman who cried earlier. He stood up, putting his hand on his buddy's shoulder. The buddy also jumped up from under the Tree and joined them. They all left together and walked towards the end of the alleyway. The Tree could still see them. They halted at the corner of a side alley, where the commander said, 'You guys all know where to stand, don't you? I'll be back in a minute with Knickers. I have to make sure he comes out soon.' As soon as his four men entered the alley, he went back to the shop, rolled up the shutter slowly and entered the shop. The shutter rolled down in one go with a shrieking rattle.

The Tree carefully followed the route that the other four men had taken towards the bazaar. When it arrived at the same place, close to the gate of the Naqib Bazaar, where it had been shot by the earlier group of gunmen, it saw a van facing away from the gate that was now open. The men were loading big boxes and bags into the back of the van.

A sudden breeze blew through the alley making the Tree quiver and sway. It hurried towards the wall beside the gate and stood still.

Two of the men came out of the back of the van and looked both ways. One of them carried a small iron box in such a way that it suggested it was very heavy. He stared at the Tree and paused a moment, thinking, then asked his mate, 'Was this tree here when we came? It looks exactly like the one you were crying under, down there.'

The man who earlier cried went back in the van and said, annoyed, 'Leave it. It's not our problem.' Then, he jutted his head out again, adding, 'And don't talk about me crying anymore. It's embarrassing, man!'

His mate, still surprised by the Tree, went back inside the van, gave the heavy iron box to him and took his position by the canvas flap at the back end of the vehicle. One of the other two men who were inside the bazaar came out with a huge box and handed it over to him, returning inside.

The man on the van's edge placed the box inside before reassuming his position, ready to receive another

Moments later, the commander and the Nickers Man came along. Just a few steps before they reached the Tree, the commander took a cigarette pack from his *sharwal's* pocket, shook out two cigarettes, gave one to the Nickers Man without looking at him and put the other one between his lips. He asked the Nickers Man for a light. The Nickers Man put his hand in the pocket of his *sharwal* and took out a lighter. With it, the knickers that he apparently had not given back to the woman, fell out on the ground, just in front of the Tree.

The Nickers Man lit his commander, then his own cigarette, producing clouds of smoke in the air.

As the commander walked towards the van, the Nickers Man bent down and picked up the knickers. The commander came back to him, snatched the knickers from his hand and tossed them high in the air. The knickers landed on one of the high branches of the Tree.

The Nickers Man grabbed at a lower branch and tried to lift himself to reach the knickers, but the commander caught his arm and dragged him towards the van, saying, 'You don't need her knickers anymore, sucker. Let's help the guys. The morning is unfolding. Hurry up, won't you?'

While the gunmen were busy loading the van with all the boxes and bags from the covered market, the Tree ran away up the alley, the knickers swaying on its branch between its leaves. It then turned right and entered another section of the bazaar, passing dozens of closed shops. At one of the covered passages, it noticed that a huge cardboard box in front of one of the closed shops was surrounded by a swarm of buzzing flies. A meowing cat jumped around, trying to catch the flies with its claws. Then, it jumped onto the box, hanging its head over the edge to look inside. It then jumped back down and started to spin crazily round the box.

When the Tree reached the box, the swarm of flies spread out and the cat ran towards the small fountain in the middle of the market square to sit down and observe the scene from there.

Mixed up in the box, the Tree saw the dismembered limbs of a naked woman and her decapitated head.

45

Early the next morning, the bell rang at the Neighbour-Girl's door. 'Come in, darling,' she said as she opened the door. It was her friend; the woman with whom she had a close friendship, although she was fifteen years her senior. The Neighbour-Girl could talk to her about everything. But the woman barely talked about herself, saying she had nothing to tell as she had led the most ordinary life. She loved to listen to the Neighbour-Girl's stories about her life and experience, she would say every time. The only thing she was delighted to do was to give her wise advice, as she was in any case older than her and could understand the world better, she would say proudly.

'Sorry, I'm still sleepy. I got home late last night,' the Neighbour-Girl said, while walking inside the *dalan*, the wide entryway between the living room and the kitchen opposite. She led her friend to her room across the central courtyard of the house that was divided into two parts: a small garden and a tiled terrace where they had a bench and a few old nylon-cord chairs. Just as they were about to enter the bedroom, Lady Journalist came out of the opposite room in a dressing gown that was obviously not hers, as she was much shorter than the Neighbour-Girl. She said good morning to them and said she would be ready in a minute.

The Neighbour-Girl introduced the two women to each other and told Lady Journalist she should stay and just leave the house when she wanted. 'I'm sorry, I have to leave,' she said. 'I'm accompanying my friend to the hospital. My mother will wake up in an hour or so and will make you breakfast.'

Lady Journalist said that she had better go to work, as she had to finish an article for the weekly paper that was due tomorrow.

When the three women came out of the house, the Photographer was at his own door. After they had wished each other good morning, the

Photographer told Lady Journalist that he was waiting for her. He wanted to go with her to her newspaper's office as he had an idea for rescuing the tree-man.

'You should write another article about him, or we can put an appeal in your paper to call on everyone, especially the authorities, not to touch this creature. We should convince them he is not harmful. And, you know, we should think about taking some kind of action. Maybe your paper could adopt it! I mean if you interview me again, I would say I will do my best to take care of him and bring him back to Qilyasan where he belongs. Or maybe—'

'I get it!' Lady Journalist interrupted him. 'It's a great idea. But I can't decide. Let's go and talk to the Editor-in-Chief.'

'Okay, guys, you go and do that. We must also leave before we end up standing in a long queue at the hospital,' said the Neighbour-Girl, avoiding the Photographer's eyes. She said goodbye quickly to Lady Journalist and walked up the alleyway, the friend following her.

The Photographer shrugged and walked down the alley with Lady Journalist, towards Serah Square.

'I don't know what I should do with him,' said the Neighbour-Girl to her friend when they walked up the road. 'I mean I don't think I can build anything with this guy. I don't know. He is so out of this world. But the thing is, he is so addictive! I can't spend a moment without thinking about him, wanting to be with him and wishing I had spent that moment with him.'

'You're head over heels for him, my dear. But what about him?' her friend said.

'I wish I knew that for sure. I mean, he is also happy to spend time with me. I have the feeling that he also tries to involve me in his interests. He took me with him yesterday evening to search for the Tree. We ended up meeting this journalist woman too.'

'Are you jealous?'

'What?' Neighbour-Girl gasped, looking at her friend. She then increased her pace, 'Ah, come on, of course not. Why should I be?'

'I don't know. You felt a bit uncomfortable when they went off together.'

'No, I'm not. It's just... You know, sometimes he just goes on with his own things and forgets me. As if I don't exist. Like with his pathetic search for this Tree, for example.'

'But you said he took you with him, yesterday.'

'Yes, only yesterday. Okay, and that night too, when we declared our admiration for each other.'

'You never told me what happened that night.'

'That's not important. I mean... I told you that we kissed, didn't I?'

'No, you didn't give me any details.'

'The thing is, he never took it any further. I know you advised me to give him a hint or something. But come on, we kissed. Don't ask me for more details, please. But that's the whole problem. How can he after...? And... Okay, honestly, we also slept together.'

'Oh, my God! How can you do such a thing? Oh, oh, oh... You mean you *slept,* slept? You really did everything?' She halted, staring at the Neighbour-Girl with exaggerated surprise, while tightening her scarf.

'I told you, don't ask me for details.' The Neighbour-Girl grabbed her friend's arm and started walking again.

'Okay, okay! But anyway, that was a huge mistake for you, girl. How could you do such a thing?'

'I said let's not talk about that. In your world and your moral hassles, that's unimaginable, I know. But... Anyway, let's not talk about this anymore. The point is that there are all these men trying it on with me. I mean, there is barely a man I meet for two minutes without his making a pass at me. And you know that I see lots of them every day. But of all the men in the world, I love this little shit of a man and he—'

'Oh, don't say that, please. He's so cute!' the woman said, laughing. She grabbed the Neighbour-Girl's arm, catching up with her. 'You walk so fast. I get out of breath, darling.'

'But we're going to be late, love,' the Neighbour-Girl said, slowing down slightly to adjust her pace to her friend's. 'You know?' she said, looking at her friend to check if she had her full attention. 'One time I had a meeting with the Minister of Culture. I could tell he caught fire immediately! He was so flirtatious. You know, he said I should definitely take part in a beauty contest for which he is soon going to be a jury member. I'd win no doubt, or so he said.'

'Oh, God, did they bring that Western farce to this country too? I think he's right though. You'll win for sure!' She looked at her sideways.

The Neighbour-Girl could see envy in her eyes. 'I don't think I will,' she said. 'I mean, I'd not attend such thing. But you know what? He also gave me his new poetry collection, signed.'

'You lucky girl, you!'

'But anyway, I wanted to say that I have all these admirers, but I am wasting my time with this guy, while he—'

'I think you should really allow him some time, and everything will—'

'Oh, come on, love!' the Neighbour-Girl interrupted her friend. 'After all that has happened between us, you want me—'

'I understand. Of course, it's him who should take the next step, but—'

The Neighbour-Girl interrupted her friend again, grabbed her by the arm and said, 'This must only be between you and me. Please! You know what would happen to me.'

'Don't worry, darling! Have you ever heard me tell anyone's secret? And you see how much I trust you too. I wanted you to come with me to the hospital. I haven't even told my mother about it,' said her friend, stopping suddenly in the middle of the road. 'By the way, you won't tell anyone about this either, will you?' she asked in a dramatic tone.

'Of course not!' the Neighbour-Girl said, grabbing her arm again, and supporting her as she walked, dragging her along. 'Let's hurry up, darling!'

They remained silent for the rest of the walk to the hospital.

46

When the Photographer and Lady Journalist reached Piramerd Street and turned right to go up the street towards the paper, the Photographer changed his mind and said that it would be better for him to go to the public garden instead. Maybe the Gardener was there, and he might know something. 'After that, I'll come to the paper. See you later!' he said and turned, walking down the street towards Serah Square.

In front of the Rashid bank, he crossed the street and walked along the *Serah*. He looked to the right and saw from above the railing that surrounded the huge courtyard, the many archways to the left and right of the entrance to the building, which, during the time of the British Mandate, was the base for the city's Rulers and Administrators. It was now used as the base for the police and the *Asayish* and other offices of the newly established Kurdish Interior Ministry.

Civil servants were making their way through the morning rush into the *Serah* to start their working day. The Photographer hurried towards the square, then turned right along the curved fence and reached the main entrance to the *Serah* courtyard. From there, he crossed the square and entered Mawlawi Street. He saw that on the other side, in front of the main entrance of Asri Bazaar, a crowd of police and *Asayish* men were blocking the entrance to the Bazaar and hindering the people walking by, asking them to cross the street and continue their walk on the opposite side – the side where the Photographer was walking.

He sped up and tried not to look to the other side, assuming that the trouble was to do with the shooting of last night. This was not the right time to be stopped and interrogated, especially as some of the *Asayish* men might recognise him. Suddenly, he remembered the three suspicious men they had seen walk out of the bazaar late last night. But for now, he had other priorities. Better go and find a trace of the tree-man. He walked fast down the street.

Halfway along Mawlawi Street, just crossing from the Dabo Bazaar, he saw the Asayish Director, accompanied by two gunmen, hurrying towards him. At once, he turned his back and started to run, but he also saw a few policemen present at the Baladiya Market and remembered how he and the girls had been walking there in the dirty puddles last night, looking for the Tree.

He ran over the bridge, took a right and entered the street parallel to Mawlawi Street. He looked over his shoulder while he was running and saw the Asayish Director and his two gunmen a hundred metres behind him. As he merged with the crowd, he was sure that the Asayish Director and the gunmen could no longer see him, so he entered an open door and ran up the many stairs that led to a huge space. As he stood at the top of the stairs, panting, his eyes scanned the place: a dozen young girls and boys sat around a table in the middle of the huge space, with hundreds of boxes of different sizes piled beside the walls up to the ceiling. Some of the young girls and boys were fixing paper bags with glue, using a brush. They dipped the brush in a tin of glue, then pasted it onto two edges of a piece of paper, folded one side of the paper over the other side, then stroked it over to make it into a bag. A couple of them were busy stapling small cardboard boxes and putting them on the floor beside the pile at their feet.

The Photographer recognised a young man whom he knew as an ambitious start-up businessman and who had told him recently that he was dreaming of starting a business in the cultural world but still had no idea what exactly it would be. The friend was picking up a bunch of the boxes from the floor in his arms when he stood up and noticed the Photographer. He looked at him surprised, then put the boxes down on the table between two of the girls who were fixing the paper bags. He greeted the Photographer quickly, grabbed his arm and led him to a narrow hall at the end of the open space. He asked him what he had done wrong this time.

'I'm going to tell you later. It's a very long story,' the Photographer said, out of breath.

At the end of the hall, the friend opened a door and pushed him into a large room that was full of small cardboard boxes in heaps, neatly piled.

'Don't worry,' the friend reassured him. 'Just hide here until you feel safe. Nobody will find you here. If you hear anyone approaching, just hide among those boxes.'

A few metres before the building where the Photographer was being sheltered, the Asayish Director and his two gunmen stopped abruptly. The Asayish Director pulled out his walkie-talkie, on which a man was shouting over the static noise, 'Sir, there is an emergency, sir.' Shhhhhhh... beep... tut...

The Asayish Director pressed a button and asked, 'What's there?' then released the button. Shhhhhhh... beep... tut...

'The Naqib Bazaar was burgled last night,' shouted the man through the static noise. Shhhhhhh... beep... tut... 'The police are there and won't allow our men to go in. It's this Patriot guy, this officer, you know? I think we should...' Shhhhhhh... beep... tut...

Pressing the button again, the Asayish Director asked, 'Where?' As he released the button, he heard: 'At the entrance of the Naqib Bazaar, sir.'

The Asayish Director immediately turned to run back to the street, his two gunmen after him. Shhhhhhh... beep... tut...

Ten minutes later, when the Photographer had heard no more from the *Asayish* men, he came out of the room that was crammed with empty cardboard boxes and walked carefully back through the hall towards the huge open space. His friend, the businessman, jumped from his chair and came to him, asking him if he was sure it was safe to come out. The Photographer said he thought so, thanked his host and hurried out of the space towards the stairs. His friend grabbed his arm, made him turn, pointed to a huge machine in a dark corner and said, 'Hey, you see that lovely thing over there? That is a printing machine, an offset. The road to the realisation of my dream. We're going to start printing soon. First, stuff for other people like paper bags and cardboard boxes. Then, maybe some books. These bags and boxes could soon be covered in text and pictures! Then we will—'

'Sorry, I really have to leave now,' said the Photographer hurriedly, freeing his arm from his friend. As he ran down the stairs, he added,

'I'll visit you soon. Thanks for giving me a hideaway!'

His friend shouted after him down the stairs, 'By the way, I have a brilliant idea. We are going to establish a newspaper with a couple of journalists. It will be the first independent Kurdish newspaper, mind you. I'll contact you when we are ready to go. Maybe you'd want to work with us?'

The Photographer had reached the bottom step. He looked up, raised his arm in the air and made a thumbs up. He then turned left and disappeared.

When he reached the side street that led back to Mawlawi Street, he took a left again. Just in front of the Post Office on the corner, where he and the two girls had decided last night to cross the street to eat chickpea soup, somebody called him. He turned to see who it was, looking for the source of the voice but no one in the crowd looked familiar. The voice called him again. He raised his head to look up to the second floor of the painting and stuffing shop on the other side of the street. He spotted the young painter who worked there, a former friend from their time together at the Art School.

The young man shouted to the Photographer, suggesting he should cross the road as he had something to tell him.

The Photographer crossed the street, and as soon as he reached the shop, the young painter appeared at the entrance, greeted him and said immediately that he had some news that would interest him.

'What could it be? Because right now there is only one thing that interests me.'

'That's what I think it is.'

'What is it, then? Say it, man. I can't wait. I'm really in a hurry.'

The painter grabbed his arm, dragged him to the wall, lowered his voice and said, 'I think I saw your Tree. If that's what deserves your attention right now.'

'It is! Tell me, where?'

'Listen, we stayed here last night to work...' He lifted his hand and nodded up to the second floor.

When the Photographer raised his head, he saw the other painter, the taller guy with the black moustache, sticking his head out of the window.

'Hi!' said the tall guy with a wide grin on his face.

'Hi!' the Photographer replied, then lowered his head again to the younger painter in front of him and asked impatiently, 'And..?'

'Well, some *Asayish* guys came in and inspected the whole shop. But then there was this tree. We didn't understand how it got into the shop, and when the *Asayish* men left, the Tree also disappeared.'

'It must be him...' the Photographer said and grabbed the painter's arm. 'But didn't you see it again after that?'

'No! It was only when we pulled down the shutter and were upstairs that we suddenly realised that the Tree was no longer there. We remembered that night at the museum gallery when you made all of us run after that Tree. I honestly didn't believe anything of it. But last night, we were both sure there was a tree up there in our workshop and that it disappeared just like that. It was actually scary.'

'Didn't you try to find it?' asked the Photographer desperately.

'Well, we ran down and raised the shutter again. We looked around in the street and in the alley back here. I think it was already too late.'

'I know. That's what always happens. Thank you so much anyway. It's important information for me.'

'You're most welcome! But tell me why you're so obsessed with this Tree?' asked the painter.

The Photographer walked off, then turned his head while walking and said, 'I'll tell you one day.' He sped up his steps and gradually started running down the street.

When he entered the public garden, he ran directly to the Gardener's office but did not find him in. He knew that he must be in the garden, as the Aladdin was on with a kettle on top. He ran around, looking for him until he found a man in his mid-fifties with a Kurdish colourful traditional hat on his head and his turban on his neck, looking around the trees, inspecting them, as if he was looking for something or someone.

'Morning, uncle!'

'Morning, my dear!' the Gardener answered without turning to him.

'You must be looking for the Tree. But I guess you know he is not a tree at this time of the day,' the Photographer said as a matter-of-factly.

The Gardener looked at him surprised and somewhat suspiciously. He waited for a few seconds, clearly not knowing what to say. Then, he smiled and said, 'Well, yes, I'm looking for the boy. For the last couple of weeks, he stayed in my office. It was a safe place for him. But I came this morning and couldn't find him. I'm so sad. Actually devastated. It feels as though I have lost a son.'

'I'm so sorry for that, uncle! I'm also—'

The Gardener did not wait for him to finish his sentence and continued, 'When he became the Tree in the evenings, he just stayed in the garden. He was my most precious tree. He could be anywhere in the garden. I could talk to him, just like I do to all the other trees and flowers. Except I was sure he heard me. He always reacted to me in his ways, with his leaves and branches. Usually when he became the boy again, he went inside the office. I always left the door unlocked for him. Oh, I'm afraid someone has done him harm. I'm so sad.' He sat down and started crying.

The Photographer stooped down, put his hand on the Gardener's shoulder and said, 'Well, I'm worried too, uncle. That's why I am here. I'm so glad I've found someone who not only believes in his existence but knows him well, too. I think we can do something to protect him if we hurry up. I have some ideas.'

The Gardener stopped crying. He stood up, loosened his *cummerbund* and wiped his eyes with its tail. He said, while fastening his *cummerbund* again, 'But how can we find him if we can't even ask anyone about him? They will think we've lost our minds. And by the way, what do you know about him and how did you know he was here?'

'It's a long story, uncle. Let's walk to your office. Wash your face, lock the door, then we will leave. I'll tell you everything on the way.' He started walking.

'Where should we go? Do you know a place where he might be?' the Gardener asked while walking after the Photographer.

'I wish I knew. But I've got an idea of how to find him or at least to make people aware that he is quite harmless. And that's how you can help. We are going now to this newspaper where I know a reporter. They will help us to put an appeal in the paper. And maybe also help us get on TV and make the appeal there too. They must know people from TV.'

'Wait a second. Now that you mention it, something's come to my mind. You can't be this Photographer guy everyone is always talking about, are you? Oh, I thought your face looked familiar.'

'Yes, that's true! It's me,' said the Photographer, looking to the Gardener to see what his reaction was.

The Gardener smiled and seemed to have relaxed. When they entered the office, he took off the kettle and put out the Aladdin.

The Photographer looked around the room for a trace of the Naked Young Man.

'This is where he spent the whole day,' the Gardener said, pointing to the bed. 'He didn't go out, didn't eat or drink anything. He just slept on that bed.'

The Photographer touched the blanket, lifted it from the bed and looked at it. Then at the mattress. No sign.

The Gardener said, 'There's nothing left of him. What would he leave? He had nothing, only this leaf around him. Oh, what an amazing thing it was! Actually, that leaf never separated from him.'

The Photographer looked at the Gardener sorrowfully, shaking his head.

'Let's go,' said the Gardener, stepping outside and waiting at the door.

When the Photographer came out, the man closed the door, then opened it again and left it ajar. 'I'm not going to lock it. Let's leave.'

They walked towards the back exit, which was closer to his office, and left the garden.

47

Around noon, the Naked Young Man woke up to the tumultuous hubbub of a screaming crowd. He was lying on his stomach on the cement floor in a room of, as he now remembered, the second story of an old building where he had taken shelter that morning. The burning sun struck his back, while a cool breeze made the sweat drops on his face, neck and shoulders feel like ice pellets. A chill ran down his spine. He remembered last night's events and a heavy grief overwhelmed him. For the first time, he felt a crushing loneliness, for he was not able to talk about the things he had been observing as a tree. He felt more than ever the need to talk to somebody. But it seemed that it was his fate to remain silent forever. He knew how powerless he was as a tree. To be a tree is to live in silence – to observe and comprehend all the secrets in the world yet to be without the words to communicate this. The sadness he now felt was different from the sorrow and distress he had been experiencing since he had left Qilyasan and started his journey to the city. Even when he became a human being in the daytime, he still was no more than the Tree. Except that it was even more difficult: as a tree it could at least blend in among the other trees, but as a man, he could not appear in public. He wished he could now look for the Photographer by himself to tell him everything he had seen since he began to wander around the city. But in the world of words and speech he was impotent; he was doomed to silence, just like any other tree.

He stood up and looked around the room, which was an abandoned dusty, dingy place with dilapidated walls, a crumbling ceiling, and all its broken windows with outworn rotten wooden frames from which the blue paint had fallen in patches. The floor was covered with his own shrivelled leaves among all the old twigs, and the straw and gravel and stone rubble fallen from the mud ceiling. He walked towards the windows and a door, from where the sunlight and clamour came. He opened the broken door and stepped outside on a narrow balcony, his long green leaf wrapping around his legs and crotch, hanging over his back and dangling over his chest. He bent over and leant on the wooden ornamented low balustrade and noticed that he was in the same building that he had seen last night, as a tree, from the muddy puddles at the empty marketplace, the place where he had then wanted to linger. Only he now found himself exposed to a crowd of noisy buyers and sellers.

He remembered how, in the first light of the morning, he had been kneeling, stunned, beside a huge cardboard box full with the dismembered limbs of a woman. He was shivering in the damp, hazy cold of the dawn, when he suddenly saw two men approaching from the other end of the covered bazaar with their rustling long-handled brooms made of twigs, sweeping the ground, walking towards him and the box. He had jumped up and run swiftly away to find himself again at the marketplace where a few men were already opening their shops and setting up their stalls with fruit and vegetables. Without hesitation, he had jumped on a bench in front of a shop, climbed the wall and reached this room via the balcony.

He rubbed his eyes and saw that down there in the market square crowds of men were looking at him, while women had lowered their heads, covering their faces with the tail of their *abba* or shawl, while the young, still without a veil or shawl, had put their hands in front of their eyes. Young girls would steal a glimpse through their fingers and watch him with a broad, shy smile on their lips. Also, most of the veiled women now removed a part of their shawl or *abba* to look at him from the corner of their eyes. He received all those gazes, astonished and not understanding why the women would sneak a glimpse while the men were looking straight at him in obvious anger.

Suddenly, an old man who was standing in front of a stall with a few huge pots of yoghurt, spat at the Naked Young Man, shouting, 'Damn you, you little bastard! What the hell are you doing over there?' His spit fell into one of the yoghurt pots and spread over the thick creamy crust on its top. The yoghurt seller shot an accusing look at the spitting customer and swept the spit off the crust with the top of his finger with a practised gesture, then rubbed his finger on his *sharwal*.

A chicken salesman, not far from the yoghurt stand, left his costumers at the big cages that were crammed with chickens and walked forward, closer to the shops under the balcony, holding a chicken in his hand, grabbing at its two wings, which he was about to weigh for a costumer. Reaching the row of fruit and vegetable stands in front of the shops, he could not go closer. Then, he directed his hand with the chicken in the air at the Naked Young Man and shouted, 'Let's drag him down, this shameless piece of shit.'

The chicken escaped from his hand and fell on somebody's head, only to jump on someone else's head, and from there on another, squawking and flapping its wings. It finally fell into a bucket of red vinegar pickles on a stall. While the salesman himself stepped back quickly, the dark-red vinegar splashed a woman's white trousers and the grey suit of a man, who, at that moment, had picked an olive from a big bowl of olives and put it in his mouth. Both the woman and the man started to complain at the top of their voices. The man pulled a handkerchief out of his pocket and the woman a tissue out of her handbag and each of them began desperately cleaning their own clothes.

Another man came out of a shop under the balcony, waving a pair of woman's knickers and shouting, while looking directly at the Naked Young Man on the balcony, 'Are you looking for these, you little devil? Are these yours, you bastard? You must have dropped them, didn't you?' He looked at the people in front of him and carried on, 'Let's get them. There must also be a woman up there. Let's catch them, men. Hurry up!' Then, he lowered his voice and said to a woman in front of him, while showing her the knickers, 'I found these this morning, in front of my shop.'

While most of the women and girls moved aside, giggling, looking partly embarrassed and partly sly, the group of men climbed the walls and jumped on the eaves above the shops to get to the balcony.

The Naked Young Man ran inside, terrified, dragging his long leaf after him over the floor. He opened the other door in the room and found himself in a hallway with several other doors. He tried to enter another room, but all the doors were locked, except one that led him to another room that looked on to the same balcony. The men were waiting for him there at the broken window on the balcony. He then ran out of the room again but saw that a couple of other men were already in the hall. He ran back into the same room and saw that the men from the balcony had climbed into that room through the broken windows. Like a trapped bird, he ran and jumped in every direction, bumping into the men and the walls. Then, he stood still in the middle of the room, wrapped his leaf around his naked body, squatted down, and begged the men with his frightened eyes not to hurt him.

The men jumped on him and started to beat him, slapping, kicking and punching him until he was crushed down to the floor. Under the knees and fists of a couple of men holding him tight, flat on the floor, the Naked Young Man heard someone shouting, 'The police are coming! They've arrived. Don't let him escape.'

48

The Photographer brought the Gardener back to the park with a taxi. They'd just made their appeal, written by the Photographer with help from Lady Journalist and the Editor-in-Chief of the paper. It would come out tomorrow morning. The Editor had also gone with them to one of the few TV stations in the city, as he knew the director, and managed to get him to agree to record the appeal so that it could be broadcast with the evening news bulletin.

'I'm glad we did this,' said the Gardener, who sat in the back seat of the taxi. 'I hope people will listen to us and will treat him reasonably.'

'Let's hope for the best,' said the Photographer, who sat in the front, looking back over his shoulder with a smile. 'We've done what we could. You were great! You became emotional and that will help. If your words don't move people, they must be heartless!'

'You don't know how much I'm longing to see him back. I miss him so much,' said the Gardener, wiping his wet eyes with the back of his hands.

The taxi stopped in front of the back entrance to the garden. The Gardener took out a five-dinar bill and reached out his hand to the driver. The Photographer pushed back his hand and said, 'It's impossible! No, no... You don't pay... No way!'

The Gardener insisted a couple of times more then gave in, got out of the car, said goodbye and went into the garden.

The Photographer shouted through the window, 'I'll visit you tomorrow. I hope with good news.'

As the car moved off, the driver asked the Photographer if that man had lost his son. The Photographer said it was actually a long story, and that they had lost a precious person. 'He was more of a son to him. But I barely knew him. It's kind of a weird story, you might not believe it.'

'Well, we taxi drivers hear all kinds of stories. I tend to believe most of the people. But we should also be careful not spread rumours. You know what I mean? We hear all kinds of gossip. Oh, I can put my finger on any corrupt politician. We hear everything about them. They tell us all the stuff themselves. I mean, one talks about the other. But what's your weird story, *kaka*?'

'You must then have heard about this Naked Young Man, too.'

'Ah, of course! They've got him—'

'They what?' asked the Photographer, shocked, looking at the driver with wide-open eyes.

'They finally arrested him. It's over.'

'Come on, seriously, where did you hear about that?'

'The radio just mentioned it. Just before you got in. I normally turn off the radio when I have passengers in the car. You know, because—'

'Can you please turn it on?' the Photographer interrupted him, pressing the knob and turning on the radio himself, unable to wait. He dialled through all the channels, but none had news at that moment, only songs or chat programmes. He left it on one of the channels and asked the driver to take a new route to a new destination. 'To Pirma Sur instead, please,' he said with resignation. 'I need to get my camera.'

'Sure, *kaka*. But I'll charge you for a double route, just so you know.'

'No problem, *kaka*. I understand. Just hurry up please!'

49

Outside the University Hospital, the Neighbour-Girl said goodbye to her friend who took the usual road back home. She herself walked down the Mahkama Street towards Mawlawi Street. After a few steps, she turned to her friend and shouted, 'Don't forget to take the yellow pill immediately after lunch and the white one tonight after dinner.'

'Sure, darling! Don't worry. I won't mix them up,' her friend shouted back.

The Neighbour-Girl hastened, making her way through the crowd, down the road. When she reached the Grand Mosque, she remembered last night's conversation with the Arab emigrants about the Tree. She changed her mind over going to Mawlawi Street and thought to take a right from there, over Kaneskan Street and to go to the public park. Maybe she would find the Gardener and be able to talk to him. He might know something about the Tree, she thought.

After walking a short way, she heard a great hubbub behind her. When she turned, she saw a large number of people were running from the Grand Mosque Square down the street towards Mawlawi Street. She was considering whether she should also rush to Mawlawi Street instead, when a big crowd of other people, mostly men, ran from the other end of Kaneskan Street, pushing her, almost forcing her to turn and run back, without hesitation.

Mawlawi Street buzzed with the sound of sirens of police cars rushing in from all the side-streets. People were shouting, 'They've got him. They've got him.'

When she could run no more and had to slow down because of the crowd, she noticed that something was happening at the Bazaar in Baladiya Square. She sensed that it must have to do with the tree-man. She then heard someone telling another that he thought they had got that naked young guy.

'Oh my God, finally! So, it was real. He *did* exist, this bastard,' said the other man.

With a lump in her throat and tears rolling down her cheeks, the Neighbour-Girl made her way through the crowd and crossed the street, but when she was at the Baladiya Bazaar, she couldn't see anything of the Naked Young Man, only hordes of people and policemen. Several men and boys were on the balcony of the almost dilapidated building of the old Farah Hotel, walking in and out of the rooms through the broken doors and windows.

Suddenly, the Asayish Director was standing in front of her. He put a hand on her shoulder as he asked her with concern, 'Why are you crying, darling? Did something happen to you? Anyone hurt you?'

'Oh, no, no! Nothing. I'm fine,' she said, taking a step backwards so that his hand had to slip from her shoulder. She looked around in the crowd for an escape route or someone to rescue her, then said nervously, 'I think I'd better go home. It's too busy today to do any shopping.'

'But you look very worried. What's going on? Shall I come with you?'

'Oh, no, thank you! I'll be fine.'

'Does it have anything to do with this tree-man hassle? You came here to see him too, didn't you?'

'Oh, no... I mean, I was around and then—'

'They've got him. The police have got him, just before my men arrived. But don't worry. If you would like to see him, you will soon. I'm going to take him over from them. He is more a matter for us than for the police, now.'

'I see,' the Neighbour-Girl said, still looking around uncomfortably. Then, she abruptly hurried off, turning her head back over her shoulder and shouted through the clamour, 'Goodbye, sir.'

The Asayish Director shouted back, 'Goodbye sweetheart! I'll let you know when I have him.'

'Oh, don't worry. I don't think I'd want to see him,' she said, elbowing her way through the crowd. But only a few steps further, she turned back and tried to reach the Asayish Director again. She saw him struggling to make his way towards his men around the entrance of the old Farah Hotel building, waiving for them to follow him.

The Neighbour-Girl shouted, 'Sir, would you slow down a second?'

The Asayish Director turned with a smile, clearly delighted. He ignored everything, even his constantly peeping walkie-talkie, and hurried back, limping, towards her through the crowd, shouting, 'Yeah darling, what would you like to say?' He stood there in front of her, his tall body projecting over most of the people, all eyes fixed on him.

'Well, if you want to do something for me, it would be great if you would help us take the Tree back to Qilyasan,' said the Neighbour-Girl, looking up at him. 'That's all you need to do with and for him. I don't think he can be of any use to you.'

She wanted to walk away again, but the Asayish Director grabbed her shoulder with his left hand, a Kalashnikov in his right hand. 'He is yours, darling. He's all yours,' he said, almost shouting through the hubbub of the market square.

The Neighbour-Girl became more nervous, not knowing what to say or do. She regretted asking him for a favour, and suddenly drew her shoulder from his hand and hurried away through the crowd without saying anything more. She walked towards Serah Square to make the Asayish Director believe she was going home.

When she reached the Serah Square and was sure the Asayish Director was not behind her, the Neighbour-Girl took a left onto the Rashid Cinema Street and walked hurriedly towards the Grand Mosque Square, planning to go from there to the public garden. Halfway, she remembered that there was no longer a need for that. The tree-man was already arrested. There was no longer any sense in searching for him. Her tears rolled down once more. Yes, it has all ended. She should now be with the Photographer and he with her. But he was chasing something else. And herself, she was being chased by someone she wished to be miles away from him. So, what was *she* chasing?

She walked back to the Serah Square and from there home, with a sense of desolation, locked in her chest. A sense of end. An end that she should declare. The end of a search that was not hers; of a love that had not even started; of chasing an illusion and being chased. She was going to put an end to all of that.

At home, she headed straight to her bedroom, took of her shoes and crashed onto her bed. She put her head under the pillow and started sobbing.

50

At the counter-crime unit, a group of five gunmen in Kurdish guerrilla fatigues brought the Naked Young Man inside and took him directly to their commander's office. The middle-aged ranking officer – a short, dark-skinned man with very short hair – sat on the edge of his small metal desk in well-ironed khaki trousers and a collared shirt with a shiny yellow star on each shoulder. When he saw the many wounds on the prisoner's face, his chest and all over his body, he nodded to his men to take him to the sofa in front of the only window in the room, which was covered by a dirty, dull, white piece of linen.

The men let the Naked Young Man sit on the sofa, and while three of them went out, the other two tried in vain to separate the huge leaf from his body. Then, they tried to dress him a shirt and *sharwal*, but that was also impossible because of the wide, long leaf around his body. The officer himself went and knelt in front of him to inspect his wounds. He fumbled with the fresh green leaf that felt somewhat viscous between his fingers. He tried to break it but noticed that it was rough and too solid to break with bare hands. He asked one of the guards to bring him an electric chainsaw and went back to his desk, picked up the phone, and dialled a number, turning the round disc with his index finger in the holes, number after number, slowly, as to give himself time to think. When the other end picked up, he ordered, 'Get me the chief!' He waited about twenty seconds and when the Police Chief came on the phone, he said, with a hesitant grin, 'Hello, sir. We've got him ... Aha, you know already ... Great ... Oh, no, no, don't worry ... No, we wouldn't give him to them, no way ... Will you call the Mayor about it or shall I try to call him? ... Oh, okay, that's great ... Bye.' He hung up.

The guard returned with the chainsaw and handed it to his commanding officer, looking at him in disbelief. The Officer plugged the saw into a socket near the sofa, pressed the button on the saw's handle and turned it on. The blade started swinging back and forth, whizzing loudly. He knelt again in front of the Naked Young Man who was looking at him frightened.

As he put the saw on the leaf at the point where the leaf turned from the crotch of the Naked Young Man onto his hip, the Naked Young Man screamed so hard that his cry could be heard over the buzz of the saw. The Officer and his two guards blocked their ears with the palms of their hands, though the Officer could cover only one. He looked at the machine in his right hand, searched nervously for the button and right away turned it off. There were now shouts and screams from the prisoners in the cells at the back of the police station.

The Officer pulled the plug out of the socket and put the chainsaw on his desk. Then, he picked up a Stanley knife from the drawer of his desk, pulled out the blade and went back to the Naked Young Man. While sweat broke out on his forehead and dropped down his cheeks and over his neck, he drew the knife with trembling hands at the point where the leaf jutted from the Naked Young Man's armpit across his chest. The Naked Young Man screamed again, even more loudly, as did the prisoners at the back of the police station.

The Officer immediately went back to his desk, put the knife back in the drawer, took a tissue out of his pocket, wiped the sweat from his face and ordered the two guards who were still in the room watching him with full attention to take a few policemen and go beat up those troublemaking prisoners. He also asked one of them to bring him a clean sheet.

When the guards left the room, the Officer closed the door and went to sit behind his desk. He saw that the Naked Young Man had noticed that all this time, a boy had been behind the open door with his face against the wall. Both his hands were tied with one end of his own *cummerbund* behind his back and his eyes covered with the other end of the *cummerbund,* a thick knot at the back of his head.

The Officer stood up again and went to the boy. He grabbed at the part of the *cummerbund* between the boy's hands and head, pulled him and dragged him to the desk. The boy fell down on his back, but was picked up halfway by the Officer who pulled the *cummerbund* further towards him until the boy's face was at the same level as his own and asked him in the calm voice, 'What have you decided chap? Confess or receive another spank?'

The boy said, weeping, 'Believe me I didn't want to break in, I just…'

Before he got the chance to finish his sentence, the Officer released the *cummerbund*, stepped back a metre from the boy, lifted his right leg horizontally in the air, then spun round on his left foot and hit the boy with a karate kick in his face, pushing him headlong down on the floor. He then yelled at him, 'I told you a hundred times to say "sir" before you say anything!'

The Naked Young Man stared silently at the boy. The Officer looked at him and shrugged.

Laying on the floor groaning, the boy said, 'Sir, I swear by God I didn't want to…' He got another kick in his stomach. He tried to cringe but could not accomplish the movement because of the *cummerbund* that tied his head to his hands.

The Naked Young Man sank back in the sofa and closed his eyes. He touched the wounds on his own face. When he opened his eyes again, he stared at the spot of blood on the toecap of the Officer's right trainer and quickly closed his eyes again. He bent his head over his chest. His leaf tightened around his body.

The Officer noticed the Naked Young Man's fear. He wiped his toecap with his trousers' hem and went to stand in front of him. He put his hand under his chin and slowly lifted his head. The Naked Young Man opened his eyes, but did not look up to the Officer's face. The Officer smiled and said in a calm voice, 'This little bastard was caught last night while trying to break into a shop, but he still doesn't want to admit it.'

Then, he turned again to the boy on the floor, went and squatted in front of him and yelled, 'You stinking idiot. I make ten of your sort per week confess. Now you think you can beat me?' He grasped the boy's hair and pulled him from the floor.

It was obvious that the boy was trying to go with the flow and stand up quickly so that pulling his hair would not hurt him much, but he could not move to make his weight any lighter. He only screamed louder. When he was finally on his feet, the Officer pushed him back towards the wall where he had been a minute ago, behind the door.

The boy stood by the wall with his head leaning back as if he knew exactly what he was expected to do.

'They're all barely out of nappies, then they begin to steal,' said the Officer, looking at the Naked Young Man. Then, he turned his head again to the boy and continued, 'And you all come from that damn same place, you motherfuckers.' He stepped towards him again, raised his arm and wanted to slap him on the back of his head but retreated to his desk, mumbling, 'I wish I could set up a checkpoint at Tasluja and prevent any bloody young man who is not from this city from coming in.' He shook his head and sat on his chair behind the desk.

One of the guards opened the door, stuck his neck in and looked around the room. The Officer nodded to him, so the guard opened the door a bit more and threw a clean white sheet into the Naked Young Man's lap.

The Naked Young Man flinched, then fumbled with the sheet, clearly not knowing if he was allowed to cover himself with it or not. He looked at the guard who was staring at him, and then to the Officer.

The guard turned to the Officer and told him that there was a doctor who wanted to examine the guy with the leaf. The Officer nodded and stood up from behind the desk to go to the Naked Young Man. He stopped in the middle of the room for a second, turned to the guard and told him that he would come to meet the doctor in a minute. The guard nodded and shut the door.

After staring at the door for a few seconds, thinking, the Officer went back to his desk, took out a pair of scissors and rushed towards the Naked Young Man. He snatched the sheet, opened it wide, then folded it in four folds and cut one of the corners. When he unfolded it again, there was a semi-round hole in the middle of the sheet, big enough for the Naked Young Man's head. Then, he dressed the Naked Young Man with it, covering his entire body from under his chin to his feet. From behind, the sheet draped over his back down to his buttocks and crumpled up on the sofa. Only his head was now visible. The Officer looked mesmerised by how few inches of the leaf jutted out of the neck hole and hung over the Naked Young Man's chest. Soon, spots of blood emerged on different parts of the sheet.

The Officer stared at him for a moment and could not believe that the Naked Young Man who was sought-after by almost the whole city for several weeks was now sitting in front of him, in his office. He turned to the other boy who was still standing with his face to the wall, moaning. Then, he looked again at the Naked Young Man who also was looking anxiously back and forth between the boy and the Officer. After another short pause, the Officer rushed out of the room and shut the door firmly behind him.

In the hallway, he paused, pondered a bit, then told one of his guards to ask the doctor if he wouldn't mind waiting a little bit longer. He then opened the door to his office again as firmly as he had shut it. The door hit the boy and pressed him to the wall. Trapped behind the door, the boy started yelling. Only after a few seconds did the Officer close the door again and the boy collapse on the floor. He tried with the support of his head and elbows to stand up again, but the Officer put his foot on his back and flattened him to the floor. He turned his head towards the Naked Young Man and saw him sitting there silently, covered with the white sheet; pink sunlight filtered through the thin linen curtain at the window behind the sofa and lit one side of his face and the outline of his shoulders. The Officer realised that he had never seen such innocent beauty in the world before. Suddenly, a poetic scene was unfolding in front of him that made him remember the poetry of his youth. He realised that he had not read a word in years. Embarrassed by this revelation, he wondered if this angel-like, Naked Young Man could also perceive what an emotional uproar was being roused inside him.

The Naked Young Man smiled and leant back on the sofa. At the same time, his leaf retreated backwards into the hole and disappeared under the sheet; a part of the sheet lifted up and revealed his left calf, wrapped with the other end of the leaf. More of the pink sunlight fell on the sheet at his knees and over the floor at his feet. The Officer noticed that reflections from a small puddle in front of the Naked Young Man were making colourful light circles dance on the ceiling.

Touched by the magic of the scenery, the Officer felt that he might as well have chosen to become a poet, if only he had made some different choices in his life. Or maybe if he'd had some luck and had grown up in a different environment. Suddenly, the moaning of the boy under his foot brought him back to reality. He looked around the room stunned, and rather shocked. An overwhelming sadness drained all moisture from his throat – a sadness that came from seeing that his office lacked any sense of poetry. He spent most of his time in this tiny room with only a metal desk, a chair, a worn-out sofa and a rusty fan suspending from the ceiling. Also, a moaning child now and then, who could not even reach out to his own face to wipe the blood from his nose, but would still beg for a crumb of kindness and clemency. And all that merely for trying, perhaps, to break into a shop while politicians were busy robbing the country and beginning to steal land and all the resources they could put their hands on.

Now, an angel was sitting on in his sofa, covered with a white sheet stained with blood. He had peed himself out of fear, and his urine was flowing to the middle of the room. The Officer could smell it now. Most of all, the terrified, shocked eyes of the Naked Young Man were hurting him. Through the expression in the Naked Young Man's eyes, he could tell that this creature could perceive the innermost thoughts and worries of this heartless, embittered Officer who stood before him.

Suddenly, a guard opened the door and politely led the Doctor in his white lab coat inside. The Officer removed his foot instantly from the back of the boy, squatted beside him and opened the knotted *cummerbund* behind his head. Then, he released his tied wrists. He stood up and ordered the guard to take care of his wounds and send him home. 'Tell him if he appears here another time, I will hang him from this fan.' When he pointed to the fan, he felt that the room was very hot; he was immersed in sweat and also noticed glistening pearls of sweat over the forehead of the Naked Young Man rolling down over his cheeks. He shook hands with the Doctor, welcomed him in. He asked one of the guards in front of the door to bring a mop and clean the floor. Then, while closing the door, he switched on the fan.

The Doctor put his leather briefcase on the desk, opened it and took out a bottle of Dettol, a bag of cotton wool, a roll of bandage, a pair of scissors and a roll of paper tape and put them all on the desk in a row.

The guard helped the boy to stand up and tighten his *cummerbund* back around his waist, while shivering. At the moment the guard opened the door to lead the boy out, the Doctor called him back. He took a chunk of cotton wool, soaked it with the disinfectant from the Dettol bottle and handed it to him, saying, without looking at him, 'You'd better use this to clean up his face.'

The guard grabbed the dressing and left the room. The boy followed him, bent over with pain. The other guard came in with a wet mop and started wiping the floor.

The Doctor approached the Naked Young Man and took the sheet from him. The leaf crawled tightly around his legs, crotch, chest and neck. With a wide-open mouth and eyes dilated in disbelief, the Doctor stood still, regarding the spectacle. Then, he quickly stepped back to the desk, dodging the guard and his mop, grasped another chunk of cotton wool, grabbed the bottle, dropped the liquid onto the cotton and went back to the Naked Young Man. This time, he almost collided with the guard.

'That's enough, brother. It's all clean now. You can leave,' the Officer said and went to sit at his desk.

The guard left the room and closed the door behind him.

Carefully, the Doctor started to clean the wounds on the Naked Young Man's face and body, stopping to remove his hand whenever the Naked Young Man twitched with pain. Then, he went back to the desk and cut the bandage and the paper tape, lining them up one by one, in a row, with one end stuck to the edge of the desk. He folded one of the lengths of bandage in four folds, soaked it with the red liquid mercurochrome, picked up two pieces of the tape and went back again to the Naked Young Man. He put the folded red bandage on the biggest wound on his face and fixed it with the tape. He then went back to the desk and treated another folded bandage with the red liquid, picked up another two pieces of tape and went back to the Naked Young Man to cover another wound on his chest. He then went back yet again to the desk to repeat the whole process over and over until he had covered all his wounds. Whenever a wound was under the leaf, the leaf would move aside by itself to make room for the Doctor. The Naked Young Man was now a body made of dozens of white-red crosses.

The whole time, while the Doctor was performing his almost ritualistic task, the Officer stood still behind the desk, with crossed arms, watching him, now and then gently shaking his head. The pink mist of light behind the curtain was changing to a dark orange, and it got darker and darker until it became more of a dark-bluish grey by the time the Doctor had finished. He then covered the Naked Young Man once more with the sheet. The leaf jutted through the hole at his neck and descended over the sheet onto his chest.

Outside, a siren was approaching loudly but when it reached the police station it stopped howling. A faint blinking red and blue light emerged through the curtain, reflecting on the walls and the ceiling.

The Officer joined the Doctor and they both grabbed each of the Naked Young Man's arms and pulled him up from the sofa. The Doctor went to the desk and started to pack his medical equipment.

A guard came in and said to the Officer, 'Sir, an ambulance has come to collect the boy. His wound was still bleeding, so we called the ambulance. If you want, we can also send this naked guy with them.'

The Doctor raised his hand and said, 'Oh, no, no... Leave this one to me. I'll take him with me to our clinic.'

While the ambulance drove away with its siren wailing, its blinking lights now replaced by the dark brown colour behind the thin linen curtain, the Doctor and the Officer each put an arm under the armpits of the Naked Young Man and took him out through the long hallway. As they reached the entrance to the police station, dusk was falling gradually.

Hundreds of people had gathered in front of the station and on the other side of the street. The Photographer, his camera dangling from his neck, leant back on the wall of a building across the road. When he saw the Naked Young Man taking his first step down the stairs at the front of the station, he elbowed his way forcefully through the crowd, trying to cross the street towards him. In the middle of the road, he got stuck, as everyone else was also trying to reach the mysterious creature. He looked up and caught the eye of the Naked Young Man. This was the first time their eyes had met, which made both of them smile. Only for a short moment, though.

Suddenly, the Naked Young Man's foot got caught in the sheet, causing him to stumble over the stairs and land on the pavement below. The Doctor and the Officer who had accompanied the Naked Young Man outside of the station instantly ran down the stairs, but both stopped on the last step.

The Photographer forced himself through the crowed, watching over the shoulders of others how tens, then hundreds of fine roots jutted from the toes and ankles of the Naked Young Man. The new growth spread out from under the sheet and over the ground. Then, the Naked Young Man's fingers turned into branches, eventually growing longer and multiplying. In a blink of an eye, hundreds of other branches jutted out of the Naked Young Man's head and torso, tearing apart the sheet in all directions; the bloody pieces of bandage were thrown around with the paper tape crosses. One of them hit the chest of the Doctor and fell at his feet, leaving a red spot on his white Doctor's coat.

In less than a minute, the whole body of the Naked Young Man was covered in bark; his legs became a trunk that grew and grew, while his arms became branches, and rapidly disappeared between dozens of other branches. Then, the branches got covered swiftly with growing green leaves. In a few minutes, there was a huge tree lying in front of the police station.

The Doctor and the Officer turned back and wanted to run away over the stairs but bumped into three guards who were in their way, one of them holding an axe in his hand. The Officer, the Doctor and two of the guards fell, landing on the Tree's trunk.

The large crowd of people swarmed the Tree. The Photographer was trying to take pictures of the chaos, when he saw the guard with the axe come into his frame, and with each spark of his flash, a shot of action was registered: the guard lifting the axe in the air behind his shoulder, then dropping it down firmly on the Tree's trunk, splitting the wood, lifting the axe once more and swinging it over again. The Photographer let go of the camera in an effort to grab the guard's arm, but when the guard lifted the axe again, the back of the blade hit the camera. The guard wrestled his arm from the Photographer's grasp and pushed him back with his elbow, all while continuing to chop at the Tree. Small splinters splashed all over the area and into the faces of the people around him, forcing them to cover their eyes with their hands. They were trying to seize a moment in which, each one, might cut a branch from the Tree.

The Doctor embraced a part of the trunk and begged the crowd, 'Leave him alone. Please, please, leave him alone, people. Have some mercy.'

The Officer stood up. His head was bleeding. He grasped the arms of the guard with the axe and shouted at him, 'You stupid bastard, this is a human being you are chopping.'

It was too late; the trunk was cut in three pieces and tens of its branches lay on the street, writhing and jumping around like fish out of water. People were picking up the branches and twigs that would, after a few seconds, stop moving, and turn yellow and die in their hands. Then, they cut off other pieces and branches with their pocket-knives, scissors, iron bars, hammers and anything sharp that they could reach at that moment. Some even tried to obtain a piece of the Tree by kicking the branches to break them or by plucking bunches of leaves.

The Photographer was running from one person to another, begging them, with tears, to leave the Tree alone. He tried to push them away, but in vain. He could not understand why they were doing this, and what they needed to do it for.

Suddenly, among the sound of hundreds of women and men, and screaming children and beeping cars, a huge, tall man with a thick black moustache snatched the axe out of the guard's hands, kicked the Doctor from the trunk and started to chop the rest of the Tree into small pieces. The Officer emerged again out of the crowd and pushed the huge man, causing him to stumble over a piece of the trunk and fall on the ground; the axe slipped out of his hands. Then, the Officer pulled out his pistol and fired three shots in the air, after which all the guards loaded their Kalashnikovs and pointed them at the frightened members of the crowd. Petrified, most of the people stood still where they were, while children clung to their parents.

At last, the crowd dispersed and left the area, leaving behind only a few small pieces of the Tree's trunk, some dried branches and twigs and hundreds of yellow, dead leaves spread over the street. Cars drove over the remains of the Tree, most of the drivers not knowing what had just happened.

The Officer put his pistol back in the holster and climbed the stairs with a bent head, but at the moment he reached the entrance of the police station, he turned to look at the Doctor.

The Doctor, looking exhausted, stood beside his car a few metres from the police station. He was wiping clean the injuries on his own face and hands with a handful of cotton wool. He then opened the door of his car and took his place behind the steering wheel. One of the guards brought his bag, opened the rear door and put it on the back seat.

The Photographer could see desperation on both their faces under the dull yellow lights – the Doctor under his car ceiling's light and the Officer under a suspended light bulb above the entrance. They both shook their heads in sorrow and waved to each other. The Doctor started his car and drove away.

After staring at the place where the whole disaster had taken place, the Officer took out his handkerchief and wiped his eyes, then turned and went back inside the police station, beckoning his guards to go in too. Only one of the guards stayed at the entrance.

At that moment, a four-by-four halted with a squeal in front of the station. The Photographer, who had gone back to his earlier place, leaning on the wall of the building across the road in an unlit spot, saw the Asayish Director and four other gunmen jump out of the vehicle. Another four-by-four arrived and six other gunmen jumped out this one. They all deployed to both sides of the police station's entrance.

The Asayish Director looked around, seemingly confused as to what had just happened and what all the wood pieces and tree branches were doing on the street. He went up the stairs and entered the station with two of his gunmen, greeting the policeman who was guarding the entrance.

'Wasn't it a bit early to arrive, schmuck?' the Photographer mumbled. 'Why do you always have to be late with everything? You and your lazy ass guys. You might have been able to rescue him.'

When he turned, he saw the Gardener crouched down beside a few pieces of the trunk, searching between the dead leaves while crying. He picked a small twig with a couple of small green leaves shining in the light from the bulb that dangled from the eave of the police station. He pulled his handkerchief out of his *sharwal's* pocket, wiped his tears with it and wrapped it around the seemingly living twig. He stood up immediately and walked away, down University Road, disappearing into the darkness.

The Photographer followed him, keeping a distance of about hundred metres behind him.

51

Four years after the ambiguous events of the tree-like man, people in the city and all over the Kurdish region were caught in the grip of ubiquitous poverty. They were busy talking about and protecting themselves against the bloody battles between armed political groups that could no longer share the nation's fortunes, and had left behind traces of their bullets and grenades on the many government buildings, the façades of the houses and in the streets and alleyways. At that time, barely anyone remembered the stories about a walking tree or a naked man who was wrapped in a leaf. Rarely anyone talked about those days anymore. Nobody any longer believed those fabulous stories. Nobody held the young Photographer responsible for anything anymore or accused him of wicked plans or conspiracies. And the Photographer himself no longer owned a camera, for since that time he no longer had taken pictures. As for the Neighbour-Girl, she still felt in limbo about their relationship, but at least she was no longer being chased by the Asayish Director – the man was killed during the infighting between his party and its rival.

In those days, one late afternoon in the early spring, as the sun was gradually going down, the Photographer sat with Neighbour-Girl on a wooden bench in the public park, under a tall, fresh-green tree, listening to the chirping of thousands of starlings and hundreds of sparrows and pigeons flying over the garden. The birds were coming in groups to nest, jumping from branch to branch, raining droppings all over the area, while the park visitors were gradually leaving. She was still in disbelief about what the Photographer had just told her. He was going to sell his house and leave the country for Europe. His father had died a few months earlier and the bloody fights were not ceasing. The situation had become so volatile that even someone like him who did not have any link to any party or political movement was not safe of the effects of the infighting. It was hard not to get involved somehow.

He took an old metal tobacco box out of the pocket of his coat, pulled out a cigarette paper, put some dry tobacco in it and rolled a cigarette. He lit it, took a puff, leant his head back towards the tree behind them, and while he blew out the smoke, said, 'If you promise me that this secret will remain between us, I'll tell you which tree this is behind us.'

The Neighbour-Girl sat upright on the bench, looked around, raised her head and stared for a while at the tree. Then, she let her head sink down and frowned at the Photographer.

The Photographer noticed a horrifying question in her wide-open eyes. He smiled, then stared at the flowers in front of them. He said, 'This secret is just between me and the Gardener. In fact, a secret shared by more than two people, even if you involve only a third, is no longer a secret. But the secret I'm now telling you, that I have a secret with the Gardener, must remain strictly between you and me.'

She stared at the large tree again. Flocks of starlings had nestled in the branches, chirping a joyous song. 'Oh my…!' she put her hand on her mouth. Then, moving her hand away, she gazed at him and said, 'Please don't tell me this is…'

The Photographer smiled.

Acknowledgements

My special thanks goes to Gillian Gee who helped so much with the first edits of this book, and my amazing editor Jessica Sanchez. And of course my partner Aleksandra Markovic for all her support. My son Sivan and his mum Hawar Qaradaghi. And to: Renas Babakir; Hermione Gee; Michaela Mongelard; Julia Sako; Ahmed Sabri; Fazil Moradi. And last but not least, I thank anyone who has, in any way, helped or will help with the promotion of this book. Reading it is part of that process.